Gone

A Pastor Missed The Rapture.
Can He Be Saved?

JOHN F. HAY Sr.

TATE PUBLISHING
AND **ENTERPRISES**, LLC

Published by Tate Publishing & Enterprises, LLC
127 E. Trade Center Terrace | Mustang, Oklahoma 73064 USA
1.888.361.9473 | www.tatepublishing.com

Tate Publishing is committed to excellence in the publishing industry. The company reflects the philosophy established by the founders, based on Psalm 68:11,
"The Lord gave the word and great was the company of those who published it."

Published in the United States of America

ISBN: 978-1-62854-867-9
1. Fiction / General
2. Fiction / Christian / General
13.08.19

While this book is a novel concerning the Second Coming of Jesus Christ through the eyes of a pastor who missed the Rapture because of a spiritual heart condition, it also includes in depth research of the following topics:

- A Biblical Discussion of Post-Rapture Salvation
- A Biblical Revelation of the great tribulation and the Antichrist
- The Fall of Babylon
- The Final Judgment
- The Final Destruction of this Earth
- The New Heaven and New Earth

Dedication

To my wife, Janet, of over fifty-nine years, who has faithfully supported and worked with me in all the various callings and ministries of my life. Her love and devotion to the work of the Lord, our two children, six grandchildren, and three great-grandchildren, along with her unwavering love and sacrifices in our ministries, has been an inspiration and steadying force in my life. I owe a great debt to her for any successes, which have come my way. Her musical talents have been a tremendous asset to the ministry in the churches we have had the privilege of serving.

Also, Janet has spent many hours assisting me with this book. She has worked diligently, correcting spelling and grammar, as well as encouraging me to complete the book. I extend sincere thanks to her for utilizing her outstanding proofreading skills helping to make this book become a reality.

Acknowledgment

To Tim Watson for extensive technical computer assistance. And to Rev. Jim Mathews, Matthew Price, and Lucy Barnes for editorial assistance and creative consultation. Also, several friends who read rough drafts of this book and strongly encouraged me to pursue having it published.

Tables of Contents

Introduction

It was an unusual, cool 1944 fall evening in Seventy Six, Kentucky, a small community about seven miles north of Albany, Kentucky. What made it so unusual was that it was the first time I ever heard anything impressionable about Jesus or who he was. Everything else about that evening was the same, usual, and uneventful.

As a six-year-old boy, I sat behind a sheet metal stove, cracking walnuts on an upturned piece of a fire log. These nut kernels would be saved and sold for a few cents at a country store some distance away. My mother was mending some clothing, my father was sitting near the stove watching me crack walnuts, and my two-year-old brother was playing with something on the linoleum-covered floor while my baby sister slept on a quilt pallet. In fact, there was little room to do much in the small three-room clapboard house built by my father with my limited assistance. It was perched upon upended parts of a large log as the foundation. There was the living room, a kitchen containing a wood cooking stove, a few crude shelves on a wall, and the homemade table with six cane bottom chairs. There was the common single bedroom for all of us in a loft-type second floor, reached by a crude ladder stairs.

In the middle of all this activity in the house, our dog, Jackie, began to excitedly bark and even howl outside. It sounded unusual for him, like an emergency. Slowly, my father cracked open the front door and cautiously crept outside. All of us anxiously awaited his explanation for the apparent alarm. Soon he returned with a troubled expression. He said, "The sky is on fire!"

Quickly, my mother and I rushed into the bare yard. Sure enough, the northerly sky was ablaze with strange multicolored moving lights. As soon as possible, we were all on our way to Grandma's, which was a little over half a mile away by a dirt wagon road. We walked quietly and quickly, often glancing at the frightening, glowing sky. We always went to Grandma's when there was trouble. When we arrived, Grandma and Granddad were standing on the long porch of the huge farmhouse, staring at the same heavenly phenomenon. Neither of them could offer any idea or meaning for what was so mystifying.

Everyone decided to climb the hill in back of the farmhouse to get a clearer view of the strange yet beautiful phenomenon. At times, it looked like moving green curtains, then streaks of light shooting almost directly overhead, constantly changing colors with indescribable shapes and forms. We were soon joined by an uncle, aunt, and three cousins near my age. Everyone was fearful and flustered by what they were viewing. I even heard my aunt begin to call upon God and pray about being ready for the return of Jesus. There was the name of Jesus in a frantic prayer about his return. That was my first introduction to that thought. Everyone else was sure that God had something to do with all this alarming yet awesome sight. All of us children were scared and bewildered because of the comments and easily sensed consternation of the adults.

In a little while, we vaguely saw another adult in the dark shadows climbing the hill to join this frightened little group. When visible, it was Aunt Mattie who was considered to be one of the godliest women in that small community. Everyone called her Aunt although she was the relative of no one there. She was also a midwife and the one who had delivered me six years earlier. Aunt Mattie was calm and serene but concerned about the fearfulness of her friends and neighbors. Someone asked her, "Is this Jesus returning to earth?"

Calmly and confidently, she said, "No, it is not Jesus returning, for the lights are not in the eastern sky." I still do not know what that has to do with the return of Jesus. However, it was accepted as Gospel truth that night.

That seemed to settle everyone, coming from such a sincere, godly lady. My aunt even stopped praying. All of us began to wonder about and enjoyed the beauty of the panorama taking place in the northern sky. Soon the little group began to break up, and everyone returned to their home.

I was too excited and filled with wonder to drop off to sleep immediately in the upstairs loft bedroom. I lay there staring into the darkness, wondering about Jesus and who he was to cause so much fear in everyone at the thought of his returning. *If he was returning, then he had been here before*, I mused. *And if he was returning, why had he bothered to go away?* Also, what did my aunt mean by praying to be ready for his return? Finally, I fell asleep wondering, *Just who is Jesus, and does all of this have anything to do with me?*

Later, I learned that the phenomenon of that night was known as the northern lights. Then much later, after moving from Seventy-Six, Kentucky, I understood that aurora borealis was the technical name for what had troubled us so greatly that night long ago.

The next day after sunup, our lives fell into the same routine, and nothing else was mentioned about Jesus or the wonders of the night before. My chores remained the same, helping my father in the tobacco and corn fields, working as a sharecropper on my grandparents' huge farm.

The name of Jesus did not come up again until several months later when my uncle Vester rode into our yard on a horse. It was strange that he was coming to see us. We always walked almost three miles to see him and Aunt Lizzie. They lived in a nice, spacious house on a hill overlooking the Seventy-Six Falls. Visiting them was always a treat, and the food was plentiful and delicious. Now, what was Uncle Vester doing here? He called Mom and Dad out to give them some grave news he had just heard on the radio. And he was about the only one in the community who had a workable radio. He said that a strange, religious group had announced that Jesus was going to return one day that next week. There was the name of Jesus again and a prediction of his return.

This was in the early summer, and along with eight other children, I was a student at the one-room Hill Top School. The school term in that community was from May through October, so we would not have to walk to school in cold weather, without shoes, which none of us wore. My walk was about three miles. Although some people think that the distance grows with the telling.

It was evident that the news from Uncle Vester terrified my parents. That struck terror in me, but I had no idea why. Every day the next week, I begged to stay home from school. I wanted to be with my parents when Jesus returned, whatever that meant. However, I was sent to school daily. Every chance I had, I looked out of a window, watching the eastern sky to see if anything different was happening, like Jesus returning. I did not know what to expect, but I watched. Of course, like many other false prophecies before and after that time, Jesus has not returned yet. But one day, he will return in the Rapture and, then in the Revelation, to reign forever.

About four years later, I began to hear more about Jesus Christ, his love for us and his willingness to save us, forgiving all our sins, cleansing our hearts, living within us, making us new persons, and preparing us to be ready to meet him in the air at his second coming. All of this began to take place after we started attending church regularly in New Castle, Indiana.

In 1944, we moved from Seventy Six, Kentucky to New Castle, Indiana, where my father, and, later, my mother worked in a defense factory. We left the three-room house in Seventy

Six and moved into a single garage located next to the last street in New Castle. Since we had not attended church regularly in Kentucky, my parents said that the first church that invited us to church is where we would attend. However, it was months before that happened. But after all, what church would look for prospective people living in a garage?

Strangely though, one Saturday afternoon, two ladies drove by and saw us three children playing in the grassless yard between the big house and our garage home. They stopped and asked us if we went to Sunday school. Of course, we answered no, almost in unison. They went to the side door of the garage to ask our mother if they could pick us up and take us to their church. Our mother told them that wouldn't be necessary, that our father and she had decided to attend the first church that invited us, so we would walk to the church, as a family. They gave directions to their church, which was many blocks away from our garage home. So that Sunday, we dressed in our best and cleanest clothes and walked to church.

One of the first things I noticed was that no one was dressed like us. Overalls and a homemade "feed sack" shirt did not seem to be the common attire. We stood out, but the people were friendly and seemed to love us, so we continued to attend. In the two years we attended there, I began to hear and learn about Jesus.

After about two years, we changed churches, mainly because I had met children in school who kept inviting me to attend church with them. Eventually, my parents gave in, and we started walking to a different church much farther away. The first Sunday there, I did not meet Jesus as my personal savior, but I saw the beautiful, young girl that I intended to marry some day although I was only twelve years old. And I did marry her in 1954.

There was more intense preaching about Jesus and the salvation he offered, along with the facts of his coming again. Soon after starting to attend that church, I repented of my sins and, by faith, accepted Jesus Christ as my personal savior. Fortunately, there were many teenagers attending that church, and we supported each other in fellowship as well as spiritually. Most of us who are still living are active in church in some way. Out of that group of young people came a missionary, preachers, gospel singers, a district superintendent, and outstanding laypeople.

After some turbulent teen years, at age of seventeen, I made a complete commitment to the Lord and accepted his call to preach his Word. That had been a growing obsession in my heart and mind for some time. My pastor insisted that I begin to preach immediately, and he helped me greatly. Soon after that, I preached a revival in my home church, and often filled in for pastors in the area many Sundays. I became a serious student of the Bible, studying for soul strength, and sermons.

Upon graduating from high school with a major in speech and mathematics, I enrolled at Olivet Nazarene University to prepare for full-time ministry. My last two years of college were completed at Trevecca Nazarene University, where I graduated in 1958 with honors, cum laude, and listed in Who's Who in American Colleges and Universities 1958.

I have been a serious student of his word across all these years, giving special attention to the second coming of Jesus Christ. I served as a pastor for over thirty-two years, as a district superintendent for nineteen years, and as an evangelist for three years. Also, I have read widely on the second coming of Jesus, endeavoring to understand all that I could about this certain coming event. I have taught extensive Bible studies on the book of Daniel and Revelation in churches I have pastored and others. In addition, I have preached scores of Biblical messages on the return of our Lord. I do not pose to be an expert on this subject, just a serious student. I have a burning desire to learn all that I can to share with others, enabling all of us to be ready for His soon appearing.

In this novel, centering upon the second coming of Jesus, I have attempted to be faithful to the Bible teaching on the subject as I understand it. I realized that there are varying interpretations of the word of God on the return of Christ, and I do not intend to be dogmatic upon what is not clear. I have also taken the liberty to delve into technology and things that might take place after the return of Jesus. You must understand that this is a story, or novel, about the return of Jesus. The main fact is that he will return. The events of this story may or may not take place as written. Also, all names used in this book are simply characters of this novel. Any similarity of the names used for individuals with similar names is accidental and without any personal intent.

The single main message of this novel is for you to be ready and watchful for the return of Jesus Christ as he announced and affirmed. Do not chance standing as Ralph Waterman did, realizing that a loved one, who was a true child of God, was gone! Madeline, his wife, was gone to be with the Lord forever.

Madeline and Millions
Gone in the Rapture

It was after 1:00 a.m. when Ralph Waterman was suddenly awakened, realizing that Madeline, his wife, had not come to bed. That was not really strange, for she often watched TV, read, or worked word games until the wee hours of the mornings. However, Ralph did quietly crack the bedroom door and saw her sitting in her leather recliner, reading. He quietly closed the door, returned to bed, and fell asleep again.

Ralph awoke again about 5:30 a.m., and Madeline was still not in bed. Now, this was a little strange. He went into the family room, and her chair was empty. He checked the extra bathroom and the two extra bedrooms, but she was gone. His heart rate began to elevate with anxiety as he rushed to the garage. Madeline's car was there. On top of all that, the exit doors were still locked from inside.

All the telephones were ringing unceasingly, but there was no time to answer them. Ralph had to find Madeline. This had never happened before, and they had been married for over fifty-five years. Also, there were no serious marital problems that would even hint that she would leave. However, it was for sure that she was gone somewhere, somehow. There was neither a note nor message of any kind.

Now, Ralph was almost hysterical and hyperventilating. He had to get hold of himself and think this thing through.

The telephones were still ringing crazily. Who could be calling so insistently at this early hour? They would just have to call back, if it was important. Ralph reasoned that he had enough issues of his own to interpret right now rather than get involved with other people's problems.

Having been a pastor, preacher, evangelist, and church leader for over fifty years, this dilemma had all the trappings of the return of Jesus in the rapture. If that was true, then he had missed it, had been left, and Madeline was gone. But he had been the preacher and pastor and had studied and preached about the return of Jesus in the rapture scores of times. With a wildly pounding, pondering heart, Ralph was trying to pinpoint a possible reason why he might have been left, missing the Rapture, if that was the reality. There were no issues that he or anyone else could identify as major sins in his life. Oh, there were blunders, errors, and mistakes, but these were part of his humanness. He had attempted to live blameless before God although he could not live faultless. And that was what the word of God had required. It was very clear, for it said in the book of Philippians,

> Do all things without complaining and disputing, that you may become blameless and harmless, children of God without fault in the midst of a crooked and perverse generation, among whom you shine as lights in the world.
>
> (Philippians 2:14–15)

Also, there is an idea of blamelessness found in 2 Peter 3:14, "Therefore, beloved, looking forward to these things, be diligent to be found by Him in peace, without spot and blameless."

Another Bible passage that seemed to literally jump onto Ralph's mind was a passage from 1 Thessalonians:

> And may the Lord make you increase and abound in love to one another and to all, just as we *do* to you, so that He may establish your hearts blameless in holiness before our God and Father at the coming of our Lord Jesus Christ with all His saints.
>
> (1 Thessalonians 3:12–13)

With this in mind, Ralph was ready to inwardly argue with God. Had God not noticed that this was the way he had endeavored to live? In addition, had God not considered all the years he had conscientiously preached and been successful in the areas of his service? Almost like a clap of thunder, Ralph was reminded that God looked more at the heart than at one's accomplishments, even in the name of the Lord. God meant what he said, "For the Lord does not see as man sees; for man looks at the outward appearance, but the Lord looks at the heart" (1 Samuel 16:7).

Ralph had read that Bible passage often, but now, it's almost like God is reading it to him. As it rang in Ralph's consciousness, he literally shuttered. Here is what God had to say about Ralph's flimsy reasoning:

> Not everyone who says to Me, "Lord, Lord," shall enter the kingdom of heaven, but he who does the will of My Father in heaven. Many will say to Me in that day, "Lord, Lord, have we not prophesied in Your name, cast out demons in Your name, and done many wonders in Your name?" And then I will declare to them, "I never knew you; depart from Me, you who practice lawlessness!
>
> (Matthew 7:21–23)

Of course, this was not the final judgment day, but in light of this Scripture, it was possible that he had missed the rapture, and Madeline was gone.

The landline telephone and Ralph's cell phone were both continuing to constantly ring. Finally, he looked at the at caller identification and recognized the callers. Reluctantly, he answered one of the telephones. That was a troubling, tragic mistake. Screaming into the receiver, someone shouted, "Reverend Ralph Waterman, what are you doing here? Haven't you heard that Jesus has returned, and we have been left? Surely you have had the TV on this morning? Our world is in complete chaos. By the way, where is Madeline? Is she still here also?" Ralph dropped the telephone. He wanted to scream or run or try to deny reality. What could he do? What could he say, or where could he go? How could he explain his personal presence in a world doomed for the wrath of God, known as the great tribulation? Maybe he should just try to disappear. He picked up the telephone and hung it up although the caller was still screaming at him. He had no answers or advice for anyone right now.

As he stared at Madeline's empty chair, he was even more stunned and troubled. The prophecy of Jesus had come to pass in his own family and life. He had read the words of Jesus often, even preached them as a solemn warning to his hearers. Now, it had become living reality. Jesus had predicted:

> But of that day and hour no one knows, not even the angels of heaven, but My Father only. But as the days of Noah were, so also will the coming of the Son of Man be. For as in the days before the flood, they were eating and drinking, marrying and giving in marriage, until the day that Noah entered the ark, and did not know until the flood came and took them all away, so also will the coming of the Son of Man be. Then two men will be in the field: one will be taken and the other left. Two women will be grinding at the mill: one will be taken and the other left. Watch therefore, for you do not know what hour your Lord is coming.
>
> (Matthew 24:36–42)

Ralph Waterman had been one of those left. He had not been watchful. He had been too busy doing good things, avoiding the big, bold sins, but he had not been watchful enough. He had evidently ignored an issue deep within his heart.

Sitting in his easy chair, with only a small table lamp separating him from Madeline's empty chair, Ralph recalled the

Bible's description of the rapture. In 1 Thessalonians, it described it clearly:

> For this we say to you by the word of the Lord, that we who are alive *and* remain until the coming of the Lord will by no means precede those who are asleep. For the Lord Himself will descend from heaven with a shout, with the voice of an archangel, and with the trumpet of God. And the dead in Christ will rise first. Then we who are alive *and* remain shall be caught up together with them in the clouds to meet the Lord in the air. And thus we shall always be with the Lord.
>
> (1 Thessalonians 4:15–17)

That's where Madeline is, and here I am left, Ralph mused mournfully. He would decide why and determine if there was anything he could do to avoid being eternally lost even though he had missed the rapture. "Can I be saved now?" Ralph mumbled hopefully to himself.

TV News Confirms Second Coming of Christ

There was the TV, but Ralph was hesitant to turn it on. For several minutes, he looked at the blank, silent screen, shrinking from what he might have to see if he turned it on. He dreaded having TV reporters inform him of the fearfully inevitable although it would be incomprehensible to them. As he fumbled with the TV remote control, contemplating whether to turn it on, both of the telephones were constantly ringing, adding to his consternation. Finally, it dawned upon Ralph that if he turned the on TV, he could see on the screen who was calling by the caller identification. Then he could respond as he desired. With shaking hands, he gripped the remote control and pushed the on button. The TV screen slowly came to life, but the picture was not a pleasant sight. Switching channels did not improve the view. On every channel, at least someone was missing. Husbands had awakened to find a wife gone, just as Ralph had found Madeline gone. Wives were awaking to find husbands and children gone. In other homes, teenagers were frantic, finding both parents gone and one parent totally distraught because the other had suddenly vanished right before their eyes. In millions of homes, all small, innocent children were missing—gone.

School officials were reporting that teachers of junior and senior high schools had vanished, leaving students sitting in their seats stunned and scared almost to death. As these students looked around, some of their classmates were gone also. Other school principals told of finding entire classrooms, in lower grade schools, empty of teachers and students. They were all gone, without any clue to what had happened. The nation was dealing with a worldwide catastrophe. The world had been stripped of thousands, no, millions of people without any apparent explanation.

Store clerks were telling of reaching to accept payment for items and individuals that suddenly vanished, leaving the money to fall on the counter. In restaurants, trays had dropped to the floor as waiters and waitresses simply disappeared. And waitresses found tables empty when they brought the food that had been ordered. In mass meeting places, seats were suddenly vacated, to the vexation of those sitting close by.

Streets were filled with frightened, frantic people trying to make some sense of what had happened. Even TV reporters had suddenly vanished before the eyes of millions of viewers. TV reporters were desperately trying to keep up with the fast moving events that were clamoring to be reported. There was worldwide pandemonium. Frantic searches were being made for those gone, but not one was ever found.

Scene after scene of tragedies were being shown in detail, one after another. There were massive automobile accidents, and strangely, some of the automobiles were unoccupied. As unbelievable as it could be, there were thousands of single automobile accidents, and no body was found in the mangled messes or nearby. It was as though the automobiles were driverless.

One of these single automobile accidents were reported by a nerve-rattled state trooper in Florida. Fortunately, or unfortunately, he had been following a late model Cadillac with two persons in the front seat, probably a husband and wife. He was driving closely enough to the automobile to notice a chrome Christian fish emblem fastened to the lower left corner of the trunk lid. "These people are Christians," the officer surmised. They were traveling north on I-4, near Orlando, Florida, at a mile or two over seventy miles per hour, which was slightly above the speed limit.

Suddenly, to the officer's dismay, both the driver and passenger simply disappeared. However, the automobile did not slow down as the cruise control evidently was engaged. The new Cadillac began to drift to the right, much to the relief of the police officer. That would keep it from crossing the median and possibly causing a head-on collision. When the front tires hit the grassy section of the roadside, it began to spin, then overturned, rolling over several times, coming to rest on its top in a clump of trees.

With his emergency lights flashing, the officer quickly began to pull to the side of the road and stopped. In the process, he radioed for a paramedic unit and a wrecker, assuming both would be needed. For a few brief moments, he forgot the shocking scene he had earlier witnessed when the driver and passenger had disappeared. Rushing to the overturned vehicle, he was preparing himself for the worst scenario. No one could survive that crumpled, mangled mass of metal. But there was no one inside! A quick search of the immediate area did not produce any bodies that could have been ejected from the wildly rolling automobile.

In a few minutes, the paramedics arrived. A diligent search of the automobile and the entire area produced no bodies. While the wrecker was hooking onto the mangled Cadillac, a confusing conversation took place between the police officer and the two paramedics. They were trying to come to some conclusions about this strange accident. The two occupants of that Cadillac were definitely gone.

The paramedics had to hasten to their vehicle as another urgent call was coming in. They couldn't help wondering if this call would be as confusing as the previous one. In fact, more emergencies were being reported than the entire fleet of paramedic units could answer. That was the situation worldwide. "What could be going on?" was the questioning paramedic's response to the urgent calls. All units were in action, and all off duty paramedics had been called into immediate service.

There were more of these tragic releases than could be related by the breathless TV reporters for multitudes of these driverless automobiles did not drift to the right but flipped across medians to be met head-on by other automobiles and trucks. In the ensuing traffic backups, there were countless driverless automobiles crashing into the vehicles in front of them. The results of all this pandemonium produced terrified passengers to relate unbelievable stories. There were many more tragedies than the mobile TV crews could cover. They found themselves stopping at horrific scenes on their way to previous assignments. *What was happening in this world?*

Aircraft accidents were beyond description in number and devastation. Pilots and/or copilots were relaying how suddenly they became aware that they were alone in the cockpit to land the aircraft without assistance. Evidently, many of the commercial aircraft crashes were the results of the cockpit becoming totally vacated leaving no one qualified to land the planes.

Air traffic controllers, whose responsibility was to maintain proper separation of all commercial aircraft, were overwhelmed with emergency calls. There was some kind of emergency on every aircraft in the air. Pilots had disappeared, or in many other cases, the copilot was gone. Pilots were reporting pandemonium in the passenger cabins as passengers had suddenly vanished. Also, the assisting crew members and flight attendants had been depleted by disappearances that could not be explained. It was quickly becoming more than what the air traffic controllers could cope with. And to add to the dilemma, many flight control terminals were empty. These strange disappearances had affected them also. In addition, many off duty controllers could not be contacted for service. They were gone as related by a wife or family member. It was like 911 multiplied by the thousands, with additional complications. Aircrafts were mysteriously disappearing from the radar screens and could not be contacted by frantically calling controllers. They were gone. This emergency had engulfed the entire world.

Quickly, the United States National Transpiration Safety Board made it a mandate that all aircraft in the air were to be directed to the nearest adequate airport and land immediately. Also, no aircraft were to be cleared for takeoff. Soon this decision spread to all air traffic control in the world. The skies had to clear of all aircraft.

The military aircraft had not been exempted from this emergency. Military controllers who were still on duty were compelled to order all aircraft to land at the nearest military airbase. If distance was a problem, they were to blend in with the civilian aircraft and land at the nearest available airport. No chances were to be taken, and safety was to be maintained without exception. Many military aircraft had disappeared from controller's radar screens, just like the civilian situation. These aircrafts were gone, probably because the pilot had vanished. The skies were soon silent, but the world was in wild worry and bewilderment. Millions were gone.

There was the consolation that there had been no more disappearances, following the first initial event. But it had totally disrupted the world order. The use of the word "consolation" was woefully inadequate in the midst of such confusion and calamity.

There were recorded conversations of flight control personnel and pilots on the ground, using cell phones, attempting to give instructions to nonqualified persons about how to fly and land unfamiliar commercial aircraft. Some had succeeded, but most had ended in massive crashes in spite of the sincere attempts of those involved.

A single engine flight instructor who had succeeded in following the ground guidance for a Boeing 737 and successfully landed it was interviewed by a TV announcer. He was surrounded by over 150 passengers who were acclaiming him a hero. Earlier, there had been pandemonium in the passenger cabin as several seats had suddenly become empty, and a flight attendant walking down the aisle suddenly vanished. It seemed as though some of the other passengers were aware of the reason for these sudden disappearances. Now, an inexperienced, jet-powered pilot was going to attempt to fly them to safety. Prayers and sobs were the prevalent sounds in the aircraft passenger cabin. He was the only other pilot of any kind aboard the aircraft.

With the assistance of an experienced flight attendant and the Boeing 737 pilot on the ground, who had been contacted to assist if possible, the process began. The instructor pilot, who was unfamiliar with the big jet, was first made aware of all the instrumentations and flight controls. "Speed control, trim attitude, sink rate, power settings, along with following heading instructions were vitally essential," he was instructed. At cruise altitude, the instructing Boeing 737 pilot guided him through the basic maneuvers to continue the flight to the nearest adequate airport. Also, he was guided through, and practiced, approach and landing techniques. With sweating palms and forehead, the single engine instructor pilot struggled to follow the instructions given.

At last, he had successfully flown the Boeing 737 to an adequate airport, a lengthy final approach, and to a beckoning long runway. The landing gears were extended, and the glowing green indicator lights confirmed they were in landing position. Power was being adjusted to the two jet engines for a proper sink rate with the nose of the aircraft pitched slightly upward. With sweat streaming down his face and sweating palms, the assisting flight attendant and the experienced ground-bound Boeing 737 instructing pilot were encouraging him. Frantically fighting the flight controls to maintain proper air speed, attitude, and heading, he wondered if he would be able to land this bucking beast. All of the souls on the aircraft, including his, depended upon that.

The landing was neither smooth nor beautiful, but after several hard bounces, he had succeeded in keeping the aircraft on the runway and bringing it to a stop just before reaching the end. What a frightening experience. It was evident that he was visibly shaken by what he had gone through. And he was deeply troubled by what had brought about the necessity of him taking over an unfamiliar aircraft type that he had never flown. All of that had been necessary because the pilot and copilot had mysteriously exited the cockpit of the 737 at an altitude of thirty-four thousand feet. They were mysteriously gone.

Ralph was transfixed by what he was viewing. He knew what had become of that pilot and copilot. They were gone, the same way Madeline had left this earth. All of this was absolute confirmation that Jesus had returned in the rapture, and along with himself, these he watched on the TV screen had been left behind.

Suddenly, the scene changed as a renowned surgeon from a famous major hospital was being interviewed by another TV reporter. Still in his blood-stained, green surgery scrub suit, he was relating how a patient upon whom he was performing delicate surgery suddenly, miraculously vanished. Pandemonium had broken out in the operating room as a scrub nurse had also mysteriously disappeared. Others in the operating room went into shock at the sight of these events.

In another operating room, the main surgeon had vanished, and although in a state of utter confusion, his assistant was compelled to complete the surgery. All other surgeries had been canceled. Besides, some of the patients scheduled for surgery were gone anyway. Speaking for the hospital administration, the surgeon related how an intense search was being made for scores of missing patients, some who were in critical condition. Ralph knew they would not be found, just as he had been unable to find Madeline. They were all gone!

Everywhere in the world and in all kinds of situations, people were reported missing. Almost everyone claimed not to know what in the world had happened, but in his sorrow, Ralph knew.

Every time the telephone rang, Ralph recognized a name on the TV screen, projected by the phone identification system. He was startled and surprised to see some of the names. *Why had they missed the rapture?* He had been the pastor of some of them. He definitely decided not to make any phone calls as many would be shocked to see that he was still here, having missed the rapture. Hopefully, he would soon determine why.

Interviews with world government leaders and scientists were contacted by TV reporters in an attempt to conclude what had caused millions of people to be missing. Most of the world leaders did not have a clue. One or two recalled hearing of the possible return of Jesus some day, but they had put no credence in it. They only believed that Jesus was a good historic man, but he had been killed by a Roman crucifixion over two thousand years ago. Why would anyone believe that he was still alive or ever be able to return again?

Of course, the scientists who were interviewed could find no scientific reason to believe in such a fantasy as the return of Jesus Christ. To them, that was only a fanatical fable. They stated that in all the years of their scientific studies and books read, nothing like this had ever been hinted. By combined consensus, the scientist interviewed could give no reason or explanation for the world's trauma.

Religious leaders who were interviewed on TV gave no better explanations than the government leaders and the scientific community. They did not believe that Jesus Christ was the divine Son of God or that the questionable Bible teachings relating to his return were reliable. It was all deception developed by uneducated disciples and followers of the man, Jesus. Their contention was that if God, assuming there was a true God, had anything to do with the trouble and consternation of the present world, it was not an act of mercy. And he had been portrayed as a merciful God by his followers. If there was a God and he had anything to do with these events, they despised him more than ever.

Ralph reasoned, "If they only knew." They had posed as religious leaders, ignoring the main textbook, the Bible. The Holy Bible was God's inspired Word to inform mankind of his being, love, mercy, power, justice, and salvation through Jesus Christ. He was the one who knew and informed mankind of the coming future events, including the return of Jesus Christ, and more.

Finally, the face of the president of the United States appeared on the TV screen. There was the same haughty, defiant, dominating expression, but today there was evident concern. He wanted to address the nation and the world, letting them know why millions of people were gone. In his former religious teaching and reliable recent information, it was a fact that Jesus Christ had returned in the air to gather all true believers to himself. Since he had evolved so far from his former religious beliefs, he was now angry at God for plunging the world into so much chaos. He also informed the world that this was not the end. The world would recover and go on. The president persisted in planning for world unity, even without God, if that is what God wanted.

Quickly, the TV picture flashed to news from Europe. A TV reporter announced that a climbing leader of the European Union had a message for the world. He was known as a powerfully gifted speaker with a charismatic personality, gaining popularity around the world. His message, attempting to console a troubled world, greatly overshadowed that of the United States president. His presence, presentation, and promises of hope, with solutions, grabbed the attention of a world in turmoil. One item common with that of the United States president was that a torn, traumatized world was the consequences of a horrible God. Strangely, TV reporters seemed to be drawn to him and directed more time to his comments. Coming as no surprise, he was a Muslim, giving him the advantageous attention of millions more around the world. He gained instant acclaim as an attractive, articulate, authoritative world leader. It was as if he had just been waiting for this moment.

A thoughtful, thorough researching TV reporter realized that there was a common denominator among those who were gone. All of them were innocent children, those incapable of rational thinking, and people who professed to be believers in Jesus Christ as savior and were living godly, Christian lives. These were the only ones gone. Lively discussions took place among TV reporters about their colleagues who were mysteriously missing, and they fit into the latter category. Although most of these in the conversation had to admit that although they had not believed in Jesus Christ as the Son of God, nor in the possibility of his return, they concluded that the rapture had probably taken place. That was the only reasonable explanation for the worldwide pandemonium.

Anger, disgust, and defiance welled up in Ralph's mind. He wanted to shout strong words at the TV, but who would hear it? Really, he was in the same situation as all of those he had listened to in disgust. He had missed the return of Jesus in the rapture and had been left with them. All of the anguish of the great tribulation loomed ahead of him. That was a terrifying thought. How could he face it?

Ralph Reviewed Bible Teachings about the Second Coming

*R*eally, *no one should have been surprised at the return of Jesus. The Bible was crystal clear on the subject,* Ralph thought to himself. He turned the TV off, for he had seen enough to convince him, without a doubt, that the inevitable fact of Jesus's return had taken place. He knew for certain why Madeline was gone. Why he had been left was not clear to him yet. He had preached so often, urging people to be ready to meet Jesus at his coming, but here he was, having missed it, left with humiliating, haunting memories and an uncertain, terrifying future.

Trudging tiredly and tormented, Ralph made his way to his study in the other end of the house. Perhaps reviewing what the Bible said about the return of Jesus would help clear his mind or give him a sense of some kind of hope. Seating himself at his desk, where he had prepared hundreds of sermons, he opened his study Bible, turning to the subject, "The Second Coming." There were scores of scriptural references on the subject. In fact, it was staggering to remember, reading from margin notes he had scribbled in his Bible, that in the 260 chapters in the New Testament there are 318 references to the second coming of Jesus. Also, his return is referred to in twenty-three of the twenty-seven books of the New Testament. And there are 1,845 references to Jesus's return in the Old Testament and New Testament.

He narrowed his review greatly. First, he wanted to reread what Jesus himself has said about his return. There it was in the Gospel of John:

Let not your heart be troubled; you believe in God, believe also in Me. In My Father's house are many mansions; if *it were* not *so,* I would have told you. I go to prepare a place for you. And if I go and prepare a place for you, I will come again and receive you to Myself; that where I am, *there* you may be also.

(John 14:1–3)

At his trial, Jesus had prophesied of his coming again with these words:

And the high priest arose and said to Him, "Do You answer nothing? What *is it* these men testify against You?" But Jesus kept silent. And the high priest answered and said to Him, "I put You under oath by the living God: Tell us if You are the Christ, the Son of God!" Jesus said to him, "*It is as* you said. Nevertheless, I say to you, hereafter you will see the Son of Man sitting at the right hand of the Power, and coming on the clouds of heaven.

(Matthew 26:62–6)4

In the Gospel of Luke, Jesus gave some of the signs of his return and a major prophecy of his coming again. Ralph read it again, in anguish of heart:

And there will be signs in the sun, in the moon, and in the stars; and on the earth distress of nations, with perplexity, the sea and the waves roaring; men's hearts failing them from fear and the expectation of those things which are coming on the earth, for the powers of the heavens will be shaken. Then they will see the Son of Man coming in a cloud with power and great glory. Now when these things begin to happen, look up and lift up your heads, because your redemption draws near.

(Luke 21:25–27)

As angels had declared the birth, or first coming of Jesus, they vividly disclosed his coming again in the first chapter of the book Acts:

> Now when He had spoken these things, while they watched, He was taken up, and a cloud received Him out of their sight. And while they looked steadfastly toward heaven as He went up, behold, two men stood by them in white apparel, who also said, "Men of Galilee, why do you stand gazing up into heaven? This *same* Jesus, who was taken up from you into heaven, will so come in like manner as you saw Him go into heaven.
>
> (Acts 1:9–11)

The manner of his return was foretold by Jesus in (Matthew 24:27), "For as the lightning comes from the east and flashes to the west, so also will the coming of the Son of Man be." It may be troubling and difficult to comprehend, but it will happen.

Also, the Apostle Paul reminded the church at Corinth, and all generations to follow, the manner in which Jesus would return, by the inspiration of the Holy Spirit:

> Behold, I tell you a mystery: We shall not all sleep, but we shall all be changed—in a moment, in the twinkling of an eye, at the last trumpet. For the trumpet will sound, and the dead will be raised incorruptible, and we shall be changed. For this corruptible must put on incorruption, and this mortal *must* put on immortality.
>
> (1 Corinthians 15:51–53)

This is precisely how millions had suddenly been taken out of this world. Right then, all of those taken were with the Lord at the marriage supper of the lamb, somewhere in the air or atmosphere above the earth. The return of Jesus Christ had been unforeseen and unexpected. And that, also, was precisely as Jesus had predicted it to take place:

Watch therefore, for you do not know what hour your Lord is coming. But know this, that if the master of the house had known what hour the thief would come, he would have watched and not allowed his house to be broken into. Therefore you also be ready, for the Son of Man is coming at an hour you do not expect.

(Matthew 24:42–44)

No one should have been surprised or uninformed about what had plunged the world into so much turmoil and trauma. The Bible had been given by the purposes of God to not only clearly give instructions how mankind could be reconciled to God, through his great salvation, by faith, but to inform mankind of the future. Also, hosts of preachers had proclaimed God's Word from pulpits and all forms of public communications. Missionaries had traveled to the far reaches of the world, preaching and teaching the Word of God. Really, no one had a legitimate excuse for being surprised at the return of Jesus to rescue his people from the torments of being left behind and the great tribulation. However, Satan had been very successful in maligning, mocking, and minimizing the Bible until mankind had ignored it to the point of being Biblically ignorant. The Bible says:

But concerning the times and the seasons, brethren, you have no need that I should write to you. For you yourselves know perfectly that the day of the Lord so comes as a thief in the night. For when they say, "Peace and safety!" then sudden destruction comes upon them, as labor pains upon a pregnant woman. And they shall not escape. But you, brethren, are not in darkness, so that this Day should overtake you as a thief. You are all sons of light and sons of the day. We are not of the night nor of darkness. Therefore let us not sleep, as others *do,* but let us watch and be sober.

(Thessalonians 5:1–6)

As Ralph read these passages of Scripture, and others, he pondered how and why he had missed the rapture. As he had preached, the signs of the soon return of Jesus were prevalent all over the world. It was evident, from the Bible teachings, that he had been living in the last days. He had not been watchful enough nor heeded the faithful working of God's Holy Spirit in his heart. He was not left by some oversight of God. Evidently, Ralph had been too busy talking the talk but failing, in some way, to walk the walk. "That was utterly ridiculous, with the signs of Jesus's soon return glaring daily in almost every form of information gleaned from the TV, radio, and newsprint," Ralph reluctantly admitted.

What Jesus Said
About His Return

One day, over two thousand years ago, some of the disciples of Jesus approached him privately, asking about the signs, which would alert them to his coming again:

> Then Jesus went out and departed from the temple, and His disciples came up to show Him the buildings of the temple. And Jesus said to them, "Do you not see all these things? Assuredly, I say to you, not *one* stone shall be left here upon another, that shall not be thrown down." Now as He sat on the Mount of Olives, the disciples came to Him privately, saying, "Tell us, when will these things be? And what *will be* the sign of Your coming, and of the end of the age?
>
> (Matthew 24:1–3)

Jesus did not ignore the questioning minds of his disciples. He revealed the answer to their three questions in detail. The disciples wanted to know about the future destruction of Jerusalem, especially the beautiful temple, the signs indicating his soon return, and about the end of the present world.

Jesus dealt with all three questions and made precise predictions of their fulfillment. One of them has already been fulfilled, for Jerusalem and the temple were utterly destroyed in AD 70, following a lengthy, devastating siege by the Roman armies under the leadership of Titus. The surviving Jews were scattered to the ends of the earth. From that time until 1948, they wandered as strangers in many nations of the world, homeless, harassed, and hated. The nations that cursed them, God cursed, and the nations that blessed them, God blessed. (Gen. 12:3) History has certainly confirmed this Biblical prediction and will continue to do so.

Definite signs of his return were numerated by Jesus. They were numerous and easily recognized. As he answered the disciples, Jesus intermingled the signs of the rapture and Revelation. Of course, these are two distinctly different events relating to his coming again. In the rapture, he returns in the heavens to instantly catch away his true followers, and they went to meet him in the air. Then, at the end of the great tribulation, Jesus Christ will literally return to this earth to reign for a thousand years as predicted in Revelation 20. That is known as the revelation of Christ:

> Then I saw an angel coming down from heaven, having the key to the bottomless pit and a great chain in his hand. He laid hold of the dragon, that serpent of old, who is *the* Devil and Satan, and bound him for a thousand years; and he cast him into the bottomless pit, and shut him up, and set a seal on him, so that he should deceive the nations no more till the thousand years were finished. But after these things he must be released for a little while. And I saw thrones, and they sat on them, and judgment was committed to them. Then *I saw* the souls of those who had been beheaded for their witness to Jesus and for the word of God, who had not worshiped the beast or his image, and had not received *his* mark on their foreheads or on their hands. And they lived and reigned with Christ for a thousand years. But the rest of the dead did not live again until the thousand years were finished. This *is* the first resurrection. Blessed and holy *is* he who has part in the first resurrection. Over such the second death has no power, but they shall be priests of God and of Christ, and shall reign with Him a thousand years.
>
> (Revelation 20:1–60)

Ralph Waterman was most concerned with reviewing the Bible passages relating to the rapture, for that is what was confronting him right now. So he searched the Scriptures, first to read again Jesus's Words about his return in the rapture. Ralph understood that the word "rapture" was not found in the Bible, but the event is clearly explained. Here, it is boldly proclaimed:

> And Jesus answered and said to them: "Take heed that no one deceives you. For many will come in My name, saying, 'I am the Christ,' and will deceive many. And you will hear of wars and rumors of wars. See that you are not troubled; for all *these things* must come to pass, but the end is not yet. For nation will rise against nation, and kingdom against kingdom. And there will be famines, pestilences, and earthquakes in various places. All these *are* the beginning of sorrows. "Then they will deliver you up to tribulation and kill you, and you will be hated by all nations for My name's sake. And then many will be offended, will betray one another, and will hate one another. Then many false prophets will rise up and deceive many. And because lawlessness will abound, the love of many will grow cold. But he who endures to the end shall be saved. And this gospel of the kingdom will be preached in all the world as a witness to all the nations, and then the end will come."
>
> (Matthew 24:4–14)

> Then if anyone says to you, "Look, here *is* the Christ!" or "There!" do not believe *it*. For false Christs and false prophets will rise and show great signs and wonders to deceive, if possible, even the elect. See, I have told you beforehand. Therefore if they say to you, "Look, He is in the desert!" do not go out; *or* "Look, *He is* in the inner rooms!" do not believe *it*. For as the lightning comes from the east and flashes to the west, so also will the coming of the Son of Man be. For wherever the carcass is, there the eagles will be gathered together.
>
> (Matthew 24:23–28)

> But of that day and hour no one knows, not even the angels of heaven, but My Father only. But as the days of Noah *were*, so also will the coming of the Son of Man be. For as

in the days before the flood, they were eating and drinking, marrying and giving in marriage, until the day that Noah entered the ark, and did not know until the flood came and took them all away, so also will the coming of the Son of Man be. Then two *men* will be in the field: one will be taken and the other left. Two *women will be* grinding at the mill: one will be taken and the other left. Watch therefore, for you do not know what hour your Lord is coming. But know this, that if the master of the house had known what hour the thief would come, he would have watched and not allowed his house to be broken into. Therefore you also be ready, for the Son of Man is coming at an hour you do not expect.

(Matthew 24:36–44)

As Ralph leaned back in his desk chair, pondering these prophetic signs given by Jesus himself, he recalled that the Gospel of Luke recorded similar words. Determined to recall all that he could about the signs he had evidently overlooked, Ralph turned to Luke 21. And there were more explicit words of Jesus:

And He said: "Take heed that you not be deceived. For many will come in My name, saying, 'I am *He,*' and, 'The time has drawn near.' Therefore do not go after them. But when you hear of wars and commotions, do not be terrified; for these things must come to pass first, but the end *will* not *come* immediately." Then He said to them, "Nation will rise against nation, and kingdom against kingdom. And there will be great earthquakes in various places, and famines and pestilences; and there will be fearful sights and great signs from heaven. But before all these things, they will lay their hands on you and persecute *you,* delivering *you* up to the synagogues and prisons. You will be brought before kings and rulers for My name's sake. But it will turn out for you as an occasion for testimony. Therefore settle *it* in your hearts not to meditate beforehand on what you will answer; for I will give you a mouth and wisdom which all your adversaries will not be able to contradict or resist. You will be betrayed even by parents and brothers, relatives and friends; and they will put *some* of you to death. And you will be hated by all for My name's sake. But not a hair of your head shall be lost. By your patience possess your souls. "But when you see Jerusalem surrounded by armies, then know that its desolation is near. Then let those who are in Judea flee to the mountains, let those who are in the midst of her depart, and let not those who are in the country enter her. For these are the days of vengeance, that all things which are written may be fulfilled. But woe to those who are pregnant and to those who are nursing babies in those days! For there will be great distress in the land and wrath upon this people. And they will fall by the edge of the sword, and be led away captive into all nations. And Jerusalem will be trampled by Gentiles until the times of the Gentiles are fulfilled. "And there will be signs in the sun, in the moon, and in the stars; and on the earth distress of nations, with perplexity, the sea and the waves roaring; men's hearts failing them from fear and the expectation of those things which are coming on the earth, for the powers of the heavens will be shaken. Then they will see the Son of Man coming in a cloud with power and great glory. Now when these things begin to happen, look up and lift up your heads, because your redemption draws near." Then He spoke to them a parable: "Look at the fig tree, and all the trees. When they are already budding, you see and know for yourselves that summer is now near. So you also, when you see these things happening, know that the kingdom of God is near. Assuredly, I say to you, this generation will by no means pass away till all things take place. Heaven and earth will pass away, but My words will by no means pass away. "But take heed to yourselves, lest your hearts be weighed down with carousing, drunkenness, and cares of this life, and that Day come on you unexpectedly. For it will come as a snare on all those who dwell on the face of the whole earth. Watch therefore, and pray always that you may be counted worthy to escape all these things that will come to pass, and to stand before the Son of Man."

(Luke 21:8–36)

The last verse that Ralph read troubled him tremendously. Tears filled his eyes as he realized that he could have been rapture ready and "counted worthy to escape all these things that will come to pass," just as Madeline had been, and was gone.

In addition to the teachings of Jesus giving the signs of his return in the rapture, as well as the Revelation, the Holy Spirit had inspired other New Testament writers to share signs of the return of Jesus for the benefit of mankind:

Now, brethren, concerning the coming of our Lord Jesus Christ and our gathering together to Him, we ask you, not to be soon shaken in mind or troubled, either by spirit or by word or by letter, as if from us, as though the day of Christ had come. Let no one deceive you by any means; for *that Day will not come* unless the falling away comes first, and the man of sin is revealed, the son of perdition, who opposes and exalts himself above all that is called God or that is worshiped, so that he sits as God in the temple of God, showing himself that he is God.

(2 Thessalonians 2:1–4)

Ralph readily realized that both the rapture and Revelation were alluded to in these verses. The "falling away" would precede the rapture and the "man of sin," or antichrist, will be revealed in the great tribulation preceding Christ's return to earth in the Revelation to reign for a thousand years.

He then turned to 1 and 2 Timothy to find additional signs of Jesus' return:

Now the Spirit expressly says that in latter times some will depart from the faith, giving heed to deceiving spirits and doctrines of demons, speaking lies in hypocrisy, having their own conscience seared with a hot iron, forbidding to marry, *and commanding* to abstain from foods which God created to be received with thanksgiving by those who believe and know the truth. For every creature of God *is* good, and nothing is to be refused if it is received with thanksgiving; 5 for it is sanctified by the word of God and prayer.

(1 Timothy 4:1–5)

But know this, that in the last days perilous times will come: For men will be lovers of themselves, lovers of money, boasters, proud, blasphemers, disobedient to parents, unthankful, unholy, unloving, unforgiving, slanderers, without self-control, brutal, despisers of good, traitors, headstrong, haughty, lovers of pleasure rather than lovers of God, having a form of godliness but denying its power. And from such people turn away! For of this sort are those who creep into households and make captives of gullible women loaded down with sins, led away by various lusts, always learning and never able to come to the knowledge of the truth.

(2 Timothy 3:1–7)

I charge *you* therefore before God and the Lord Jesus Christ, who will judge the living and the dead at His appearing and His kingdom: Preach the word! Be ready in season *and* out of season. Convince, rebuke, exhort, with all longsuffering and teaching. For the time will come when they will not endure sound doctrine, but according to their own desires, *because* they have itching ears, they will heap up for themselves teachers; and they will turn *their* ears away from the truth, and be turned aside to fables. But you be watchful in all things, endure afflictions, do the work of an evangelist, fulfill your ministry.

(2 Timothy 4:1–5)

As Ralph researched the Bible further, he came to an important passage concerning the signs of Christ's return in 2 Peter and Jude:

> Beloved, I now write to you this second epistle (in *both of* which I stir up your pure minds by way of reminder), that you may be mindful of the words which were spoken before by the holy prophets, and of the commandment of us, the apostles of the Lord and Savior, knowing this first: that scoffers will come in the last days, walking according to their own lusts, and saying, "Where is the promise of His coming? For since the fathers fell asleep, all things continue as *they were* from the beginning of creation."
>
> (2 Peter 3:3–4)

> But you, beloved, remember the words which were spoken before by the apostles of our Lord Jesus Christ: how they told you that there would be mockers in the last time who would walk according to their own ungodly lusts. These are sensual persons, who cause divisions, not having the Spirit.
>
> (Jude 1:17–19)

Signs of the nearness of Christ's return were so prevalent that they could not be ignored. Jesus said that when days like the days of Noah were duplicated, you will know that his coming is near. Then, he related the trends of Noah's day:

> But of that day and hour no one knows, not even the angels of heaven, but My Father only. But as the days of Noah *were,* so also will the coming of the Son of Man be. For as in the days before the flood, they were eating and drinking, marrying and giving in marriage, until the day that Noah entered the ark, and did not know until the flood came and took them all away, so also will the coming of the Son of Man be.
>
> (Matthew 24:36–39)

History reveals that there have been some signs of Christ's return in every generation or age. However, Jesus said that there would be a single generation that would behold all the stated signs of his return. Ralph looked at the Words of Jesus again, trying to ascertain their significance:

> So you also, when you see all these things, know that it is near—at the doors! Assuredly, I say to you, this generation will by no means pass away till all these things take place.
>
> (Matthew 24:33–34)

And the Gospel of Luke records the pointed words of Jesus concerning the same period of which to be aware:

> Then He spoke to them a parable: "Look at the fig tree, and all the trees. When they are already budding, you see and know for yourselves that summer is now near. So you also, when you see these things happening, know that the kingdom of God is near. Assuredly, I say to you, this generation will by no means pass away till all things take place. Heaven and earth will pass away, but My words will by no means pass away."
>
> (Luke 21:29–33)

Many Bible scholars believed that the fig tree was a reference to Israel. They also believed that when they were revived as a nation, it would mark the beginning of the final generation leading up to the return of Christ. And that took place May 14, 1948, when Israel was recognized as a viable nation by the United States and the United Nations.

Of course, the disciples of Jesus assumed that he was assuring them of his return in their generation. However, beyond question, that is not what Jesus was teaching. "Many generations have passed, and Jesus had just returned today," Ralph regretfully remembered. Everything had been fulfilled, enabling Jesus to return in the clouds of heaven and catch away his true followers, today.

Ralph went back over the Scriptures he had just read, jotting down the evident signs related by Jesus and the other New Testament authors. It was a staggering summary. Jesus spoke of wars and rumors of war, civil strife as kingdom opposes kingdom, great earthquakes in various places, famines, pestilences or outbreaking diseases, along with persecution of the righteous. Also, Jesus said to watch for hatred, murders and betrayal of one another, many false prophets arising deceiving many, lawlessness abounding, and the love for God growing cold in hearts and lives of multitudes. In addition, mankind will see fearful sights and signs in the heavens, men's heart failing them for fear of things coming upon the earth, and distress of nations with perplexity. That means that there will come a time when there are unresolved issues between nations and within them as well. Jesus said to expect the sea and waves to be roaring, the budding fig tree, and all the trees, indicating the birth of many new nations; these were signs that his return was near. The budding fig tree was referring to the revival of Israel as a nation. Again, Ralph was reminded that the repeated conditions of Noah's day were a conclusive sign of the near return of Jesus. "And when the gospel is preached in all the world, the end will come," Jesus promised.

The Apostle Paul, Simon Peter, and Jude gave additional signs of the return of Jesus as inspired and instructed by the Holy Spirit. His return will be preceded by a great spiritual falling away as many will depart from the faith, and many will sear their conscience against the truth of God's Word. Perilous times will be prevalent, and people will become lovers of pleasure more than lovers of God. Also, people will have a form of godliness but deny its power, not enduring sound doctrine, but run after preachers who are praise seekers. And tragically, the day will come when there will even be scoffers mocking the very idea of the return of Jesus Christ.

As Ralph thought on this, he concluded that in his lifetime he had literally beheld all the prophetic signs of Jesus's return, but he had not taken it seriously enough. That final generation that would see all these things probably began with the restoration of Israel or the budding fig tree. Ralph remembered that he was old enough to recall that event although he was a child. It was commonly discussed how strange it was that after thousands of years, the Jews were being given back part of the very lands that God had promised to Abraham and his descendents through Isaac. Possibly, the generation referred to by Jesus included many of those who were alive when Israel again became a nation and would live to see the rapture and beyond.

He was staring out his study window, and a chill shook his whole body, realizing that for some definite reason he had been left, and Madeline along with all the good, godly people of the world were gone.

Thinking along this line, Ralph recalled that the Bible described clearly how the rapture would take place:

> But I do not want you to be ignorant, brethren, concerning those who have fallen asleep, lest you sorrow as others who have no hope. For if we believe that Jesus died and rose again, even so God will bring with Him those who sleep in Jesus. For this we say to you by the word of the Lord, that we who are alive *and* remain until the coming of the Lord will by no means precede those who are asleep. For the Lord Himself will descend from heaven with a shout, with the voice of an archangel, and with the trumpet of God. And the dead in Christ will rise first. Then we who are alive *and* remain shall be caught up together with them in the clouds to meet the Lord in the air. And thus we shall always be with the Lord.
>
> (1 Thessalonians 4:3–17)

Then, Madeline had heard "the trumpet of God," along with every other prepared child of God. As was the case with millions of the world's population, Ralph had not heard the sounding trumpet because he was not ready to meet the Lord. She was gone, and all of them were left. Since there had been no phone calls from their two children or grandchildren, Ralph concluded that fortunately they were also gone. That thought brought some consolation to his troubled mind.

Madeline and many of his friends and family members were not all that was gone. All who were left behind had no hope of evading the torturing torments of the great tribulation into which they were now thrust. Ralph lamented this greatly, but it was too late to alter that troubling fact. There would be no secondary rapture. The parable Jesus gave of the wise and foolish virgins in Matthew 25 convincingly established that truth:

> Then the kingdom of heaven shall be likened to ten virgins who took their lamps and went out to meet the bridegroom. Now five of them were wise, and five *were* foolish. Those who *were* foolish took their lamps and took no oil with them, but the wise took oil in their vessels with their lamps. But while the bridegroom was delayed, they all slumbered and slept. And at midnight a cry was *heard:* "Behold, the bridegroom is coming; go out to meet him!" Then all those virgins arose and trimmed their lamps. And the foolish said to the wise, "Give us *some* of your oil, for our lamps are going out." But the wise answered, saying, "*No*, lest there should not be enough for us and you; but go rather to those who sell, and buy for yourselves." And while they went to buy, the bridegroom came, and those who were ready went in with him to the wedding; and the door was shut. "Afterward the other virgins came also, saying, "Lord, Lord, open to us!" But he answered and said, "Assuredly, I say to you, I do not know you."

> Watch therefore, for you know neither the day nor the
> hour in which the Son of Man is coming.
>
> (Matthew 25:1–13)

Reading this, Ralph sensed that panic was setting in. He had preached all of this, but now he was experiencing the horrors of missing the rapture. Even though he could not escape the inevitable approaching events prophesied concerning the great tribulation, could he be saved and get right with God? "Can I be saved? Can anyone left be saved?" Ralph shouted. Then, as though he thought someone might have heard his frantic shout, he slowly he looked around. Of course, he was still alone and becoming more panicky.

He would have to delve into that thought later. God's Word certainly would clarify that for him. But right now, he had to get out of this house and take a drive his truck, trying to clear his mind of some of the confusion confronting him.

Ralph Discovers Why
He Missed the Rapture

S omberly, Ralph Waterman was determined to get out of that quiet, lonely house, but where could he go or what should he do? He definitely did not want to see anyone who would recognize him. That would be too embarrassing and emotionally draining. Almost everyone Ralph knew would expect him to be gone, but here he was. He would disguise himself as much as possible, for he had to get out of that house, where he was alone with too many haunting thoughts.

Going to a closet, where Ralph had hung some old clothing, he selected a dark-colored coat and an ancient hunting hat. Putting on the coat, turning up the collar, and pulling the old hat down over his forehead, he glanced in a full-length mirror to determine if he was disguised enough. He was.

Ralph trekked to the garage where he got into his recently purchased truck. Backing out of the garage and heading slowly down the street, he became aware that many more people were gravely concerned about recent events. It was evident that many of them were in total confusion, not having the slightest idea of what had happened. Ralph drove slowly, avoiding many people in the streets, but he did not stop to make any inquiry. Farther on, in another neighborhood, there was pandemonium everywhere. People were running wildly in all directions, as if on a wild search. He wanted to stop and shout, "They are gone!" But he kept driving toward the seclusion of the open country to be able to pour over the thoughts that were flooding his mind and causing his racing, pounding heart.

Not seeing other perplexed people along the country road did calm him some. However, it did not change his dilemma. He had missed the rapture and had been left. As he passed a few houses, he noticed that on the porches or in the yards, there seemed to be frantic activity of some kind taking place. He could have stopped and solved their questioning minds, but he kept on driving. Another reminder of the sobering facts that faced all of them did not add any solace to Ralph.

Since he was driving in the direction of the church, where he had pastored last, he would drive by the church and observe what might be going on there. "But someone might see me and recognize me or my truck," he mumbled. However, he became convinced that everyone would be so overwrought with their own turmoil that they would not even notice him. Also, only a few people of his acquaintance even knew about his new truck as it was a very recent acquirement. As far as he knew, those he knew or knew him, would probably be gone, at least he hoped so. Just as he had done hundreds of times during the years he was pastor, Ralph drove on toward the church. But this drive was different.

When Ralph arrived in view of the church, he observed that there was strange activity. The parking lot was filled with vehicles, and parked vehicles lined the sides of the highway. People were milling everywhere. Evidently, the church building was packed with people, some of whom had probably never been there before. In the years Ralph pastored there, he had never seen this many people attend church. Much to his surprise and dismay, he recognized a few of them. Hopefully, none of them would recognize him. That was unlikely since he was in a steady line of slowly moving traffic approaching the church building.

Suddenly, he had to come to a stop since a vehicle in front of him was attempting to find a parking place. "This is not good," he wanted to shout at the traffic ahead of him. He simply wanted to drive by and not stop, but he had no choice.

Begrudgingly, sitting there in the traffic, he noticed that the people outside the church building were gathering in small groups, seriously discussing something. Ralph had little wonder as to what they were discussing. His attention was drawn to a small group of four couples clustered close together talking. Instantly, he recognized them without any delight. Before he thought, he muttered in disgust, "Now there are people who deserve to be left to face the wrath of the great tribulation. What did I just say?" Ralph asked himself. "Why would I even have such a thought, much less speak the words? It was because of what they had done to me and had attempted to do," Ralph was saying, still surprised by his outburst. Like a bolt of lightning, it struck him, as he sat there in his idling, stopped truck. "Forgiveness!"

It's all about forgiveness, no, the lack of forgiveness. That's the reason he had missed the rapture. He had not forgiven them as he thought he had. He sensed his heart racing wildly as a heated feeling flooded his neck and face. When he looked into the rearview mirror of the truck, his face was almost bloodred. At times, these same emotions gripped him when he read the Bible about forgiveness, but he convinced himself that he had forgiven them. He recalled that when he had preached about forgiveness, he had done so cautiously. The words of the Bible seemed to almost shout at him, remembering the parable of Jesus about forgiveness:

> Then Peter came to Him and said, "Lord, how often shall my brother sin against me, and I forgive him? Up to seven times?"
>
> Jesus said to him, "I do not say to you, up to seven times, but up to seventy times seven. Therefore the kingdom of heaven is like a certain king who wanted to settle accounts with his servants. And when he had begun to settle accounts, one was brought to him who owed him ten thousand talents. But as he was not able to pay, his master commanded that he be sold, with his wife and children and

all that he had, and that payment be made. The servant therefore fell down before him, saying, 'Master, have patience with me, and I will pay you all.' Then the master of that servant was moved with compassion, released him, and forgave him the debt.

"But that servant went out and found one of his fellow servants who owed him a hundred denarii; and he laid hands on him and took *him* by the throat, saying, 'Pay me what you owe!' So his fellow servant fell down at his feet and begged him, saying, 'Have patience with me, and I will pay you all.' And he would not, but went and threw him into prison till he should pay the debt. So when his fellow servants saw what had been done, they were very grieved, and came and told their master all that had been done. Then his master, after he had called him, said to him, 'You wicked servant! I forgave you all that debt because you begged me. Should you not also have had compassion on your fellow servant, just as I had pity on you?' And his master was angry, and delivered him to the torturers until he should pay all that was due to him.

"So My heavenly Father also will do to you if each of you, from his heart, does not forgive his brother his trespasses."

(Matthew 18:21–35)

It was verse 35 that rang in Ralph's consciousness with heartbreaking, haunting effect. He had been left because he had not forgiven their trespasses "from his heart." In fact, he continued to be unforgiving, or he would never have thought that they deserved to miss the rapture. Their missing the rapture may have had nothing to do with things done against him, although none of them had ever asked to be forgiven.

But why should he miss the rapture and be left because of what he considered one minor issue? He wasn't sure, but what he resented was the fact that he had been left over one single thing. Evidently, his often quoted statement, to console himself, was not satisfactory. It seemed sensible to say, "I will forgive but never forget." He had remembered and recalled it so much that it was ingrained in his mind. Really, he had no one to blame but himself. He was the one who had harbored resentment and lack of forgiveness in his heart.

Another powerful Scripture about forgiveness is found in Ephesians, "Let all bitterness, wrath, anger, clamor, and evil speaking be put away from you, with all malice. And be kind to one another, tenderhearted, forgiving one another, even as God in Christ forgave you" (Ephesians 4:31–32). Ralph had to consider this nagging truth of the Word of God.

On more than one occasion, Madeline had asked Ralph, "Are you sure that you have forgiven that bunch for what they attempted to do to you? It was a vicious act against you, but you can certainly have victory over it."

And Ralph thought that he did have it all settled. Recalling the resultant facts drove him to prayer many times. He thought that he had given up all his grudges and had gotten victory over grief and guilt.

"What is true forgiveness?" Ralph questioned. Oh, yes, he knew what it meant for he had studied the Bible commentaries and dictionaries often. It meant, "To grant a full pardon for any wrong done to you." It also meant to give up all claim of getting even with or demanding punishing for a transgression. And forgiveness meant to cease feeling resentment toward those who had wronged you and to stop being angry toward an evildoer. Finally, and most importantly, it meant to let go of it all, not constantly contemplating it or discussing it.

Honestly, Ralph could not claim to have done much of the above although he had convinced himself that he had.

Thinking along this line brought to Ralph's mind the encounter of the rich, young ruler, in conversation with Jesus, in the tenth chapter of the Gospel of Mark. Jesus explained the requirements for having eternal life, about which the rich, young ruler inquired. The conclusion of the matter troubled Ralph as much as the rich, young ruler:

> Then Jesus, looking at him, loved him, and said to him, "One thing you lack: Go your way, sell whatever you have and give to the poor, and you will have treasure in heaven; and come, take up the cross, and follow Me."
> But he was sad at this word, and went away sorrowful, for he had great possessions.
>
> (Mark 10:21–22)

"If 'one thing' outside the will of God would keep a person from enjoying 'eternal life,' then one thing would cause anyone to miss the rapture," a conscience-stricken Ralph concluded. Also, there was a solemn warning regarding this in James 2:10, "For whoever shall keep the whole law, and yet stumble in one *point*, he is guilty of all."

Being unforgiving was not considered to be a major sin. In fact, no one else even suspected that he was guilty of not forgiving the personal injuries that had been inflicted upon him. It was very evident that being unforgiving was not a minor issue with God.

Truly, Ralph did sense guilt because of his attitude toward those who had tried to destroy him and his ministry. He had been deeply hurt. Actually, he had told others, even the official church board, that he had forgiven those who had wronged him. But it did not come from his heart, only from his lips.

He had been viciously lied upon and accused of actions, which church records substantiated to be false. If the lies were true, Ralph would have been guilty of a major crime. But the records of the church board conclusively proved that the accusations were not true. However, the lies would not die. More and more members of the congregation began to think, *Where there is smoke, there might be some fire?* or truth to the false rumors. And there were a few church members who enjoyed being members of the rumor mill.

In spite of the facts that proved him innocent, not one church board member came to the Ralph's defense. And that hurt him almost as badly as the vicious falsehood. One board member could have put it to rest with a simple statement. However, nothing was ever said by anyone. Ralph could not believe the unconcerned attitude of the church board members, and he continued to hurt.

He contemplated resigning as pastor and letting it all go, but that did not remedy anything. Actually, that would look like he was guilty and was running from it. He remained as pastor, and the church continued to grow, in spite of about twelve people who resigned and left the congregation, attempting to get others to follow them. None did. Ralph saw this as an affirmation of his leadership and their confidence in him.

The small group Ralph was watching had gone to higher church leadership, attempting to have him removed as pastor. Church leaders were told that Ralph was destroying the church and that it would be closed within a year since this group of twelve had left. Ralph knew all this because copies of the accusing letters were sent to him. Since they could not shatter his leadership, the accusers claimed that it was Ralph's church. They continued attempting to get others to follow them to different churches but without success.

Surprisingly to many, the church did not die. Actually, growth accelerated after the exit of the false accusers. Four years later, when Ralph resigned as pastor, the church attendance and finances were at an all-time record high. The church and Pastor Ralph had received numerous growth awards during the ensuing years. All of that was gratifying to Ralph. No one could claim that the ministry of Ralph Waterman was ineffective or insignificant.

Now Ralph sat staring at these same people since he was stuck in a traffic jam, just north of the church building, which he had simply wanted to drive past. Worst of all, those troublesome thoughts were racing through his mind again. He had not let go of it. He had not forgiven them, and he was left with them to encounter the great tribulation.

What a price to pay for one sin not forgiven. And all who thought that world conditions could get no worse, were tragically mistaken. The worst was just beginning to unfold. Jesus described it, "For then there will be great tribulation, such as has not been since the beginning of the world until this time, no, nor ever shall be" (Matthew 24:21).

Ralph was suddenly shocked back into present reality by the moving traffic ahead of him and blaring horns behind him. Pulling his coat collar higher and the brim of the old hat lower, he moved forward with the traffic now approaching the church building. No one even looked his way, for which he was thankful. The milling multitude was too freaked out by the turmoil facing them to care who was driving by. All of them were alike, in that Jesus had returned, and they had been left.

Having successfully passed the church building and the meandering people, Ralph began to seek a way to move into the left lane of traffic. He desperately wanted to make a U-turn and return to his house.

There was praying and more Bible researching to do. He must find out, from the Word of God, if there was any hope of being saved and becoming a believer after having missed the rapture. Would God hear his prayer of repentance now? Because he never intended to be left, he had not spent much time thinking about post-rapture salvation. Now it must be considered conclusively.

Does the Bible Address
Post-Rapture Salvation?

At last, after passing the church building, Ralph was able to ease into the left lane of bumper to bumper traffic. Finding a median crossover, he headed north toward his house. He was anxious to get to his study and into the Bible, searching for answers to mind-boggling questions. Could anyone be saved after the return of Christ in the rapture? What faced those who were left in the great tribulation? What kind of world order was predicted by the Word of God? The Bible was the only reference book to answer these baffling questions. Ralph was going to dig into it seriously.

The traffic seemed to be creeping along, and Ralph was overly anxious to get home. Horn-honking did not hurry anyone along. He had to resolve himself to patiently go with the flow of the traffic. No one was in a mood to be pushed today. Everyone else was as anxious and bewildered by today's appalling events as Ralph. There were also important persons gone from their lives.

Finally, Ralph was able to turn off the busy four-lane highway onto the street leading to his house. He breathed a sigh of relief that was short-lived. By missing the rapture, he had been ushered into the unknown. "I should have been ready." He sighed.

There were still confused people wandering on the street leading to his house. Neighbors were gathered in yards talking. Ralph was sure of what they were discussing. And he was fearful of what he would find in the Bible about the future for all of them, including himself.

Turning into the driveway, pushing the automatic garage door opener, closing the door behind him, and leaning forward toward the steering wheel of the truck, he sighed, thankful to be home. But he was tormented by the thoughts of the empty house, without Madeline. "How foolish I have been," he mournfully mumbled as he slammed the truck door and headed to the entrance of the lonely house, which had once been a happy home. He was hungry but had no desire to eat anything. Hanging up his coat and old hat, he slumped down into his favorite easy chair. A horrible sensation crept over him. There was no one in the other matching easy chair. He was alone. Madeline definitely was gone for good. But Ralph realized that he was not home to continue lamenting having been left behind but to attempt to discover if there was any hope of being restored to eternal life. In other words, could he be saved now? Again, he reminded himself that the only place to resolve that issue was in the Bible.

Wearily arising from his chair, he again headed toward his study. On the way, passing through the kitchen, he prepared coffee to brew, thinking perhaps that would relieve some of the mental fatigue. Stepping into his study, seating himself at his desk again, he turned to the index of his study Bible to find references to "post-rapture salvation" but soon discovered they did not exist. Ralph lifted his head and stared out the window again, bewildered. Was everything going to continue to be this difficult and delusional? Where would he look now?

The only thing Ralph knew to do was to turn to the Book of Revelation in the Bible. That book was all about the future, revealed by Jesus Christ and angelic beings. Surely there would be something about salvation, following the rapture of the righteous, if that was a possibility. But where should he look? Since he had not spent adequate time reading the book of Revelation, he could not recall any specific Scripture relating to the serious subject in mind. "I will begin and read it all, recording important passages and information," Ralph said out loud to himself.

Remembering the brewing coffee, he headed back into the kitchen and poured himself a cup of black coffee. Sipping the hot coffee, he slowly walked back to his study to delve into some of the most important Bible study of his entire lifetime. His major concern was, "Can I be saved after Jesus has returned and the church is gone?"

Quickly thumbing through the New Testament, to the last book, he began to scan verses to find the subject matter most important to him. However, he stopped that process straight away. He decided that he needed to take time to read every word, fearful that he might overlook an important promise of God concerning post-rapture salvation, and that was his greatest desire. How rewarding it was when he read the encouraging words from Revelation 1:3, "Blessed *is* he who reads and those who hear the words of this prophecy, and keep those things which are written in it; for the time *is* near."

The blessing Ralph wanted from God was to be forgiven and to be saved. He would read on word for word. *If I can find evidence of others being saved in the great tribulation, then there is hope for my salvation*, he thought with renewed anticipation.

In Revelation 3, Ralph was brought face-to-face with what he had missed, in the message to the church in Philadelphia. There it was in bold print:

> Because you have kept My command to persevere, I also will keep you from the hour of trial which shall come upon the whole world, to test those who dwell on the earth. Behold, I am coming quickly! Hold fast what you have, that no one may take your crown. He who overcomes, I will make him a pillar in the temple of My God, and he shall go out no more. I will write on him the name of My God and the name of the city of My God, the New Jerusalem, which comes down out of heaven from My God. And *I will write on him* My new name.
>
> (Revelation 3:10–12)

This passage of God's Word related to what Ralph found later in Revelation 19:

> Then he said to me, "Write: 'Blessed *are* those who are called to the marriage supper of the Lamb!'" And he said to me, "These are the true sayings of God."
>
> (Revelation 19:9)

In addition, Ralph recalled important words of Jesus in Luke 21 relating to Christ's warning to prepare to be ready for his return and to avoid the things coming upon the earth:

> But take heed to yourselves, lest your hearts be weighed down with carousing, drunkenness, and cares of this life and that Day come on you unexpectedly. For it will come as a snare on all those who dwell on the face of the whole earth. Watch therefore, and pray always that you may be counted worthy to escape all these things that will come to pass, and to stand before the Son of Man.
>
> (Luke 21:34–36)

Madeline and all the missing who had gone to meet their Lord at the marriage supper of the lamb were going to avoid the terrible tortures and testing of the great tribulation. Thoughts of what he understood of the tribulation period struck terror to his soul. He could have been an overcomer and kept from the hour of trial, which shall come upon the whole world. But that was only a haunting memory. If he can just get back to God and be saved was paramount at the present. So he kept on reading.

Revelation 6 brought a ray of hope to Ralph, which read:

> When He opened the fifth seal, I saw under the altar the souls of those who had been slain for the word of God and for the testimony which they held. And they cried with a loud voice, saying, "How long, O Lord, holy and true, until You judge and avenge our blood on those who dwell

on the earth?" Then a white robe was given to each of them; and it was said to them that they should rest a little while longer, until both *the number of* their fellow servants and their brethren, who would be killed as they *were,* was completed.

(Revelation 6:9–11)

Ralph was convinced that some of the souls of these martyrs had given their lives because of their faith in God during the great tribulation. It was very evident that more would be martyred for their testimony of faith in God in the future, and that was after the rapture. All he wanted to do was get right with God and have an inner resolve and robustness to be one of them, if required to do so. Eagerly, he read on, as the Word of God was igniting hope within him.

In the very next chapter of Revelation, Ralph read extremely exciting words telling of a great multitude that were saved during the great tribulation:

> After these things I looked, and behold, a great multitude which no one could number, of all nations, tribes, peoples, and tongues, standing before the throne and before the Lamb, clothed with white robes, with palm branches in their hands, and crying out with a loud voice, saying, "Salvation *belongs* to our God who sits on the throne, and to the Lamb!" All the angels stood around the throne and the elders and the four living creatures, and fell on their faces before the throne and worshiped God, saying:
> "Amen! Blessing and glory and wisdom,
> Thanksgiving and honor and power and might,
> *Be* to our God forever and ever.
> Amen."
> Then one of the elders answered, saying to me, "Who are these arrayed in white robes, and where did they come from?"
> And I said to him, "Sir, you know."

So he said to me, "These are the ones who come out of the great tribulation, and washed their robes and made them white in the blood of the Lamb. Therefore they are before the throne of God, and serve Him day and night in His temple. And He who sits on the throne will dwell among them. They shall neither hunger anymore nor thirst anymore; the sun shall not strike them, nor any heat; for the Lamb who is in the midst of the throne will shepherd them and lead them to living fountains of waters. And God will wipe away every tear from their eyes.

(Revelation 7:9–17)

Ralph was determined to be one of that number, for if they could be saved, so could he. For sure, he could not escape the time of trouble coming upon the world, but he could escape the final doom of hell. He could spend eternity with his Lord and would! Whatever the cost, he would meet those conditions and be saved!

Revelation 9 revealed that there were people with the mark of God upon their forehead and those without it. That surely meant that some were right with God, while multitudes were not. For the demonic locust-like creatures, released from the abyss, were commanded not to harm or hurt those who were right with God. No doubt, this will incur additional persecution and passionate ire from the ungodly and their leaders.

Then the fifth angel sounded: And I saw a star fallen from heaven to the earth. To him was given the key to the bottomless pit. And he opened the bottomless pit, and smoke arose out of the pit like the smoke of a great furnace. So the sun and the air were darkened because of the smoke of the pit. Then out of the smoke locusts came upon the earth. And to them was given power, as the scorpions of the earth have power. They were commanded not to harm the grass of the earth, or any green thing, or any tree, but only those men who do not have the seal of God on their foreheads. And they were not given *authority* to kill them, but to torment them *for* five months. Their torment *was* like the torment of a scorpion when it strikes a man. In those days men will seek death and will not find it; they will desire to die, and death will flee from them.

(Revelation 9:1–6)

That was one torment that Ralph was determined to avoid, for he was going to get right with God, whatever it might take. He astutely observed that those having the seal of God, must have been saved after the rapture, for all who were right with God at the time of Christ's return, were taken to the marriage supper of the lamb. Only the lost were left.

He was now convinced that those who had missed the rapture could be saved. According to the Bible, multitudes would get right with God and maintain a testimony of faith in God, even at the cost of their lives. However, he wanted to read on and see what else God's Word revealed about post-rapture salvation.

Ralph was reminded in Revelation 11 that there would be two outstanding witnessing prophets proclaiming the Word of God and performing miraculous feats. It is almost an unbelievable utterance, but the following is a true prophecy of God:

"And I will give *power* to my two witnesses, and they will prophesy one thousand two hundred and sixty days, clothed in sackcloth."

These are the two olive trees and the two lampstands standing before the God of the earth. And if anyone wants to harm them, fire proceeds from their mouth and devours their enemies. And if anyone wants to harm them, he must be killed in this manner. These have power to shut heaven, so that no rain falls in the days of their prophecy; and they have power over waters to turn them to blood, and to strike the earth with all plagues, as often as they desire.

When they finish their testimony, the beast that ascends out of the bottomless pit will make war against them, overcome them, and kill them. And their dead bodies *will lie* in the street of the great city which spiritually is called Sodom and Egypt, where also our Lord was crucified. Then *those* from the peoples, tribes, tongues, and nations will see their dead bodies three-and-a-half days, and not allow their dead bodies to be put into graves. And those who dwell on the earth will rejoice over them, make merry, and send gifts to one another, because these two prophets tormented those who dwell on the earth.

Now after the three-and-a-half days the breath of life from God entered them, and they stood on their feet, and great fear fell on those who saw them. And they heard a loud voice from heaven saying to them, "Come up here." And they ascended to heaven in a cloud, and their enemies saw them. In the same hour there was a great earthquake, and a tenth of the city fell. In the earthquake seven thousand people were killed, and the rest were afraid and gave glory to the God of heaven.

Revelation 11:3–13)

Ralph had to pause and think about this prophetic passage. Reaching for Bible commentaries, he wanted to survey what learned men concluded concerning this particular Scripture. First of all, who were these two witnesses? No one could be sure since the Bible did not identify them. However, there seemed to be general consensus that they were possibly either Moses and Elijah or Enoch and Elijah since neither of these had physically died. It seemed more likely that it was the spirit of Moses and Elijah that rested upon these two men of God. That made sense to Ralph since the Bible taught that John the Baptist was the forerunner of Jesus, with the spirit of Elijah resting upon him. And Jesus had identified John as the promised Elijah, in Matthew 17:10–12.

Whoever they will be, they will be God-appointed, God-anointed, God-affirmed, and with God's authority. Their message will be one of warning, condemning sin, and proclaiming salvation through Jesus Christ, accompanied with miraculous signs and wonders. They will prophesy for three and one half years. God will raise them up specifically for a great tribulation prophecy and ministry. Since their ministry will be so effective, the Antichrist and his followers will be enraged against them. But these men of evil will be unable to hinder their words and work or hurt them for their appointed time of ministry. In fact, it is probably because of their effective witnessing that 144,000 Jews are converted, as recorded in Revelation 7.

Prime-time TV will be interrupted by the two witnesses worldwide warning people of the impending wrath of God, wooing them to repent of their sinfulness, and turning to God by faith in Jesus Christ the Lord. TV personnel will have no power to black out their messages as they are under the mastery of God. The Word of God will be spreading to the ends of the earth, and many will become genuine believers.

Although the evil authorities will have no power over God's two witnesses, many believers will be martyred because of their testimony of faith. But that will be deliverance from a world reeling under the curse and wrath of God in tribulation like never has been. And every martyred soul will go to be with the Lord forever.

When the proclamations of the two witnesses are completed, they will be killed in the city of Jerusalem. No doubt, the whole world will witness this dastardly deed by TV. Their enemies will leave their dead bodies in the street for three and one half days to be viewed by the world. Rejoicing will break out because of their death but impending doom awaits these mockers. After three and one half days, the world will view the strangest reality scene ever played out on TV. The two bodies of the slain witnesses will begin to stir, shaking off death, and come to life to the utter unbelief of their enemies and the Antichrist. An even more fearful sight grips the worldwide viewers when the two witnesses ascend into the heavens. That is immediately followed by a mighty earthquake, killing seven thousand people.

Turning to Revelation 13, Ralph discovered more evidence that people could and would be saved in the great tribulation. There will be those in the tribulation whose names will be recorded in heaven:

> It was granted to him to make war with the saints and to overcome them. And authority was given him over every tribe, tongue, and nation. All who dwell on the earth will worship him, whose names have not been written in the Book of Life of the Lamb slain from the foundation of the world.
>
> If anyone has an ear, let him hear. He who leads into captivity shall go into captivity; he who kills with the sword must be killed with the sword. Here is the patience and the faith of the saints.
>
> (Revelation 13:7–10)

The above passage is referring to the Antichrist's hatred and ultimate victory over righteous believers. However, there will be those whose names have been written in the Book of Life because they remained true to their faith in God, refusing to worship the haughty Antichrist. They must have been saved in the great tribulation, for at the time of Jesus's return in the rapture, all the saved on earth were caught up to meet him in the air. Ralph was becoming more encouraged as he continued reading the Word of God in Revelation. He became determined that his name would also be recorded in the lamb's Book of Life.

Revelation 14 enlightened and encouraged Ralph even more. God will not only empower his two witnesses to preach the gospel, but he will commission angels to do the same. He was filled with incredible joy as he read the following verses:

> Then I saw another angel flying in the midst of heaven, having the everlasting gospel to preach to those who dwell on the earth—to every nation, tribe, tongue, and people—saying with a loud voice, "Fear God and give glory to Him,

for the hour of His judgment has come; and worship Him who made heaven and earth, the sea and springs of water."

And another angel followed, saying, "Babylon is fallen, is fallen, that great city, because she has made all nations drink of the wine of the wrath of her fornication."

Then a third angel followed them, saying with a loud voice, "If anyone worships the beast and his image, and receives *his* mark on his forehead or on his hand, he himself shall also drink of the wine of the wrath of God, which is poured out full strength into the cup of His indignation. He shall be tormented with fire and brimstone in the presence of the holy angels and in the presence of the Lamb. And the smoke of their torment ascends forever and ever; and they have no rest day or night, who worship the beast and his image, and whoever receives the mark of his name."

Here is the patience of the saints; here *are* those who keep the commandments of God and the faith of Jesus.

Then I heard a voice from heaven saying to me, "Write: 'Blessed *are* the dead who die in the Lord from now on."

(Revelation 14:6–13)

It was self-evident that if there was not hope of being saved, there would be no need for an angel to preach the gospel to every nation, tribe, and people. Nor would there be any reason for an angel to warn mankind about receiving the mark of the beast. That one act seemed to be the final test of faith for mankind. Receiving or not receiving the mark of the beast will be a personal choice that will determine one's eternal destiny.

God seemed to be using a final, spectacular means to save mankind. Many are converted because of the angelic message, but multitudes will reject God's efforts, receiving the mark of the beast, sealing their eternal doom forever. Also, God is reminding mankind that world conditions and torments are going to become so bad that death, as a martyr, will literally be a blessing.

Without any further searching, Ralph Waterman was thoroughly convinced that he could be saved, along with any others who would turn to the Lord. He knew the plan of salvation well, for he had presented it repeatedly during his time serving as a pastor. Sitting with his head in his hands, he thought in his mind that he was going over what the Bible said about being saved.

"Repent therefore and be converted, that your sins may be blotted out" (Acts 3:19) immediately came to mind. That was exactly what he needed and desired. Then Ralph recalled 1 John 1:9, which said, "If we confess our sins, He is faithful and just to forgive us *our* sins and to cleanse us from all unrighteousness." He was also blessed by the words of Jesus to Nichodemus in John 3:

> For God so loved the world that He gave His only begotten Son, that whoever believes in Him should not perish but have everlasting life. For God did not send His Son into the world to condemn the world, but that the world through Him might be saved.
>
> (John 3:16–17)

God offered salvation in a simple yet effective way. It included confession of one's sins or admitting to the wrongness of acts of sin. So without making any personal excuses, Ralph confessed to having handled a bad situation wrongly.

Now there was the need for repentance, asking for God's forgiveness, including a willingness to turn from his sins. His repentance included asking forgiveness for harboring hurt feelings and resentments for so long. Ralph also he repented of self-denial when God's Holy Spirit dealt with him about that issue.

The final step he must take involved believing the Word and work of God through Jesus Christ by faith. Those three steps appropriated the saving grace of God. Ralph had done that before, finding forgiveness and acceptance by God. He would do that again, right now, for there were no exceptions as to time or place to be saved. There was nothing he had found in the Bible that limited being saved in the great tribulation. In fact, everything he found in the Bible encouraged mankind to turn to God even then.

Remorsefully and tearfully, Ralph slipped out of his chair, knelt with his head buried in his hands, and began to pray to God. He confessed his wrong attitude and not forgiving those who had insulted and injured him. He repented in sorrow for allowing such insignificant insults to become sin in his heart. Vocally, he expressed faith and confidence that God was hearing him and believing with all his heart that God saved him right then. How could God's Word be any plainer than revealed in 1 John 5?

> Now this is the confidence that we have in Him, that if we ask anything according to His will, He hears us. And if we know that He hears us, whatever we ask, we know that we have the petitions that we have asked of Him.
>
> (1 John 5:14–15)

Looking up toward the heavens, through his tears, Ralph thanked God for hearing him and saving him. Wiping tears from his face, sensing a heavy load had been lifted from his heart, he became conscious that the long pent-up, passionate resentment was melting away. Actually, he felt like a new man, and he was.

Suddenly, he realized that he was no longer alone in that big house. God was with him. His responding to God, confessing, and repenting meant spiritual victory, but that likely meant persecution and possibly death at the hands of the Antichrist and his followers. Being saved did not remove him from the horrors of the great tribulation, but it did extract the hatred and lack of forgiveness from his heart. Along with the inner peace and joy, there was a burning desire to share what God had done for him with others. He must find a way to help others experience the saving grace of God.

It was quite possible that many others were not sure if they could be saved after the rapture, like he had been. Many preachers had preached that there was no hope of salvation after the return of Jesus in the rapture. Much of that was due to a misunderstanding of Matthew 25 concerning the shut door. The shut door simply meant that there will be no one taken in rapture, after the second coming of Christ. Also, the repeated emphasis of Jesus, stressing being ready and watchful for his return, caused some to conclude that there probably was no post-resurrection salvation. Jesus wanted people to be ready for the rapture, to avoid the horrors of the great tribulation, and to participate in the blessings of the marriage supper or the lamb.

Since Ralph had delved deeply into the Word of God, he had discovered and personally experienced God's great salvation. He must share it. Ralph had carefully noted the Scriptures that had convincingly given him spiritual insight, the hope of being saved, and that led him back to God. It was this Biblical good news that was driving him to find a way to share it.

Ralph Addressed Concerned People about Being Saved After the Rapture

Ralph decided to take another drive in his truck, not to simply get out of the lonely house; he was on a mission. He was going to drive back to the church he had once pastored. It was the same church he had driven past just a few hours earlier. However, this time he would not be a mere observer nor would he have condemnation for anyone he might see. He had a message of hope from the Word of God to share with anyone present.

That trip to the church was like old times. He had a message to deliver. It was late in the afternoon as Ralph drove south toward the church building. Traffic was not as terrible as it had been earlier that morning. Evidently, people were beginning to accept the reality of what had taken place and were going on with their lives the best they could. Little did they know how life-changing the major event of that day would be.

When he arrived in the vicinity of the church building, it was evident that many people were gone, for there were no vehicles parked everywhere. But as he turned into the driveway of the church, the parking lot was partially filled. For some reason, several people were still present.

Ralph sat in the silence of his parked truck, wondering what effect his presence would have upon the people in the church. He even wondered what effect it would have upon him. Swinging himself out of the truck, he slowly walked toward the front door of the church.

No one was outside to be seen or to see him. Ever so slowly he opened one of the glass doors and stepped into the foyer. It was empty, but the sanctuary doors were open. The sanctuary was almost filled with bewildered, brokenhearted people, some of whom he recognized. Again, he sensed surprise at seeing that they had been left but not nearly as surprised as they would be at seeing him. Almost every head was bowed in prayer or deep thought. Many heads were resting on the back of the pew in front of them. A few were staring straight ahead as if their vision was transfixed on the large wooden cross affixed to the front wall behind the platform. One could only wonder what they were thinking. It was not a pleasant sight. The only sounds were sobs, moans, and, once in a while, even a wail. This was a troubled confused congregation.

Ralph quietly stepped into the sanctuary and slowly walked down the far right aisle where he planned to be seated on an empty front pew. As he passed by the ends of the pews, on his way down the aisle, he heard murmuring and saw them elbowing one another, drawing attention to his presence. He could only guess what they were thinking and whispering.

As he first entered the sanctuary, he had spotted two of the couples who had done him so much harm. They were sitting about midway in the center section of pews. Strangely, there were no feelings of resentment or disgust welling up within him. Instead, there was a longing to help them and a feeling of love and respect for them. All of that was a definite confirmation of a radical change in the heart of Ralph Waterman. He truly was a converted man. The experience alone with God in his study a few hours earlier had been effective.

Suddenly, someone shouted, "Pastor Ralph, what are you doing here? Why are you not gone, like our pastor? Don't you know Jesus has come, and all of us have been left?"

As he scanned the congregation, Ralph stopped momentarily and simply glanced at the shouter who was standing. In that scan of the congregation, he spotted the other couples who had attempted to destroy him and his ministry. He had no hatred toward them. He even felt sorrowful that they had been left to encounter the great tribulation, like himself. But he continued onto his destination on the front pew. He did not respond to the shouter. All he wanted to do was help the entire congregation to understand that they could get right with God and be saved, just as he had. There would be a proper time for explanations. That congregation was gathered out of fear and frustration as to what to do or expect. They desperately desired hope and help, and fortunately, Ralph had that to offer them through the grace of God.

Ralph sat alone on the front pew, staring at the pulpit from which he had preached in days past. Quietly, someone sat down beside him, saying nothing for several minutes. Finally, the person whispered, "Pastor Ralph, our pastor is gone. We are left without anyone to give us directions or explain what we should do. Could you help us, or is there any help or hope left for us, Pastor Ralph?" Wiping tears and staring hopefully at Ralph, he awaited an answer. *But was there an answer?*

"Yes, I have a message of hope, which I found in the Bible earlier today. Alone, since Madeline is gone, I desperately searched the Word of God, determined to find out if our dire situation is fatal, and I found the answer," Ralph replied. He continued, "Do you think it would be all right to speak to the people? After all, I'm not the pastor any longer. However, since your pastor is gone, no doubt in the rapture, he will not be back. He is with the Lord, but we are not fatally lost without hope of salvation. For sure, we have missed God's best plan for us and face some tortuous days, but we are not forgotten by God. We can be saved!"

"Oh, please do," his friend responded. "We have been here all day waiting for help, but none of us knows what to do. God must have sent you back here to speak to us and give us instructions," the friend said hopefully.

Pastor Ralph reached into an inside pocket of his jacket, taking out a piece of paper on which he had jotted down notes from his search of the Bible earlier that day. Glancing at them momentarily, he slowly stood and headed for the steps leading to the platform and familiar pulpit desk. He had taken this short journey often before but under much better circumstances. Back then, the congregation had expected him. Today the congregation is greatly surprised and shocked that he is there. All eyes of the silent congregation were now fixed upon him. *He should be gone!* they were thinking.

When Ralph stepped behind the pulpit desk, there arose a murmur from the crowd. What it meant, he could not comprehend. All he knew to do was raise his hand in an effort for silence so he could speak to them. Silence suddenly settled in. The weary, confused congregation was ready to hear what Pastor Ralph had to say.

First of all, he apologized for being a disappointment to them in even being here, asking for their forgiveness. Then, he related how surprised he was at being present as he had honestly surmised that he had been ready to meet the Lord in the rapture. He confessed to sensing serious feelings of resentment about wrongs, which had been done against him, from time to time. However, he had not considered it serious enough to be a sin, but it was, and he had been left. He explained how the shocking truth had dawned upon him as he passed the church earlier that day. There had been a bitter attitude welling up inside of him when he saw certain people left and gathered in the driveway. It had suddenly dawned upon him that he was guilty of the sin of not forgiving. Yet he had concluded his pastoral prayer each Sunday morning with these words from the Lord's Prayer, "And forgive us our trespasses, as we forgive those who trespass against us." But he had not forgiven from his heart. However, today he could honestly say, "It is all forgiven, and I have experienced confirmation of that fact."

He then asked forgiveness of those he had not forgiven prior to the rapture. He had let go of it all and had peace within his heart where there had previously been hurt and hate. Ralph encouraged everyone to examine their heart and honestly determine why they had been left. He admitted to them how painful that might be but emphasized it must be done. That had been the beginning point of his return to a right relationship with God.

Further, referring to his scribbled notes, he went on to share with the congregation how he had come to the conclusion that he could be saved even though the Lord had returned and the saints were gone. Ralph asked the people to share the pew Bibles with one another and follow along with him as he read the Word of God. Hopefully, they would see and understand that they could be saved just as he had a few hours earlier. He began to read from the Bible the results of his search to determine whether or not he could be saved now. As they read passage after passage, he could sense light and hope dawning upon the congregation. Tears of joy could be seen on many faces while others wiped their eyes to be able to see the Word of God more clearly. It was obvious that many of the people were ready to become born-again believers, and that overjoyed Ralph.

He concluded his brief message by relating how he had knelt in prayer to God, confessing his desperate need of him, and the hidden sin of his heart. Along with acknowledging his sin, he sincerely repented, seeking God's forgiveness. Finally, Ralph said, "I put complete confidence in God and his Word, believing with all my being that he heard my prayer and saved me! When I did that, I became aware of a heavy burden of guilt and condemnation lifted from my heart. Now I can confidently say that God saved me through the blood of his son, the Lord Jesus Christ. I do not know what I may face in this time of turmoil and tribulation, but I am confident that God will be with me, giving me courage and enabling me to be victorious."

Pausing as if overcome with joyous emotion, Ralph looked at the audience with sympathy and encouragement. He said, "All of you can be saved today if you will turn to the Lord with all your heart and follow his simple plan of salvation. If you now understand that you can be saved and urgently desire to get right with God today, please stand. Then, I will ask you to pray a simple, sincere sinner's prayer with me, from your heart. I will pray the prayer, a phrase at a time, giving you time to sincerely pray, following me."

There was a shuffling of feet, as almost everyone in the congregation stood, ready to follow Ralph in prayer. For many, it would be the first time they had ever prayed such a prayer or prayed at all. Giving them time to get adjusted, Ralph encouraged them to follow every word of the prayer in which he would lead them. They were to pray vocally, focusing upon the desire and intent of their heart, which was to be saved by the grace of God.

With his head bowed in humility, Ralph began to pray, pausing between every phrase to give the people opportunity to think and pray sincerely. "Oh, God, I come to you today in prayer, admitting that I am a lost sinner…I cannot recall every sin I have ever committed, but I am sorry for them all…I confess my need of your forgiveness…I also confess all of my sins and sinfulness to you…I do this because the Bible tells me that you love me and desire to forgive me…your Word clearly says, 'If I will confess my sins, You will forgive me of my sins, and cleanse me from all unrighteousness.' God, not only do I confess my sins, I regret them greatly and repent with godly sorrow…I am willing to turn from all my sins and live for you as a new person by your grace… today, by faith, I claim you as my personal Savior and Lord…I open the door of my heart and invite you to come in and live within me…I do not know what the days ahead hold for me… but I will continue to live for you, believing in you as Savior and Lord of my life…thank you, Lord, for saving me right now, by faith…I am yours, and you are my God! Amen and amen!"

Ralph heard sobs of joy, a chorus of sincere "amens," and even several shouts of praise. Hearts and lives had been changed. People had been saved, in spite of the turmoil in which they found themselves. Every person who knew, by faith, that they were now saved was asked to raise a hand of praise as a testimony to God's saving grace. Hands shot up all over the sanctuary. Ralph was overjoyed to see the upraised hands of the eight people he had not forgiven before. Tears of joy streamed down their faces. He was able to smile at them for the first time in several years, and they returned his smile. Spontaneously, a song began, and almost everyone seemed to be singing, "Jesus saves, Jesus saves."

It was decided that they would meet again next Sunday at 10:30 a. m., and Ralph was to preach. Again, the congregation wanted him to encourage and enlighten them and requested that he again explain that others who had missed the rapture could turn to God and be saved.

After the benediction, four couples quickly made their way to Ralph, asking forgiveness for all the trouble they had caused him and the church. He assured them that they were forgiven, and he meant it from his heart. They were deeply hurt at being the cause of him missing the rapture and being left, and they openly wept about it. Ralph assured them that they were not the cause, personally taking responsibility for not forgiving them, even though they had not sought his forgiveness before. Although he thought he had forgiven them, it had not been from his heart, and that was not their fault. He did not want that thought to enter their minds again.

Later, two of the couples became volunteers for training that would prepare them to teach other believers, led by Ralph's efforts to win and encourage as many as possible in these days of tribulation. In spite of all the turmoil of a troubled world that was reeling without God and under the wrath of God many more might be saved.

The next Sunday, the church building was overflowing with people. And most of those who had been present for the first service had returned. They brought family members and friends with them. In his message, Ralph wanted it clearly understood that this was not God's intended best plan for them. Jesus had preached and urged people to be prepared for his return, enabling them to avoid the horrors of the great tribulation. Although now saved, they must live in a world that was going to be shaken by unimaginable torment and tribulation. Also, as believers, they could expect persecution and, possibly, violent death at the instructions of the Antichrist and his followers. However, he assured them of God's grace to make them victorious rather than mere victims. For evil men could not destroy the soul of a believer in Christ, and to die for one's faith and in faith will instantly usher one's soul into the presence of the Lord. These made up the great multitude that John could not identify in Revelation 6 and 7. Ralph repeated the reading of this important, reassuring Word of God:

> When He opened the fifth seal, I saw under the altar the souls of those who had been slain for the word of God and for the testimony which they held. And they cried with a loud voice, saying, "How long, O Lord, holy and true, until You judge and avenge our blood on those who dwell on the earth?" Then a white robe was given to each of them; and it was said to them that they should rest a little while longer, until both *the number of* their fellow servants and their brethren, who would be killed as they *were,* was completed.
>
> (Revelation 6:9–11)

> After these things I looked, and behold, a great multitude which no one could number, of all nations, tribes, peoples, and tongues, standing before the throne and before the Lamb, clothed with white robes, with palm branches in their hands, and crying out with a loud voice, saying,

"Salvation *belongs* to our God who sits on the throne, and to the Lamb!" All the angels stood around the throne and the elders and the four living creatures, and fell on their faces before the throne and worshiped God, saying:

"Amen! Blessing and glory and wisdom,
Thanksgiving and honor and power and might,
Be to our God forever and ever.
Amen."

Then one of the elders answered, saying to me, "Who are these arrayed in white robes, and where did they come from?"

And I said to him, "Sir, you know."

So he said to me, "These are the ones who come out of the great tribulation, and washed their robes and made them white in the blood of the Lamb. Therefore they are before the throne of God, and serve Him day and night in His temple. And He who sits on the throne will dwell among them. They shall neither hunger anymore nor thirst anymore; the sun shall not strike them, nor any heat; for the Lamb who is in the midst of the throne will shepherd them and lead them to living fountains of waters. And God will wipe away every tear from their eyes.

(Revelation 7:9–17)

When Ralph concluded his message, an invitation was given for anyone who wanted to be saved to move forward to the front of the church to pray. "You need to confess your sins to God, repent of them, and believe upon the Lord Jesus Christ as Savior," Pastor Ralph told them. Many responded, and Ralph prayed the sinner's prayer with them, and by faith, they accepted the Lord Jesus Christ as their personal Savior. Some were kneeling at the church altar, but space was limited; many more stood praying sincerely from their heart. The position of the body does not matter. It is the attitude of one's heart in confession, repentance, and faith in God's promise to save, which appropriates the saving

83

grace of God. Testimonies of spiritual victory were shared by many who were saved.

Before the service was dismissed, there was a chorus of unified prayer to God for grace, strength, and perseverance to live faithful to him in a world that was purposefully turning more and more against him and his followers. Acts of tribulation were taking effect.

They also agreed to meet together for prayer on Wednesday at 6:00 p.m. This would be a time to support each other and encourage new believers. In addition, there would be another church service the following Sunday at 10:30 a.m. At that time, Pastor Ralph would bring another message to inform and inspire them in their journey through the great tribulation with God as their guide and guardian.

Upon leaving, it was evident that they were being observed carefully by a stranger in a strange automobile. He passed the church several times while the congregation vacated the building and parking lot. "Now what could be the significance of that action, if anything?" many of them speculated, including Pastor Ralph. The strange actions did deserve some consideration. Why would they be spied upon? How could they forget the fearful age in which they were now living?

The Wednesday evening prayer service took place uneventfully without any interruptions from outsiders. The congregation left the meeting more determined to maintain their faith in God and live faithfully for him. However, none of them could predict the pathetic events facing them the following Sunday.

The Rise of the Antichrist

World events were changing radically, even unrealistically. The formerly unnoticed European Muslim leader was rising to power in unimaginable proportions. His charismatic personality, powerful speaking ability, problem solving, self-elevation without major objections, and acceptance by most other world leaders were making his words the laws of the world. Very subtly, he was assuming world leadership by intrigue. His face, fame, and words were constantly appearing on every TV screen around the world. In fact, the entire world seemed to be holding him in awe.

As Ralph watched this troubling news on TV, he recalled that Europe was the location of the old Roman Empire. That was significant, for the prophet Daniel had prophesied that the Antichrist would arise from that kingdom. Ralph turned to his study Bible and found the following words literally unfolding before his eyes through the news broadcasts. It is the rise of the Antichrist, who will rule in the great tribulation, empowered by Satan himself:

> Then I wished to know the truth about the fourth beast, which was different from all the others, exceedingly dreadful, *with* its teeth of iron and its nails of bronze, *which* devoured, broke in pieces, and trampled the residue with its feet; and the ten horns that *were* on its head, and the other *horn* which came up, before which three fell, namely, that horn which had eyes and a mouth which spoke pompous words, whose appearance *was* greater than his fellows.

I was watching; and the same horn was making war against the saints, and prevailing against them, until the Ancient of Days came, and a judgment was made *in favor* of the saints of the Most High, and the time came for the saints to possess the kingdom.

"Thus he said:
'The fourth beast shall be
A fourth kingdom on earth,
Which shall be different from all *other* kingdoms,
And shall devour the whole earth,
Trample it and break it in pieces.
The ten horns *are* ten kings
Who shall arise from this kingdom.
And another shall rise after them;
He shall be different from the first *ones,*
And shall subdue three kings.
He shall speak *pompous* words against the Most High,
Shall persecute the saints of the Most High,
And shall intend to change times and law.
Then *the saints* shall be given into his hand
For a time and times and half a time."

(Daniel 7:19–25)

And in the latter time of their kingdom,
When the transgressors have reached their fullness,
A king shall arise,
Having fierce features,
Who understands sinister schemes.
His power shall be mighty, but not by his own power;
He shall destroy fearfully,
And shall prosper and thrive;
He shall destroy the mighty, and *also* the holy people.
Through his cunning
He shall cause deceit to prosper under his rule;
And he shall exalt *himself* in his heart.
He shall destroy many in *their* prosperity.

He shall even rise against the Prince of princes;
But he shall be broken without *human* means.

(Daniel 8:23–25)

Ralph was also directed to the book of Revelation, which foretold of the rise of the Antichrist following the return of Christ in the rapture:

Then I stood on the sand of the sea. And I saw a beast rising up out of the sea, having seven heads and ten horns, and on his horns ten crowns, and on his heads a blasphemous name. Now the beast which I saw was like a leopard, his feet were like *the feet of* a bear, and his mouth like the mouth of a lion. The dragon gave him his power, his throne, and great authority. And I saw one of his heads as if it had been mortally wounded, and his deadly wound was healed. And all the world marveled and followed the beast. So they worshiped the dragon who gave authority to the beast; and they worshiped the beast, saying, "Who *is* like the beast? Who is able to make war with him?"

And he was given a mouth speaking great things and blasphemies, and he was given authority to continue for forty-two months. Then he opened his mouth in blasphemy against God, to blaspheme His name, His tabernacle, and those who dwell in heaven. It was granted to him to make war with the saints and to overcome them. And authority was given him over every tribe, tongue, and nation. All who dwell on the earth will worship him, whose names have not been written in the Book of Life of the Lamb slain from the foundation of the world.

(Revelation 13:1–8)

Studying these Scriptures, Ralph noted several important items he must call to the attention of the congregation at church on Sunday. He must tell all believers to expect severe persecutions and fearful outbreaks of conflict as the Antichrist subdues nation after nation. And there will be changing of times, or the calendar, along with changing of all laws as the Muslim calendar, and laws were instituted by the Antichrist. As a Muslim, the Antichrist will instill the Islamic law of Sharia, which no believing Christian can follow.

Not only has this self-acclaimed world leader assumed control of the European Union, but he is now turning his attention to the United Nations. Many world leaders of the United Nations were already lending strong support to his leadership. Of course, all Muslim nations are the first to follow and support the Antichrist. Even the president of the United States has publicly given a televised speech, supporting this new world leader. Every United State citizen is urged to follow the new directives of the Antichrist as the laws of the land.

The president further declared, administratively, that the new laws of the emerging, changing United Nations will, without question, become the laws of the Unites States of America. The United Nations is soon to become the New World Order led by the Antichrist. This world leadership is achieved by more intrigue and scheming by the Antichrist, who is an empowered genius politically, diplomatically, and as a leader.

Ralph Waterman was amazed that he is seeing all of this developing exactly as the Word of God had predicted. Most of all, he could not believe that he had missed the return of Christ in the rapture and was having to live through this tribulation. But he was, and there was no way to get around it. The saddening thoughts were that it was going to get worse.

God had revealed to the prophet Daniel that the great tribulation would last for seven years, and Jesus, in his preaching, supported the prophecies of Daniel:

> Seventy weeks are determined
> For your people and for your holy city,
> To finish the transgression,
> To make an end of sins,

To make reconciliation for iniquity,
To bring in everlasting righteousness,
To seal up vision and prophecy,
And to anoint the Most Holy.
Know therefore and understand,
That from the going forth of the command
To restore and build Jerusalem
Until Messiah the Prince,
There shall be seven weeks and sixty-two weeks;
The street shall be built again, and the wall,
Even in troublesome times.
And after the sixty-two weeks
Messiah shall be cut off, but not for Himself;
And the people of the prince who is to come
Shall destroy the city and the sanctuary.
The end of it *shall be* with a flood,
And till the end of the war desolations are determined.
Then he shall confirm a covenant with many for one week;
But in the middle of the week
He shall bring an end to sacrifice and offering.
And on the wing of abominations shall be one who makes desolate,
Even until the consummation, which is determined,
Is poured out on the desolate.

(Daniel 9:24–27)

The seventieth week referred to is the final week, each day equaling a year prophetically. Also, the covenant, or peace treaty between the Antichrist and Israel is the same seven-year period of the great tribulation.

It was interesting to Ralph to recall that prior to the return of Christ in the rapture; the self-acclaimed Muslim European leader had been able to broker a peace treaty between Israel and her surrounding Muslim national neighbors. With part of the European Union supporting Israel and the verbal alliance of the United States, Israel relaxed. At last they had peace. They had ignored the word of God, which warned them of impending destruction, recorded in 1 Thessalonians 5:

> But concerning the times and the seasons, brethren, you have no need that I should write to you. For you yourselves know perfectly that the day of the Lord so comes as a thief in the night. For when they say, "Peace and safety!" then sudden destruction comes upon them, as labor pains upon a pregnant woman. And they shall not escape.
>
> (1 Thessalonians 5:1–3)

One of the first items of business for the Antichrist was to sign a seven-year peace treaty with Israel. However, all nations will not be pleased or in compliance with that action. Russia, formerly Gog and Magog, along with Iran, known as Persia until March, 1935, and their allies will be bitter against the Antichrist and Israel over their peace treaty.

Strangely, Israel will not be troubled by the threats of these nations. They feel protected by the European Union, led by the Antichrist, along with the verbal alliance of the United States of America to help defend them if attacked. But will either of these world powers aid them? Iran considered the United States as Big Satan and Israel as Little Satan. Put another way, would it be possible for the Antichrist and his partial control of the European Union and the United States to defend Israel against a massive Russian/Islamic attack?

All of these matters and questions were discussed daily by TV news commentators. The world is watching and waiting to see the outcome. The world, as a whole, is not aware of what God has said about this whole situation in Ezekiel 38 and 39. Actually, the Word of God is never considered by world leaders. The Bible is seen as an archaic book of superstitions, believed only by the less intelligent, unlearned Christians. *What a tragic error.*

The news media reminded the world again of the threat by Iran to wipe Israel off the map. Now that Iran is allied with Russia, they seemed more determined to follow up on this long-standing threat. In spite of all the saber rattling, Israel revels in peace and a false sense of security. For the first time since they miraculously became a revived nation in 1948, they are enjoying peace. All the while, Russia and Iran were planning to attack Israel with a massive army, including their Muslim allies. Their goal was to kill and plunder the riches of Israel rather than destroy with a nuclear attack.

The nuclear attack was intended for the United States. In fact, numerous suitcase nuclear bombs developed by Russia have already been hidden in key cities of the United States. These have been secretly shipped into the United States, hidden in massive ship pallets. It is very evident that every ship pallet cannot be inspected on the shipping docks of the United States. These nuclear suitcase bombs will be detonated simultaneously with the ICBM attack, which evades the massive antimissile system of the United States. From experience, it is known that the antimissile system cannot take out every incoming missile, especially in a massive attack.

Now consider what God says about the imminent attack upon sleeping Israel, who is claiming peace and safety in these early days of the great tribulation. As Ralph read the following Scriptures, he understood that most Bible commentaries and Bible scholars agree that Gog and Magog referred to Russia. The other nations identified are mostly self-evident. So the impending attack upon Israel will be a Russian/Islamic invasion. The prophetic Word of God described this inevitable attack upon Israel very vividly:

"Therefore, son of man, prophesy and say to Gog, 'Thus says the Lord God: "On that day when My people Israel dwell safely, will you not know *it?* Then you will come from your place out of the far north, you and many peoples with you, all of them riding on horses, a great company and a mighty army. You will come up against My people Israel like a cloud, to cover the land. It will be in the latter days that I will bring you against My land, so that the nations may know Me, when I am hallowed in you, O Gog, before their eyes." Thus says the Lord God: "Are *you* he of whom I have spoken in former days by My servants the prophets of Israel, who prophesied for years in those days that I would bring you against them?

"And it will come to pass at the same time, when Gog comes against the land of Israel," says the Lord God, "*that* My fury will show in My face. For in My jealousy *and* in the fire of My wrath I have spoken: 'Surely in that day there shall be a great earthquake in the land of Israel, so that the fish of the sea, the birds of the heavens, the beasts of the field, all creeping things that creep on the earth, and all men who *are* on the face of the earth shall shake at My presence. The mountains shall be thrown down, the steep places shall fall, and every wall shall fall to the ground.' I will call for a sword against Gog throughout all My mountains," says the Lord God. "Every man's sword will be against his brother. And I will bring him to judgment with pestilence and bloodshed; I will rain down on him, on his troops, and on the many peoples who *are* with him, flooding rain, great hailstones, fire, and brimstone. Thus I will magnify Myself and sanctify Myself, and I will be known in the eyes of many nations. Then they shall know that I *am* the Lord."

(Ezekiel 38:14–23)

"And you, son of man, prophesy against Gog, and say, 'Thus says the Lord God: "Behold, I *am* against you, O Gog, the prince of Rosh, Meshech, and Tubal; and I will turn you around and lead you on, bringing you up from the far north, and bring you against the mountains of Israel. Then I will knock the bow out of your left hand, and cause the arrows to fall out of your right hand. You shall fall upon the mountains of Israel, you and all your troops and the peoples who *are* with you; I will give you to birds of prey of every sort and *to* the beasts of the field to be devoured. You shall fall on the open field; for I have spoken," says the

Lord God. "And I will send fire on Magog and on those who live in security in the coastlands. Then they shall know that I *am* the Lord. So I will make My holy name known in the midst of My people Israel, and I will not *let them* profane My holy name anymore. Then the nations shall know that I *am* the Lord, the Holy One in Israel. Surely it is coming, and it shall be done," says the Lord God. "This *is* the day of which I have spoken."

(Ezekiel 39:1–8)

The prophetic attack upon Israel must be early in the great tribulation because God's Word says that it will take Israel seven years to burn the military equipment left by the defeated armies. That is why Ralph realizes the massive attack upon sleeping Israel is imminent.

This act of war and Russian/Islamic attack upon Israel is most likely the same war that is described in Revelation 9:

Then the sixth angel sounded: And I heard a voice from the four horns of the golden altar which is before God, saying to the sixth angel who had the trumpet, "Release the four angels who are bound at the great river Euphrates." So the four angels, who had been prepared for the hour and day and month and year, were released to kill a third of mankind. Now the number of the army of the horsemen *was* two hundred million; I heard the number of them. And thus I saw the horses in the vision: those who sat on them had breastplates of fiery red, hyacinth blue, and sulfur yellow; and the heads of the horses *were* like the heads of lions; and out of their mouths came fire, smoke, and brimstone. By these three *plagues* a third of mankind was killed—by the fire and the smoke and the brimstone which came out of their mouths. For their power is in their mouth and in their tails; for their tails *are* like serpents, having heads; and with them they do harm.

But the rest of mankind, who were not killed by these plagues, did not repent of the works of their hands, that they should not worship demons, and idols of gold, silver, brass, stone, and wood, which can neither see nor hear nor walk. And they did not repent of their murders or their sorceries or their sexual immorality or their thefts.

(Revelation 9:13–21)

Note that verses 17 through 19 gives a perfect description of ICBM (intercontinental ballistic missiles) warfare. If you have ever watched a rocket launch, this Scripture has to leap to your mind. The smoke or vapor trail certainly resembles a snake. And the driving power is in the tail of the rocket, while the destructive power is in the head, where the nuclear device is attached. John, the revelator, had no idea of all that was involved, but God, who revealed his Word to him, understood it perfectly. And Ralph, along with all mankind remaining upon the earth, is just weeks, or at the most months, away from this catastrophic conflict. Getting right with God is vitally important in the face of this inevitable encounter when millions will die.

As Ralph studied and attempted to honestly apply these Biblical prophecies, which were beginning to take place before his eyes and being constantly reported by all means of communication, his reference study Bible referred him to Zechariah 13:

"And it shall come to pass in all the land,"
Says the Lord,
"*That* two-thirds in it shall be cut off *and* die,
But *one*–third shall be left in it:
I will bring the *one*–third through the fire,
Will refine them as silver is refined,
And test them as gold is tested.
They will call on My name,
And I will answer them.
I will say, 'This *is* My people';
And each one will say, 'The Lord *is* my God."

(Zechariah 13:8–9)

Although God will use a multinumber earthquake on the Richter scale, fire and brimstone from heaven, mighty storms, great hailstones, darkness, and confusion among the coalition forces, causing them to literally kill one another, as they attempt to decimate Israel, whom will suffer astounding losses. God said that two thirds of the Jews would be killed. However, God's weapons of nature will destroy the invading forces. One day soon the smirky, defiant smile will disappear from the face of the Russian president. News will be relayed to him of the total decimation of his armies. The coalition forces of evil will be destroyed by the God, which they deny.

God goes on to describe the completeness of the defeat and destruction of the Russian/Islamic armies on the hills and plains of Israel:

> Then those who dwell in the cities of Israel will go out and set on fire and burn the weapons, both the shields and bucklers, the bows and arrows, the javelins and spears; and they will make fires with them for seven years. They will not take wood from the field nor cut down *any* from the forests, because they will make fires with the weapons; and they will plunder those who plundered them, and pillage those who pillaged them," says the Lord God." "It will come to pass in that day *that* I will give Gog a burial place there in Israel, the valley of those who pass by east of the sea; and it will obstruct travelers, because there they will bury Gog and all his multitude. Therefore they will call *it* the Valley of Hamon Gog. For seven months the house of Israel will be burying them, in order to cleanse the land. Indeed all the people of the land will be burying, and they will gain renown for it on the day that I am glorified," says the Lord God. "They will set apart men regularly employed, with the help of a search party, to pass through the land and bury those bodies remaining on the ground, in order to cleanse it. At the end of seven months they will make a search. The search party will pass through the

land; and *when anyone* sees a man's bone, he shall set up a marker by it, till the buriers have buried it in the Valley of Hamon Gog.

(Ezekiel 39:9–15)

Israel will be shocked and stunned that the United States does not come to their aid nor does the Antichrist, who has signed a peace treaty with Israel, who lend help. Perhaps he has not acquired enough military power at this time to confront the invading forces. However, as observed from the Bible, God will come to the aid of Israel.

The United States will cease to have the blessings and protection of God because of their rejection of Israel in their hour of dire need. God had established his attitude and actions toward nations who deny or desert Israel. Genesis 12:1–3 revealed God's changeless covenant. The Word of God is:

Now the Lord had said to Abram:
"Get out of your country,
From your family
And from your father's house,
To a land that I will show you.
I will make you a great nation;
I will bless you
And make your name great;
And you shall be a blessing.
I will bless those who bless you,
And I will curse him who curses you;
And in you all the families of the earth shall be blessed."

(Genesis 12:1–3)

It has become obvious from verbal threats made by Iranian and Russian leaders that they intend to destroy Big Satan and Little Satan at the same time. News reporters are constantly cautioning both Israel and the United States of an impending attack. But it is obvious that the leaders of both nations have been lulled into complacency. They have been threatened before, without follow-up. However, catastrophic conditions are confronting them sooner than they can imagine. Ralph wondered if he would survive the awesome calamity.

Ralph had read the above prophetic Scriptures before but had not paid much attention to them since he had no intention of being on the earth when they were fulfilled. Now, here he is living in the turmoil of the great tribulation. He knows for sure that he is saved, but there is no safety or security in this troubled, tormented world. Many wonder why the strongest, mightiest nation in the world, the United States of America, is not mentioned in the end time prophesies. Considering this, Ralph is convinced that when the Russian/Islamic armies mount a conventional attack against Israel, simultaneously a nuclear attack will take place against the United States. The major cities of the United States will be incapacitated by nuclear explosions. The United States government will be destroyed as Washington, DC, is hit. The financial system of the country will go up in smoke as New York City takes major hits along with Chicago. All major shipping centers like Miami, Los Angeles, New Orleans, Galveston, Philadelphia, and others will be incapacitated by direct nuclear strikes.

The retaliatory strikes by the United States and their allies, from submarines, ships, and land based ICBMs (intercontinental ballistic missiles) will be devastating to Russia, Iran, and the other invading nations. It will be a fulfillment of Ezekiel 39:

> "And I will send fire on Magog and on those who live in security in the coastlands. Then they shall know that I *am* the Lord. So I will make My holy name known in the midst of My people Israel, and I will not *let them* profane My holy name anymore. Then the nations shall know that I *am* the Lord, the Holy One in Israel. Surely it is coming,

and it shall be done," says the Lord God. "This *is* the day of which I have spoken."

(Ezekiel 39:6–8)

It should not be surprising that Revelation 9:18 predicts that one-third of mankind will be killed in this conflict. From that point on, the United States of America will be powerless and posed no threat to the conquests and sovereign reign of the Antichrist. In fact, that early war in the tribulation period will enhance the speedy takeover by the Antichrist since the two major military powers of the world have been all but destroyed.

Antichrist Troubled by Believers
and Closes All Churches

Ralph got up from his desk and walked into the family room to view the latest TV news. The first major news item was the report of a disturbing worldwide spiritual awakening. It seemed to be a spiritual revival of major proportions. That was causing major concern to the emerging Antichrist. To his disgust, thousands were being saved. What had been happening in the church where Ralph was ministering seemed to be taking place around the world. Evidently, millions had been awakened to their spiritual needs but in a terrible time. And immediate steps were being taken to stop this spiritual movement. First of all, every church or meeting place of believers was to be closed immediately, and there were to be no gatherings of believers anywhere.

In addition to ordering all churches closed, there could be no proselytizing. The Antichrist had decreed that anyone caught proselytizing would be punished by death. He was the only one to be worshiped, and his word was the final authority worldwide.

The Antichrist could close the churches and squelch much of the witnessing for Christ, but he could not silence God's two witnesses for three and one half years. Much to his dismay, the gospel will continue to be proclaimed worldwide. TV screens around the world will blink a few times during prime time, and there will be one of God's witnesses proclaiming the gospel. No station managers, nor the Antichrist, are able to cancel the programs and messages nor can the TV sets be turned off. This is the Lord's doing, and his message is going to be proclaimed. As all powerful as the Antichrist thinks himself to be, he can only do what God permits.

Ralph turned his thoughts to the Sunday service that has already been scheduled. Will they be allowed to have one final service? There is so much that he needs to share with the believers, alerting them to major upcoming events of the great tribulation. They must prepare themselves for turbulent days ahead. There will be no hope for spiritual weaklings as all the forces of Satan will be unleashed against them through the growing power and authority of the Antichrist. Every day more of the world is turning to him as their leader.

Sunday arrived, and Ralph readied himself to drive to the church. Would anyone be present since they had seen and heard that all churches were to be closed? When he drove within view of the church, much to his delight, there were several vehicles in the parking lot, and more were arriving. Upon entering the church, the foyer was empty. But as he entered the sanctuary, he was pleased to see that it was already half filled, and it was thirty minutes before starting time.

Ralph was anxious for the service to begin as he had prepared well to alert and assist the congregation. By 10:30, the sanctuary was almost filled. Sitting on the platform, Ralph scanned the audience to see if there were any strangers who should have his special attention.

During the first congregational song, two strange men walked into the sanctuary, seating themselves separately on either side of the church. Ralph noticed that they were observing everyone present with special interest. They were also constantly writing notes on legal pads. They stood out and were cautiously observed by everyone sitting around them. It was evident that no one knew who they were. Ralph could tell that there was fear in the eyes of many.

The church service continued uninterrupted through the singing, prayer, and a special solo by a member of the congregation.

When Ralph stood to speak, the two men stood and walked defiantly to the front of the sanctuary. They motioned for Ralph to be seated and took their places on either side of the sanctuary, facing the people. Suddenly, cameras appeared, and there were the repeated flashes of light as the entire congregation was photographed. One of the men began to speak in a demanding, defiant tone, "How many of you knew that all church services have been canceled?" He almost shouted. There was complete silence. "I must assume that you are cowardly and will not answer my question, but I'm sure you heard the news repeatedly this week," he continued. With all the authority he could muster in his voice, he declared, "This church is closed as of this minute, and all of you are guilty of ignoring the ultimatum decreed by the Antichrist, our world leader, including you, Mr. Pastor." He turned to stare at Pastor Ralph.

Ralph was too stunned to speak.

"All of you are to leave this so-called church building immediately," he sternly announced. "Anyone lingering will be arrested and face the ultimate punishment for defying the absolute orders of our world leader," he cautioned without any mercy in his voice. "You so-called Christians must understand that the days of religious freedom are only a memory. Public worship by believers is banned forever," he said gleefully. As both men glared at the frightened congregation, they had one final demand to make. "Everyone stand and leave this building quickly and quietly. There is to be no conversing with anyone. And that goes for you also, Mr. Pastor," both men almost shouted in unison. The order was followed quickly, and the church building was vacated for the last time as a place of worship. "What is ahead of us now?" they asked themselves.

Driving home, Ralph sadly observed that there was no activity at any church he passed on his way. It was evident that the days of the church as an organization of believers were over. Satan had finally accomplished one of his goals, to silence the church.

Ralph's mind was awhirl with troubling thoughts as to how to communicate with the newly saved believers, sharing with them what the Bible said they would face and preparing them for it.

Ralph had no way of knowing what would happen to him or his friends who had become strong believers in Christ. One thing he did know was that they were despised by the emerging Antichrist and all his dedicated followers.

Two days later, one of the men of the church mustered the courage to simply drive by the church building. He observed a beer truck, along with a furniture truck, in the driveway, and men were wheeling and carrying their contents into the building. Tears filled his eyes as he drove on, realizing that his church had become a simple storage building. All of the church furnishings had been tossed out and would probably be burned or done away with in some way. Saddened, he thought, "This really is the great tribulation."

Ralph Finding a Way
to Assist Believers

Ralph was watching the rearview mirror as he drove home from church for the last time ever. He suspected that he was being followed by a strange automobile. To verify his suspicion, he circled to the right a couple blocks and began to return his route. Sure enough, there was the same vehicle and driver. Realizing that he could probably not shake the follower, he circled left for a few blocks and then returned to his normal route home. *That same automobile is still back there*, he thought to himself. Oh, well, why worry; he was doing nothing wrong, just going home.

As Ralph turned into his driveway and into the open garage door, that same automobile passed his house slowly. Several times, the stranger drove by from both directions. Ralph could see through the one-way glass windows of his house, but as long as he had no lights on, he could not be seen. For some reason, he was definitely being scrutinized by someone.

He seated himself in his favorite easy chair again. From the position of the chair, he could observe the street in front of his house. Several times the rest of the day, his observer drove by ever so slowly. Fortunately, all of the windows were protected by heavy drapes so that when it was necessary to have lights on, no one could see in. He could thank Madeline for insisting upon this protection when she was decorating their home.

One of the main issues facing Ralph is to find a method to communicate with other believers. At first, he considered a home Bible study, but that would be a violation of the law against believers gathering. With his house under observation, he gave up on that idea. Phoning them would not work either for he was sure his telephone was tapped, and that would be interpreted as proselytizing. The punishment for that was death. At least he could purchase a prepaid cell phone that could not be traced to any specific person. And that's what he did. Now, he could be in limited contact with people, without imminent danger of detection.

Evidently, it was going to take time to figure out the dilemma of communication with needy new believers. He could call upon them personally, but that posed two problems. First, it would be too time consuming, and it would delay him in getting to everyone. Also, he was sure of being followed, which would endanger the persons he visited. He would think this over for the next few days.

Other problems facing Ralph were the upkeep of the house and eating properly. He was not the best at housecleaning or cooking. A casual observation of his trash can would reveal numerous frozen TV dinner boxes, along with a host of frozen pot pie containers. Of course, he was often eating out at fast-food restaurants. Once in a while he went to a good restaurant and had an adequate meal. However, his retirement income was limited, so he had to be frugal.

One day as he was thinking about these two problems, he hit upon a promising idea. *Why not have a retired couple who did not own a home but was renting move in with me?* he thought. Almost instantly, his mind went to a couple who had been saved at the first meeting he had at the church, Todd and Faye Summerfield. They had once been vital Christians and actively involved in the work of their church. For some unknown reason, there came the time when they began to withdraw from their church responsibilities and finally dropped out of church altogether. In spite of repeated efforts by Ralph to win them back to the Lord and the church, he had failed.

As soon as Todd and Faye realized that the rapture had taken place and they had been left, they rushed back to the church from which they had drifted a few years ago. They were among the first to respond to the invitation of Ralph to be saved, following his first message. What a relief to them to understand that they could be saved in spite of their spiritual failures and after the rapture. They had also been faithful in attendance to all the following services.

Faye could care for the house cleaning and do the cooking while Todd could care for the yard and minor house repairs. If they could do that, there would be no monetary outlay for them. The more Ralph considered this idea, the more it seemed like a realistic possibility. He would explore the idea with them in the next day or so. This arrangement would free Ralph to have more time to study and be ready to teach, encourage, and prepare as many as possible for the turmoil of the great tribulation.

The house was well suited for more than one family. There were three bedrooms, along with two and one-half bathrooms. And the rooms were situated so that there could be adequate privacy for everyone. Now, if they were interested in this arrangement, it would be advantageous for all of them. Ralph looked forward to the possibility. He would not be alone anymore, would have someone to talk with, and house work and eating habits would be greatly improved. They would also be excellent sounding boards for any new ideas that came to his mind. "Madeline had been an expert at this across the years, but now she was gone," Ralph somberly reminisced.

As thoughts turned to Madeline, Ralph realized how much he missed her. He was sure that she had gone to be with the Lord she loved in the rapture and was now rejoicing and enjoying the marriage supper of the lamb. All that was comforting to him, but he still missed her greatly. Their love for each other had been strong and true. The one consolation is that she has been kept from the turmoil and terrible tribulations that are increasing in magnitude in the world from which she is gone.

Daily TV newscasts reported mounting pressure and persecution against believers or followers of Christ. Minor infractions of the Antichrist's infallible instructions were being treated as major crimes, and merciless executions were common daily. Common, minor infractions of the Antichrist's commands needed constant causalities to remind people of serious consequences if they were caught. Demands were being made that Christians could not follow. Instant arrests were being made, and many of those were never seen again. To resist the Antichrist or his directives was death, without appeal, for believers.

Ralph recalled that his Scripture studies revealed that the time would come when anyone not pledging allegiance to the Antichrist would not be able to buy or sell anything. That would include renting property to believers. It will be called the mark of the beast. Perhaps if they could feel clear to accept it, his offer to Todd and Faye would spare them an inevitable eviction. All of them could be better off.

A few days later, Ralph drove to the home of Todd and Faye. All the way he was watching the rearview mirrors of his truck. He was not being tailed for which he was thankful. After a welcome and casual conversation, Ralph presented the proposed plan of them moving into his house with him. The work entailed for the privilege of having a home in which to live did not concern them at all. In fact, they seemed to be excited about the prospects of such an arrangement but wanted a few days to consider the matter and pray about it. Not foreseeing any immediate emergency, Ralph was content to wait a few days for a decision.

While he was there, he shared some of his grave concerns for believers in the coming days of the great tribulation. Scriptures were shared with them, which they read together, and were noted for further study by Todd and Faye. Their faith seemed to be strong and unmoved by the prospects of severe persecutions.

Also, they promised to pray with Ralph about the matter of sharing important tribulation information from the Bible with as many believers as possible. This was an urgency with Ralph. It was vitally important that all believers be prepared to face severe persecutions and death victoriously. After having prayer together, Ralph left. He was greatly encouraged.

Driving home was uneventful, and there was no one following him. Maybe the opposition was going to leave him alone for a while. However, he could not become too relaxed and reckless about the matter. Often each day he surveyed the entire neighborhood to be sure there was not a spy lurking somewhere.

Ralph realized that he must do some much needed house cleaning before Todd and Faye made a decision to move in with him. "Seeing this mess would discourage the most desperate of needy persons," he muttered jokingly. For the next three days, he spent every spare minute cleaning, washing, sweeping, and arranging things as he remembered Madeline doing. At the end of all his efforts, he looked over his accomplishments with pride. However, he was hoping and praying that Todd and Faye would accept his offer soon before the house was a mess again.

Four days later, there was a knock at his door in the early afternoon. Hesitantly, he approached the door, looking through the viewer in the door. Much to his delight and relief, it was Todd and Faye. Opening the door, welcoming them in, and having them to be seated, he awaited a response from them. They were all smiles about something. Faye was scanning the house to appraise its size and condition. "It doesn't look like you need a housekeeper, Ralph," she said with a broad smile.

Ralph thought, *If you only knew, dear one.* The house had been carefully cleaned to impress them and help convince them to accept his offer.

It had worked. They informed Ralph that they would thankfully accept his offer and conditions. It would be possible for them to move in one month. Although their landlord was exerting pressure upon them because they were believers, they felt it only fair to give a one month notice of their moving. Ralph was overjoyed and looked forward to the arrangement with great anticipation. He would have more time to study and prepare for whatever method materialized to communicate with as many believers as possible and by the most effective means.

The month passed quickly, and Todd and Faye arrived with their clothing and a few personal items. Since there was no need to bring furniture, they sold what they had in a yard sale. The arrangement seemed to be a perfect match for them all. And the fellowship was enriching, especially for Ralph. He had become weary of talking to himself. Now, meals were not just a time for eating but also for happy conversations. The vast improvement in the quality of the cooking and overall conditions at the home of Ralph Waterman had improved tremendously.

Russia and Iran Begin
Threatening Israel and the USA

Regretfully, Ralph observed that conditions in the world were quickly deteriorating. The Antichrist was becoming more powerful and obnoxious all the time. There was constant antagonistic action being taken against believers in every manner possible. It seemed to be the goal of the Antichrist and his followers to make the lives of Christians as miserable as practicable. If so, the goal was being achieved.

In addition, there was more severe saber rattling by Russia and Iran, along with their allies against Israel and the United States. It had become more than threats. United States spy satellites surveying Russia, Iran, and the Muslim nations were beaming back troubling information. Massive troop and military equipment movements were taking place especially in Russia and Iran. Russia was moving a massive army and armaments to their Southern border. At the same time, Iran was making major movements toward their Western border. That is bringing them closer to Israel, which seems to be the targeted area. *Are they planning to wipe Israel from the face of the earth?*

Along with rocket areas in Iran, the spy satellites were relaying strange, readying action around known ICBM areas in Russia. In spite of this unquestioned action, neither Israel nor the United States were doing anything to offset a major attack. It has been reported that the president of the United States believed that negotiating was the only way to deal with a troublesome enemy. And Israel was reveling in the peace they have been granted by the Antichrist. There is little, or no, sense of alarm.

Both Israel and the United States leaders seemed to take the attitude, "They will not dare." They will do more than dare. They will attack with fury upon Israel and nuclear fire upon the United States. Big Satan and Little Satan are under the guns of a Russian/Islamic attack. They have no intention of stopping for a party at their borders.

All modes of news media are screaming alarms but to no avail. The Antichrist was worried but powerless to protect Israel at this time. He was too busy amassing power for himself. And the United States seemed indifferent to any kind of support for troublesome Israel. That is how Israel has been described by the United States administration. Little does the administration realize that the massive Russian nuclear ICBMs are aimed at the major cities in the United States. Millions were going to die in a very short time. God foretold of this conflict in Ezekiel 38 and 39, along with Revelation 9, all of which have been quoted earlier in this narrative.

Realizing and understanding these world conditions and the fatality of them, Ralph was desperately trying to come up with an effective way to communicate with the believers for whom he felt responsible. Various possibilities were often discussed with Todd and Faye. Something must be decided soon for time was of serious essence. World conditions were deteriorating fast, and persecution of Christians was mounting. It was tragic that the new believers might not be aware of the trauma to be expected in the great tribulation. How would they face it or survive without adequate knowledge and instructions? Sadly, many of them will not survive with their lives. Above everything else, they must be sure of a right relationship with God and ready to face death. Thousands or perhaps millions of believers will face instant death at the hands of the Antichrist or as innocent casualties of the terrible conflicts ahead. All believers must be reminded that instant death will be instant glory into the presence of the Lord.

The Apostle Paul had reminded all believers of this fact as he wrote to the church in Corinth:

> Therefore we are always confident, knowing that, whilst we are at home in the body, we are absent from the Lord:
> (For we walk by faith, not by sight:)
> We are confident, I say, and willing rather to be absent from the body, and to be present with the Lord.
>
> (2 Corinthians 5:6–8, KJV)

The new believers must be made to understand that instant death, by any method, will be to exchange the rags of this life for pure, white robes in the presence of the Lord. Over two thousand years ago, God revealed this fact to John the revelator, and he actually saw those white-robed saints. Every believer can face death with faith and confidence in the Word of God. Ralph himself was looking forward to this tremendous transition.

One night, Ralph was suddenly awakened, his mind alert with thoughts and ideas flowing one after another. There was a method to multiply communication with the new believers for whom he felt tremendous responsibility. He could teach leaders to teach others, in their homes, without attracting undue attention by the officials of the Antichrist. "Why have I overlooked this method that the Apostle Paul used in spreading the gospel in the early church?" Ralph sat up wondering aloud.

He could hardly wait for Todd and Faye to get up so he could consult with them about the new method of communicating with believers. In fact, he was fully dressed, sipping from a cup of hot, black coffee when Todd and Faye appeared. Before Faye could even prepare breakfast, Ralph had to bounce the matter off of them. As they listened, nodding their heads in agreement, Todd expressed that the idea must have come from God. So Ralph began planning to implement that method.

First of all, ten or twelve key leader/couples must be identified and informed of the importance of communicating the Word of God and encouragement to distraught but faithful believers. Todd and Faye would be very helpful in that process. They had lived in the community for many years and knew the people better than Ralph.

Breakfast being finished, the three of them sat down to the serious business of coming up with at least twelve leading couples who could be taught to teach others. The names and qualifications of many people were considered. They were not being judgmental but honestly seeking out the persons most qualified to carry out this important mission.

After between two and three hours, twelve couples were selected to be trained by Ralph to teach other believers. Faye, Todd, and Ralph were in agreement with the list of possible teachers. It would be necessary for them to risk teaching in their homes. The next step was to contact these twelve couples to enlist their participation.

Ralph used his prepaid cell phone most of the afternoon in conversation with the twelve couples selected to participate in the plan. Interestingly, all twelve agreed to become involved. They would come to Ralph's house in evenings, four couples at a time, to avoid as much suspicion as possible. A schedule was established, and three evenings of the following week, Ralph would be teaching them. He would provide printed study materials for them to share in their own homes on three evenings of the week after the trainings session held at Ralph's home. Ralph cautioned them to host not more than eight persons at a time.

It was established that four of the twelve leader/teacher couples would come to Ralph's house Monday evening at seven o'clock, prepared to spend at least two hours in study and training. Then, four more would attend on Wednesday evening, and the final four on Friday evening. The training would be the same for all of them. Ralph would provide each one of them with a copy of the material to be covered, and they could copy it to distribute to those they trained. It was to be carried inside a pocket or hidden within their clothing. In case they were being observed, they were to leave his house without any visible items.

These teachers were to telephone at least four families and invite them to their house for food and refreshments. Of course, these were to be provided so there would be no deception. But the main reason for their attendance was to receive the much needed training and encouragement that would help them cope with the fast moving events of the great tribulation. Absolutely nothing was to be discussed over the telephone concerning the training sessions. The followers and officials of the Antichrist were doing everything possible to identify all believers. It was obvious why this was being done as persecutions were being planned for everyone not in sympathy with the Antichrist.

Those attending any and all training sessions were to park their vehicles in random, inconspicuous places in the neighborhoods where the sessions were to be held. Not more than one vehicle was to be parked at the designated house where training was to take place. All of these were for apparent reasons.

The plan was now in motion to equip believers to become aware of what to expect in this time of tribulation as revealed in the Bible. Ralph wanted them to be able to face it with an unwavering faith, trusting God for his guidance. And they must be adequately prepared for major, unbelievable conditions confronting them.

Significance of Ezekiel 38 and 39

It had been predetermined by Ralph, in his conversation with those he was to teach, that they were to drive by his house at a normal speed, and if his porch light was on, they should keep on driving and not come in for training. They were to go to some store for a minor purchase before returning home. Ralph had often noticed a strange automobile with two unknown men driving by his house at different times of the day. Also, several times, he had spotted the same vehicle parked in obscure places but always where the occupants could view his house. Once, he drove by in his truck and noticed two men seemed to be studying a map or at least trying to hide behind it. Ralph was sure that his house was being watched for any suspicious meetings of believers. This apparent surveillance activity continued for days. Those he was to teach were instructed to return the following designated weeknight if his porch light was on. And he staggered the nights his porch light was on so no one would detect a set pattern.

The first week for training arrived, and Ralph's porch light was on every night. Those he was to train followed his instructions carefully, returning to their own homes. It was obvious that Ralph's house was still being observed. For two weeks, there could be no training because of the enemy tail. Finally, the watchers evidently became weary or convinced that nothing unusual was going to take place at the home of Preacher Ralph. However, his house was watched closely every Sunday, but there was never any unusual activity.

The third Monday evening arrived, and so did the first four couples who were to become voluntary trainers. All of them arrived at different times but by the designated time of seven o'clock. Only one automobile was parked in Ralph's driveway, and none of the four couples had any indication of attracting undue attention from anyone. Together, they enjoyed the refreshments Faye had prepared. Todd and Faye were going to sit in on the teaching for they were interested in finding out all they could about what faced them in these troublesome times.

The first lesson prepared by Ralph dealt with actions believers should be taking immediately in their neighborhoods. Then, the imminent threat of attack upon Israel, which would probably involve the United States, would be dealt with. There were also important matters that believers needed to begin caring for as soon as they could afford to do so. Every item to be considered and from which they would later be teaching would be Bible-based and well outlined. A copy of the lesson plan was presented to each person present, both for discussion and from which copies were to be made to distribute to the persons they would teach the following week.

In order not to attract attention, the lights were turned low and limited to one room in the house. Of course the porch light was off. A second inspection was made of the drapes to be sure no light would escape or permit outsiders to see inside the house. It was vitally important that no detection of the plan be discovered early in the program.

Ralph turned to the words of Jesus, which may have been difficult to understand previously. However, they were vitally important to believers living in the great tribulation.

These words of Jesus are profound and purposeful:

> So the master commended the unjust steward because he had dealt shrewdly. For the sons of this world are more shrewd in their generation than the sons of light.
> "And I say to you, make friends for yourselves by unrighteous mammon, that when you fail, they may receive you into an everlasting home."
>
> (Luke 16:8–9)

With the tragic events unfolding during the great tribulation, what an advantage it will be for believers to have reliable friends as neighbors. As the Antichrist unleashed an unimaginable assault upon believers, they could be trusted to assist one another. For instance, when the mark of the beast is refused by believers and they cannot buy food or anything else, friends could help by making purchases for them.

Right now, friends could help in the training gatherings. Ralph has been personally working on this in his neighborhood. He has close, dependable, honest friends living within the block where he lived. They are not believers, but they respect him and would do anything to help him. Actually, two of the couples who are to attend the training sessions will first go to the house next door to Ralph's house. There is a safe, secure rear entrance to both houses, making it all but impossible for anyone to be observed going from house to house. These two couples will appear to be visitors of Ralph's neighbor. A few minutes after their entry into the neighbor's home, they will transition to Ralph's house. They will depart by the same method.

Since the time was approaching when only those who have received the mark of the beast or have pledged allegiance to the Antichrist will be able to buy or sell, there are several things believers need to be doing to prepare for that terrible time. It is true that many will not even survive to that time, but some will. Death and dying will be widespread during the entire period of tribulation. Due to conflicts, persecutions, famine, along with the woes of God, the world population will possibly be reduced by possibly 50 percent. It must be remembered that during the great tribulation, this world will be under the wrath of God. It will be like God wants to get even with a world that rejected his Son, shed his blood, spurned his love, and determined to continue in their gross sinfulness. In fact, an angel declared in Revelation 16:6 that sinful mankind is worthy of the vials of God, which are poured out without mercy.

When the mark of the beast was required worldwide, food and water will become vital issues for believers. Right now, believers should be storing up nonperishable food to last for several months, even as much as two or three years. "When food cannot be purchased, what will you do?" Ralph asked his students. Having made friends among the unsaved might help. Some of them might be willing to purchase food for believers, but it could not continue without serious suspicions. "Purchasing extra food now and storing it safely and secretly is the best solution," Ralph insisted.

Along with the food, bottled water must be stored in large quantities. "Why would water be a problem?" someone asked.

"It will be a problem because the utilities of every believer will be cut off, for that is considered buying," Ralph reminds them. Another possibility for water is to have a well drilled and install a hand pump. The hand pump will be absolutely essential since believers will have no electrical service, which will also be terminated as a sales item.

Thinking of all the normal household items that would no longer be useful because of no electrical power brought on a lengthy discussion by the group. Neither the portable gasoline electrical generator nor the large automatic natural gas powered units were options. Battery-powered lights and an adequate supply of all sizes of batteries needed to operate them should be stored safely and securely. In addition to the battery powered lights, large quantities of candles should be purchased.

Gasoline would not be sold to believers since they did not have the mark of the beast. Besides, it would be too dangerous to store large amounts of gasoline. And natural gas is one of the utilities that will be cut off as demand by officials of the Antichrist. With natural gas and electrical power gone, cooking, lighting, heating, air-conditioning, and keeping food cool or frozen will be impossible. How they would cook or preserve food was a major concern.

Having thought through most of this, Ralph reminded them that it was nonperishable food that must be stored in quantity. In addition, he strongly recommended that every believing family purchase a good, reliable charcoal grill, along with adequate charcoal and lighter fluid, and a huge store of matches, enough to last for many months. This was not the normal way to prepare normal food, but it would have to be done the best way possible. He let it be known that he was open to any other suggestions to pass along to all believers as the upcoming conditions would be desperate.

Transportation will be another major problem, also, as it will not be possible to purchase gasoline or any kind of fuel for vehicles. That is another area where unsaved friends can greatly help believers by providing rides by to places they need to go. This goes back to the instruction of Jesus, to make friends of unbelievers so they will help in the time of need. For obvious reasons, traveling will be limited to a local area. Under the rule of the Antichrist, walking or bicycling will be the main modes of travel for believers.

Don't forget to consider what will be needed for the exterior upkeep of their property. A hand-pushed lawnmower, along with all kinds of hand-operated trimming tools, must be available. An unkempt yard and shrubbery would draw too much attention to those living there. Everything that was done to prepare for the inevitable future of tortuous turmoil must be done as discreetly as possible. Under no circumstances do they need any unknown outsiders snooping around in or near their dwellings.

Being cautious, careful, and thorough must be paramount in preparing to survive as long as possible under the inescapable, tormenting rule of the Antichrist. Ralph reminded them that it was too late to bemoan the fact that they had been very foolish in not being saved before the rapture and ready to meet the Lord. All they could do now was make the best of the adverse circumstances in which they now found themselves, knowing many of them would not survive.

Rummaging through garbage cans for food will be a normal practice for those who do not prepare. Starvation will be common after the mark of the beast is instituted. However, their hope was not in this world but in the Lord, who would meet them at the ending of their lives here on earth. For some of them, the emotional damage was enormous.

The entire group was aware of the rumblings of war, seen and heard in most of the TV news reports. Russia and Iran were continuing to threaten Israel and the United States if they became physically involved with Israel. Not only were there threats and mockery, but troop and military equipment are continuing to move toward Israel. In addition, the spy satellites indicate that Russian ICBMs were in readiness for launching. War seemed to be inevitable and imminent. To deny that fact in the face of overwhelming evidence was foolish. In spite of all these facts, both Israel and the United States apparently continued to be indifferent to what is shaping up.

Ralph wanted to conclude the session with a brief survey from the Bible that had prophesied the very things that are taking place. He urged all of his students to carefully study Ezekiel 38 and 39 along with Revelation 9 before teaching their groups the following week. He was insistent that they understood that God had predicted these very events over twenty-six hundred years earlier:

> Now the word of the Lord came to me, saying, "Son of man, set your face against Gog, of the land of Magog, the prince of Rosh, Meshech, and Tubal, and prophesy against him, and say, 'Thus says the Lord God: Behold, I *am* against you, O Gog, the prince of Rosh, Meshech, and Tubal. I will turn you around, put hooks into your jaws, and lead you out, with all your army, horses, and horsemen, all splendidly clothed, a great company *with* bucklers and

shields, all of them handling swords. Persia, Ethiopia, and Libya are with them, all of them *with* shield and helmet; Gomer and all its troops; the house of Togarmah *from* the far north and all its troops—many people *are* with you.

"Prepare yourself and be ready, you and all your companies that are gathered about you; and be a guard for them. After many days you will be visited. In the latter years you will come into the land of those brought back from the sword *and* gathered from many people on the mountains of Israel, which had long been desolate; they were brought out of the nations, and now all of them dwell safely. You will ascend, coming like a storm, covering the land like a cloud, you and all your troops and many peoples with you."

'Thus says the Lord God: "On that day it shall come to pass *that* thoughts will arise in your mind, and you will make an evil plan: You will say, 'I will go up against a land of unwalled villages; I will go to a peaceful people, who dwell safely, all of them dwelling without walls, and having neither bars nor gates'— to take plunder and to take booty, to stretch out your hand against the waste places *that are again* inhabited, and against a people gathered from the nations, who have acquired livestock and goods, who dwell in the midst of the land. Sheba, Dedan, the merchants of Tarshish, and all their young lions will say to you, 'Have you come to take plunder? Have you gathered your army to take booty, to carry away silver and gold, to take away livestock and goods, to take great plunder?'"'

"Therefore, son of man, prophesy and say to Gog, 'Thus says the Lord God: "On that day when My people Israel dwell safely, will you not know *it?* Then you will come from your place out of the far north, you and many peoples with you, all of them riding on horses, a great company and a mighty army. You will come up against My people Israel like a cloud, to cover the land. It will be in the latter days that I will bring you against My land, so that the nations may know Me, when I am hallowed in you, O

Gog, before their eyes." Thus says the Lord God: "Are *you* he of whom I have spoken in former days by My servants the prophets of Israel, who prophesied for years in those days that I would bring you against them?"

(Ezekiel 38:1–17)

Everything prophesied was being reported daily by all forms of public news communications. Of course the Antichrist and his followers were editing the reports at will. The massive Russian/ Islamic army, which seemed ready to move, so far outnumbered Israel that it was inconceivable that Israel could survive. There was still no indication that the Antichrist or the United States had any intentions of helping Israel. The only hope of Israel's survival would be special intervention by God and looking ahead in the prophecy that is precisely what God said he would do:

And it will come to pass at the same time, when Gog comes against the land of Israel," says the Lord God, "*that* My fury will show in My face. For in My jealousy *and* in the fire of My wrath I have spoken: 'Surely in that day there shall be a great earthquake in the land of Israel, so that the fish of the sea, the birds of the heavens, the beasts of the field, all creeping things that creep on the earth, and all men who *are* on the face of the earth shall shake at My presence. The mountains shall be thrown down, the steep places shall fall, and every wall shall fall to the ground.' I will call for a sword against Gog throughout all My mountains," says the Lord God. "Every man's sword will be against his brother. And I will bring him to judgment with pestilence and bloodshed; I will rain down on him, on his troops, and on the many peoples who *are* with him, flooding rain, great hailstones, fire, and brimstone. Thus I will magnify Myself and sanctify Myself, and I will be known in the eyes of many nations. Then they shall know that I *am* the Lord."

(Ezekiel 38:18–23)

While the United States, who was supposed to be a supporter of Israel, turned its back upon this highly important ally, seemingly unconcerned and complacent, God will intervene and conquer the entire Russian/Islamic armies. And God will not forget the actions, or inaction, of the United States. Again, even though God spared Israel, but not without tremendous losses, God's Word revealed the devastation of that brief war in Revelation 9:

> Then the sixth angel sounded: And I heard a voice from the four horns of the golden altar which is before God, saying to the sixth angel who had the trumpet, "Release the four angels who are bound at the great river Euphrates." So the four angels, who had been prepared for the hour and day and month and year, were released to kill a third of mankind. Now the number of the army of the horsemen *was* two hundred million; I heard the number of them. And thus I saw the horses in the vision: those who sat on them had breastplates of fiery red, hyacinth blue, and sulfur yellow; and the heads of the horses *were* like the heads of lions; and out of their mouths came fire, smoke, and brimstone. By these three *plagues* a third of mankind was killed—by the fire and the smoke and the brimstone which came out of their mouths. For their power is in their mouth and in their tails; for their tails *are* like serpents, having heads; and with them they do harm.
>
> (Revelation 9:13–19)

Ralph and those entering the discussion were now aware that this conflict could start any day, and there was the strong possibility that some of them will not survive the attack. The massive military attack against Israel will be by armies, while the attack against the United States, or Big Satan, will be by nuclear missiles.

Following a brief discussion since the two hours had slipped by quickly, the four couples left Ralph's house just as cautiously as they entered. They would study and be prepared to teach their groups the following week. Nothing was to be mentioned of these study groups to anyone outside the group of believers. After believers were alerted and trained, they may contact friends and family members at their own risk of being charged with proselytizing. Secrecy was essential because of the wrath of the Antichrist against followers of Christ. The various groups would meet again at the same time two weeks later to receive additional training from Ralph.

The Antichrist
Definitely Revealed

During the intervening two weeks while preparing for the next sessions with those who had been selected to teach, Ralph would be praying for those he taught to be safe and effective in teaching the information they had just learned. At the time of the next session with the twelve trainer/couples, he was going to deal mainly with Bible prophesies from the book of Daniel, the book of Revelation, Ezekiel, and others. For God had chosen to reveal detailed information to the Apostle John about what would transpire in the great tribulation. Ralph thought that it was important that believers not be surprised nor traumatized as unbelievable events began to take place in their tormented world. He felt like he was a messenger on a mission for his master. By word of mouth, he had learned that others were spreading the gospel message of salvation by various methods around the world. Fortunately, this had not yet been picked up by the news media.

Many things prophesied by God's Word were beginning to take place, angering the Antichrist even more against God, and he was letting that be known in public statements. Also, his followers, now most of the world population, were enraged against God. As suffering increases, the multitudes are even cursing God. One must remember that the reason they are still on this planet is that they were living godless lives when Jesus returned in the rapture. Now that there is no restraint, they have become more godless. Ralph is desperately trying to influence everyone he can not to be influenced by this godless attitude. Believers must be alerted to the fact that, according to the Word of God, much more severe conditions are to follow. These are just the beginnings of sorrows that began even before the rapture (Matthew 24:8). He is very interested that as many as possible be informed and encouraged. However, he does not want believers to be dominated by fear and depression. God is their hope and help, and they must constantly turn to him in prayer for assistance.

Two weeks later on Monday evening, the same four couples arrive at Ralph's home but at different times and having parked in other locations. No one seemed to have observed them. They were able to report good results in attendance along with discussions and sincere appreciation for the training. Their spirits were high and hungering for further Bible truth and training.

While Faye and Todd distributed the lesson plan, Ralph asked those gathered how it was going in laying aside extra food, water, and necessary supplies. There was silence for a minute or two. Finally, more than half of them confessed that they had not yet gotten around to this matter. Ralph was a little stunned by their statements. He warned them that there was imminent danger due to the threats of the Russian/Islamic armies to attack Israel and probably the United States. When that takes place, there would be grave shortages of everything on their list. He urged them to immediately give serious attention to the matter. Their survival was at stake as well as the important matter of spreading the gospel. At this time, secret, secluded believers were the only ones seeking the salvation of the lost.

In addition, Ralph informed them that the meeting days for training would be altered to Tuesday, Thursday, and Saturday at 7:30 p. m., two weeks from now. He wanted to make the change to avoid establishing a set pattern of when people might be seen coming to his house. He also suggested that they alter the teaching days at their homes. Secrecy and security was vital to the continuation of training and reaching lost loved ones.

The material planned by Ralph would take at least two sessions to present. This posed no problem to the people attending. They understood that the events of the great tribulation were going to be abundant and awesome. And they were aware that they would not escape the terror of the unfolding developments. Only those who were ready to meet the Lord in the rapture were spared the coming wrath upon mankind.

So Ralph plunged into the prophecies of God to Daniel, John the revelator, the prophet Ezekiel, and others. Much of the material was in figurative language and presented in words understood in a much earlier age. It was not that God did not know how to explain matters plainly, but people of that age could only understand in terms of their experiences and knowledge. Ralph reminded them that Jesus had promised that the Holy Spirit would guide in revealing truth and understanding when he came. "These things I have spoken to you while being present with you. But the Helper, the Holy Spirit, whom the Father will send in My name, He will teach you all things, and bring to your remembrance all things that I said to you" (John 14:25–26). Jesus also promised help from the Holy Spirit in understanding the future. "I still have many things to say to you, but you cannot bear *them* now. However, when He, the Spirit of truth, has come, He will guide you into all truth; for He will not speak on His own *authority*, but whatever He hears He will speak; and He will tell you things to come" (John 16:13).

Ralph assured his hearers that he was not posing as an expert on prophecy or things to come but simply trying to make the Word of God clearer to them. The Apostle Paul explained to the young pastor Timothy that this was one of his responsibilities when he said, "Be diligent to present yourself approved to God, a worker who does not need to be ashamed, rightly dividing the word of truth" (2 Timothy 2:15). That meant that the Word of God is to be subjected to sound exegesis and the correct meaning be properly ascertained. In all his study and preparation, Ralph had diligently endeavored to follow this exhortation from the Bible.

One of the main events of the great tribulation had already taken place. The Antichrist had been revealed. That one thought of who the Antichrist would be has caused as much speculation in the past as almost anything in the Bible. He was not to be revealed until after the rapture. God's Holy Spirit revealed the following inspired Word to the Apostle Paul:

> Now, brethren, concerning the coming of our Lord Jesus Christ and our gathering together to Him, we ask you, not to be soon shaken in mind or troubled, either by spirit or by word or by letter, as if from us, as though the day of Christ had come. Let no one deceive you by any means; for *that Day will not come* unless the falling away comes first, and the man of sin is revealed, the son of perdition, who opposes and exalts himself above all that is called God or that is worshiped, so that he sits as God in the temple of God, showing himself that he is God.
>
> Do you not remember that when I was still with you I told you these things? And now you know what is restraining, that he may be revealed in his own time. For the mystery of lawlessness is already at work; only He who now restrains *will do so* until He is taken out of the way. And then the lawless one will be revealed, whom the Lord will consume with the breath of His mouth and destroy with the brightness of His coming. The coming of the *lawless one* is according to the working of Satan, with all power, signs, and lying wonders, and with all unrighteous deception among those who perish, because they did not receive the love of the truth, that they might be saved. And for this reason God will send them strong delusion, that they should believe the lie, that they all may be condemned who did not believe the truth but had pleasure in unrighteousness.
>
> (2 Thessalonians 2:1–12)

The Apostle Paul was reassuring the church at Thessalonica that the Lord had not returned. There was confusion because some false teachers were teaching that Christ had already returned because of persecutions the church was encountering. Also, Paul wanted it understood that the man of sin, or the Antichrist, would not be revealed before the day of the Lord. It was the Holy Spirit who was restraining the revelation and takeover by the Antichrist before the rapture. In fact, the Antichrist would not be revealed and empowered until the Holy Spirit is taken out of the way. And that will take place when Jesus returns in the rapture. The Holy Spirit indwells human hearts, and every true believer, whose heart is right with God, will be gone. So then, the Holy Spirit is taken out of the way.

Ralph thought that it was important to consider again the prophetic words given to Daniel regarding the rise of the Antichrist in the great tribulation:

> "I, Daniel, was grieved in my spirit within *my* body, and the visions of my head troubled me. I came near to one of those who stood by, and asked him the truth of all this. So he told me and made known to me the interpretation of these things: 'Those great beasts, which are four, *are* four kings *which* arise out of the earth. But the saints of the Most High shall receive the kingdom, and possess the kingdom forever, even forever and ever.'
>
> "Then I wished to know the truth about the fourth beast, which was different from all the others, exceedingly dreadful, *with* its teeth of iron and its nails of bronze, *which* devoured, broke in pieces, and trampled the residue with its feet; and the ten horns that *were* on its head, and the other *horn* which came up, before which three fell, namely, that horn which had eyes and a mouth which spoke pompous words, whose appearance *was* greater than his fellows.
>
> "I was watching; and the same horn was making war against the saints, and prevailing against them, until the

Ancient of Days came, and a judgment was made *in favor* of the saints of the Most High, and the time came for the saints to possess the kingdom.

"Thus he said:
'The fourth beast shall be
A fourth kingdom on earth,
Which shall be different from all *other* kingdoms,
And shall devour the whole earth,
Trample it and break it in pieces.
The ten horns *are* ten kings
Who shall arise from this kingdom.
And another shall rise after them;
He shall be different from the first *ones,*
And shall subdue three kings.
He shall speak *pompous* words against the Most High,
Shall persecute the saints of the Most High,
And shall intend to change times and law.
Then *the saints* shall be given into his hand
For a time and times and half a time."

(Daniel 7:19–25)

Daniel further describes the Antichrist in these words:

And in the latter time of their kingdom,
When the transgressors have reached their fullness,
A king shall arise,
Having fierce features,
Who understands sinister schemes.
His power shall be mighty, but not by his own power;
He shall destroy fearfully,
And shall prosper and thrive;
He shall destroy the mighty, and *also* the holy people.
"Through his cunning
He shall cause deceit to prosper under his rule;
And he shall exalt *himself* in his heart.
He shall destroy many in *their* prosperity.

He shall even rise against the Prince of princes;
But he shall be broken without *human* means."

(Daniel 8:23–25)

Then the Apostle John recorded these words regarding the rise of the Antichrist as inspired and revealed by the Holy Spirit:

> Then I stood on the sand of the sea. And I saw a beast rising up out of the sea, having seven heads and ten horns, and on his horns ten crowns, and on his heads a blasphemous name. Now the beast which I saw was like a leopard, his feet were like *the feet of* a bear, and his mouth like the mouth of a lion. The dragon gave him his power, his throne, and great authority. And I saw one of his heads as if it had been mortally wounded, and his deadly wound was healed. And all the world marveled and followed the beast. So they worshiped the dragon who gave authority to the beast; and they worshiped the beast, saying, "Who *is* like the beast? Who is able to make war with him?"
>
> And he was given a mouth speaking great things and blasphemies, and he was given authority to continue for forty-two months. Then he opened his mouth in blasphemy against God, to blaspheme His name, His tabernacle, and those who dwell in heaven. It was granted to him to make war with the saints and to overcome them. And authority was given him over every tribe, tongue, and nation. All who dwell on the earth will worship him, whose names have not been written in the Book of Life of the Lamb slain from the foundation of the world.

(Revelation 8:1–8)

From the Scriptures given above and the mysterious, greatly troubling dream, which Nebuchadnezzar could not recall but was revealed and interpreted by God through Daniel, the Antichrist was to arise from a revived Roman empire. And that was the geographic area of modern Europe. The legs of the great image were of iron, representing the original Roman empire. The final kingdom on earth was represented by the toes of the image, which were a mixture of iron and clay. There would be strength and weakness due to that mixture, which is the structure of Europe today. "Is it any wonder that the main spokesman for the world today is a selfish, charismatic, self-appointed, powerful speaker, clamoring for world domination has arisen from the European Union?" Ralph asked.

According to the Word of God to Daniel, one of the first official actions of the Antichrist was to sign a peace treaty with Israel: "Then he shall confirm a covenant with many for one week; But in the middle of the week He shall bring an end to sacrifice and offering. And on the wing of abominations shall be one who makes desolate, Even until the consummation, which is determined, Is poured out on the desolate" (Daniel 9:27).

"That treaty has been confirmed," Ralph affirmed. And that is why Israel is indifferent to impending danger from the Russian/ Islamic armies. Israelites are calling out to each other, "Peace and safety, for we have a peace treaty with the powers that be," while armies are amassing against them.

Another observation Ralph had detected while delving into the prophetic writings was that angels played a prominent role in all of the acts of the great tribulation. He reminded his trainees that this should come as no surprise since God has utilized the service of angels, seen and unseen, throughout the history of mankind. The Bible is filled with examples of the angels of God carrying out his will and work in the world he created. And the Bible clearly defined the role of angels to mankind:

> And of the angels He says:
> "Who makes His angels spirits
> And His ministers a flame of fire."
>
> (Hebrews 1:7)

Angels, seen and unseen, will be carrying out the will of God in the great tribulation. At times, in the book of Revelation, the word "angel" is referring to an especially designated human being to be used by God in his overall prophetic plan. Ralph wanted it understood that every action of an angel is due to God's will and empowerment. Angels do not act on their own authority.

In his introductory remarks, Ralph shared another insight from the book of Revelation. Most of the main events of the tribulation period center around the opening of seven seals by the Lamb of God, seven trumpet blasts by angels, and the seven final vials, or bowls, of the wrath of God poured out upon the earth by angels. However, there are important in-between events that must be considered.

By this time, almost two hours had elapsed, and along with lively discussion, the group of trainers still had questions to be answered. The great tribulation was not some far distant event for them. They were now living in that terrible time of tribulation, having not been ready to meet the Lord in the rapture. What a horrible price to pay for a few, or even one, harbored sin in their hearts or lives.

Following the discussion and instructions from Ralph, they had fervent prayer together, seeking the assistance of God for another week. They were reminded again that the next training session would be one week from next Tuesday at 7:30 p.m.

The other two training groups met with Ralph on Wednesday and Friday, covering the same lesson material they were to teach to their trainees the following week.

Trouble Moves in Close to Ralph as the Antichrist Increased in Power and Influence

The following week was very stressful for Ralph. As he dug deeply into the Scriptures concerning the events of the great tribulation, it was difficult to keep from becoming depressed. "Just think I could have missed all of this turmoil if I had only listened to my heart," he said over and over to himself. He knew that he was saved, but that did not erase all the human hurt and haunting memories. At times, it was difficult to stay focused on the formidable task at hand. Before, he had casually read the alarming Scriptural events of the great tribulation but without having to face their actual trauma.

Bowing his head on his desk in prayer, Ralph pleaded with God in prayer to calm his mind and emotions, enabling him to prepare to help other believers who were depending upon him so desperately. Gradually sensing some settling peace, he pressed on in the Word of God and its teachings about a period of time he wished he could simply forget and certainly wishing he never had to personally experience. But the facts could not be ignored.

As he studied and prepared for the following week, he had the strange feeling that he was being watched by someone. Often he scanned the space surrounding his house but could see no intruder. But that strange sensation would not subside. He asked Faye and Todd to keep a close watch on any unusual activity by anyone near the house. Often, they both scanned the one-way windows but saw nothing. Perhaps Ralph was just being overwrought by the ponderous revelations of his study and preparation for lessons to be taught. Time would certainly tell, but caution was not to be cast aside. Feeling that adequate observation techniques had been taken, he attempted to continue studying, preparing for the following week. However, concentration was too ponderous and producing little for all the effort. Ralph decided that he must take a break.

Not able to escape the strange emotional sensation of being watched, he put aside his Bible and study materials. He decided that a drive through the community again could either calm him or alert him to dangers that might have triggered his strange concerns. On the way, he would stop and get a cup of coffee. That might help.

Backing out of the garage and starting down the driveway, Ralph caught the image of a person sitting on the neighbor's porch across the street. He stopped the truck momentarily, pretending to adjust the side mirror. While doing this, he studied the person on the porch. What made it so strange was that last week, his neighbor had come over to tell him that he was going to New Jersey to be with family members in these troublesome times. The neighbor asked Ralph if he would keep an eye on his house for at least the month or more that he would be gone. "Now, who was this man sitting on the neighbor's porch?" Ralph questioned. To make it even stranger, the man was dressed in some of the neighbors clothing. Ralph wondered how all of this could simply be incidental? "Who else knew that my neighbor was going to be gone for a while?" Ralph mouthed silently.

"Come to think of it," Ralph recalled, "there had been lights on in the neighbor's house last night." *Why did that not arouse my suspicion?* Ralph thought with alarm. After adjusting the mirror and backing into the street, he drove slowly away, as if nothing was amiss. As he drove away, watching the mirror and the image of the man on the porch, he became even more troubled when he saw that binoculars were trained on his truck. Or was it the lens of a telephoto camera? A sudden chill ran down Ralph's spine and goose bumps appeared on both arms. His face was also burning like fire. These unexplained events only agitated his feelings of anxiety. It was evident that he was being watched for some reason, and he was afraid he knew why.

After slowly driving all the streets of his housing development and purchasing the much needed coffee, he headed directly home. When he came in view of his house and that of his neighbor, there were two people on the neighbor's porch. *Things certainly were not improving*, he thought as he drove onto his driveway and into the garage. He found Faye and Todd, explaining the strange situation to them and asking that they watch the activity across the street. Ralph was certain that some unusual events at his house had raised suspicion among the foes of the believers. That must be thought through before next week's training sessions.

Sipping his coffee, Ralph went back to his desk, gathering the study material. Again, he tried to concentrate on the studies for the following week. The material to be considered was from the Bible, describing the unthinkable events that were in store for mankind, those who had been left to face the horrors of the great tribulation, was to be considered. These filtered through his mind for a few seconds. They were as excruciating as the events taking place across the street. There was no way to ignore or evade the Biblical prophecies. They were just over the horizon and could be expected to happen exactly as God had foretold them, in all their unimaginable horrors. However, the more he attempted to concentrate on the lesson he was to teach, it seemed trite compared to the predicament in which he was finding himself. Of course, turmoil and tribulations like this were to be expected. He must not forget that this is the great tribulation and calmness and serenity are gone. He, along with everyone else, must understand that these are the days of the unexpected.

To add turmoil to trouble, Jim, the man who was to have taught believers at his house the night before, dropped by to consult with Ralph about an unusual event that had taken place. All these believers supposedly had slipped into his house without being noticed or without raising any outside suspicion. While he and his wife Sue and four other believing couples were enjoying refreshments and fellowship, there was a loud knock at their door. When he went to the door, there was a strange man and woman, claiming to be a new neighbor from the next street over. "Since we saw several people coming to this house, we wondered if we could join the party," they nonchalantly asked. Then they both suddenly stepped around Jim and into the room, much to his surprise and concern. It was evident that they were very pushy and not to be trusted or turned away. However, both of them were served refreshments, and they entered into the conversations without any reserve. *Who were they? Why were they there?* All these questions, and many others, were racing through the minds of the believers.

The presence of these two strangers presented a dilemma. Should they continue with the training, or was it wise to let this be a simple party as the visitors had said they suspected? Looking around the room, Jim saw no evidence of the training materials, which could have raised questions from the visitors. Wisely, nothing was mentioned about the planned study by anyone. This was taken as a signal to forgo all training for the evening.

It was difficult to be jovial during the party and time of fellowship. There were too many uncertainties and questions about the visiting couple. After about an hour of talk about nothing in particular, the party began to break up as couples began to leave. The visitors asked if a party was planned for the following week. They were informed that nothing was planned here for next week. They said they would be watching, and if people began to gather again, they would join in the food and fun. The remaining guests stood stunned and bewildered, looking at these uninvited guests. Silently, they thought, *Then, we are being watched.*

There had been similar intrusions at other homes as training had been interrupted by perplexing, uninvited visitors. Fortunately, all teaching and discussion of the lessons were halted when visitors ventured into a home. Ralph wondered if they were being suspected of proselytizing believers.

These were troubling, uncertain days, but the new believers were determined to stand firm and unfaltering in their faith. *Oh, that we had followed this relationship with the Lord prior to the rapture*, they mused.

"And for some reason, we thought it was too difficult to be a Christian back then," Jim lamented. Thoughts like this sent chills up and down their spines, remembering they had been spineless to matters of salvation prior to the second coming of Christ.

Finally, Jim related that he feared that he had been followed as he had driven to Ralph's. He had taken a roundabout route, but the same car was always there in his rearview mirror. About that time, Todd rapped on Ralph's study door before stepping briskly into the room to inform them that a black Lincoln, with a man and a woman inside, had slowly passed the house several times. Jim flinched at the information. "It was a black automobile that was following me," he blurted out with alarm. Wide-eyed, Ralph wondered if things were coming to a head with them and their endeavors. It was certainly a reminder that they were living in the great tribulation, and followers of Christ were not condoned by the Antichrist or his followers. No stranger could be trusted, even as they appeared to befriend believers.

Jim left after he, Todd, and Ralph had joined hands, praying for protection, courage, and perseverance in the face of a powerful enemy. When Ralph was alone, he sat down in his desk chair, swinging his feet to rest upon his desk and staring out the window. Looking at nothing in particular, he pondered what should be done about further training. He decided to call off all training sessions for at least two weeks. Perhaps enemy surveillance would dwindle or die out if they did not observe further regular gatherings by the believers.

Although the new believers were hungry for the Biblical truth and encouragement Ralph was providing, he could not unduly expose them to imminent danger or death. In the meantime, he would use his prepaid cell phones to make limited contact with as many believers as feasible. He wanted to keep their spirits as high as possible and their faith unwavering. Severe times of testing were ahead for all of them, Ralph concluded, as he sat with his feet on his desk, staring out the window, meditating, praying, and trying to think as clearly as possible for some time.

This had not been a good day for study and preparation of lesson material. In fact, it had not been a good day at all. But then, good days had not been promised for the tribulation period. Finally, Ralph put away all of his study materials, closed the window blinds, shut the door behind himself, and headed for the main part of the house. The extra days before any further training would give him plenty of time to prepare the next lesson, if it could ever be presented.

Perhaps it would be wise to check the news, as tainted as it might be by the Antichrist, to see what was taking place in a world cursed by constant turmoil. The TV news might not be totally reliable, but then when had it ever been? Maybe he could get a hint of important happenings that might affect him and all believers.

As he slipped into his easy chair, trying to relax, Todd and Faye joined him. They were concerned about Ralph and the turmoil he was experiencing. If they could be a comfort to him, without intruding, they wanted to do so. Ralph was pleased with their presence and support.

Reaching for the TV remote control, he turned it on, surfing the channels for the most reliable news. Settling back in the easy chair, he watched and listened to the world events that were being reported. He was confident that everything was not being made public, especially the subtle, underhanded takeovers by the Antichrist. Although his influence and power was creeping around the globe, he had not been addressed publicly as the Antichrist. However, anyone knowing anything about Bible prophecy recognized that fact. Evidently, there was an apparent attempt to keep that fact a secret. Does he even know who he really is? More than likely, he does know.

Who gave him his awesome abilities, masterful intrigue, ready acceptance, and power, along with other unbelievable characteristics? No one on earth was claiming responsibility for bringing him into such a position of prestige and importance. He is acting like a Messiah or special gift to a troubled world. Ralph suddenly recalled the answer to the question, which is in so many minds. It is clearly stated in the Bible:

> Then I stood on the sand of the sea. And I saw a beast rising up out of the sea, having seven heads and ten horns, and on his horns ten crowns, and on his heads a blasphemous name. Now the beast which I saw was like a leopard, his feet were like *the feet of* a bear, and his mouth like the mouth of a lion. The dragon gave him his power, his throne, and great authority.
>
> (Revelation 13:1–2)

God revealed to the apostle John the rise of the Antichrist and the source of his powerful authority. The dragon, who is the devil, empowered the Antichrist to fulfill his onslaught against Israel and all who become believers. As God empowered his followers with the fullness of the Holy Spirit to spread the gospel to the ends of the earth, Satan will empower the Antichrist with the evil spirit and power to control the world and mock God. For seven years, the Antichrist will reign over the entire world: "It was granted to him to make war with the saints and to overcome them. And authority was given him over every tribe, tongue, and nation" (Revelation 13:7). He will become so powerful that he will decide that he is God.

Actually, Satan offered Jesus Christ this role and the alarming responsibility of becoming the Antichrist:

> Then the devil, taking Him up on a high mountain, showed Him all the kingdoms of the world in a moment of time. And the devil said to Him, "All this authority I will give You, and their glory; for *this* has been delivered to me, and I give it to whomever I wish. Therefore, if You will worship before me, all will be Yours."
>
> And Jesus answered and said to him, "Get behind Me, Satan! For it is written, 'You shall worship the Lord your God, and Him only you shall serve.'"
>
> (Luke 4:5–8)

Jesus Christ resisted and rejected the temptation of Satan, which the Antichrist has embraced. In fact, the Satan-empowered Antichrist will lead the major part of the world population to worship the devil. As unbelievable as it may seem, devil and Antichrist worship will become the trend of the day in the great tribulation:

> All who dwell on the earth will worship him, whose names have not been written in the Book of Life of the Lamb slain from the foundation of the world.
>
> (Revelation 13:8)

Anyone not willing to worship the devil and the Antichrist will incur the wrath of both. Finally, Satan has found someone who will totally sell his soul, and being to him, in worship and following. Satan will display his power, rage, and abilities against God through the Antichrist. However, it will not be absolute power and working of his will. He and the Antichrist will accomplish only what God permits. Ralph decided that he will deal with these issues in more detail as he prepared the printed material to be presented to the trainers, if that is ever possible again.

He is shocked back to present reality by what is being reported on TV and an outcry from Todd and Faye. A full screen image of the Antichrist was shown, and he was speaking to the world. He has a solemn warning for Russia, Iran, and all the Islamic alliance with them. Their troop movements were to cease and withdraw to their own former bases while comforting words are given to Israel, reminding the world that a seven year peace treaty has been signed and confirmed by the Antichrist and his present followers (Daniel 9:27). Actually, it is this peace treaty that has enraged the leaders of Russia, Iran, and other radical Muslim nations. The Antichrist was demanding a speedy confirmation from the Russian/Islamic powers that his commands will be complied with immediately. In addition, the world was reminded that the mighty United States of America had been a long-standing ally of Israel. But nothing was mentioned about any interventions by the United States.

Christian believers were not ignored in this worldwide speech. They were reminded again that all gatherings of believers were forbidden and will be severely punished if there was failure to obey. For emphasis and warning to believers, examples of arrests of Christians were flashed on the TV screen from around the world. They were roughly pushed and shoved into police vans by agents wearing the emblem of the Antichrist, and the vans displayed the same image. This is probably the last time these particular believers will ever be seen or heard of. Under the rule of the Antichrist, it is evident that it will be fatal to become a believer or follower of Christ. They are reminded that hosts of undercover agents are diligently enforcing the desires of the Antichrist against believers. Homes were being barged into where small groups have gathered, and everyone present was carted off into oblivion. People were being arrested on the streets for witnessing to unbelievers, many of whom turned out to be members of the undercover agency. Any and all who were arrested were gone.

There was a new demand by the Antichrist. All Bibles, or portions of the Bible, were to be taken to centers in every city to be burned. In the event that a Bible was found in a home or the person of anyone, the punishment will be severe. "The Bible is a book of nonsense and needless demands of a wrathful God. And its historic statements and prophetic declarations are not dependable," the Antichrist announced. This new notification created an unbelievable dilemma for Ralph. It is the Bible that revealed all the dastardly deeds of the Antichrist and an alert to the world of what to expect. It is also the only literature of hope for believers. The risks may be extensive, but Ralph established the fact that he will not be deprived of his study Bible. It has been the comforting, counseling, challenging, chastising, consistent Word of God to him too long to be separated from it.

In this age of the tribulation, freedom is only gained by agreeing with the Antichrist and his godless policies. Many who have lived in democracies and have enjoyed so many freedoms find this dictatorial practice difficult to comprehend. Ralph stared at the TV, wondering how much longer he may have to live. That is a valid thought considering, the strangers across the street. He thought that at least two more sessions with his trainees would enhance the cause of believers. The fewer shocking surprises of the events they will face could intensify their preparation and strengthen their faith. Hopefully, that will be possible. He was encouraged by the fact that some of those he was training were former vital Christians but for some reason had become church dropouts. From the discussion periods, Ralph detected that they were very knowledgeable about the end time prophecies. They could carry on with the mission if he could just have time to prepare the final lessons. He would be sure to accomplish that, if at all achievable.

The Antichrist rambled on for several minutes, but much of it was repetition of what had been heard before. Ralph was sure that he was using brainwashing techniques to condition the world for even more startling statements in the near future.

Taking a break from the TV, Ralph stood, stretched, and stepped over to a position where he could observe any strange activity at his neighbor's house. Almost as if on cue, a black Lincoln swung into the neighbor's driveway and parked. A man and woman stepped briskly out of the automobile and entered the house, without even knocking. "Now what could that mean?" Ralph whispered to himself. He demonstrated such shocking surprise that Faye and Todd quickly rushed to his side, inquiring about what had happened that was so troubling to him. Briefly, he explained the entry of two more people into an already desperate dilemma, pointing out the black Lincoln. He reminded them that it had been a black Lincoln, with a man and woman, that had followed Jim to his house. Could this be the same couple that had barged into Jim's house the night before?

After about half an hour, the couple came out of the house, stopping on the porch to stare at Ralph's house, giving it serious study. Ralph was sure that they were part of the undercover agents alluded to by the Antichrist in his rambling speech. Extreme caution was going to have to be the rule of every day. He decided to postpone the training classes to be held at his house for two more weeks. That would give a total of four weeks to break up trends that might be counted upon by any observers.

Ralph decided to call his neighbor at a telephone number he had given him in New Jersey. He wanted to determine if the neighbor had given permission to anyone to use his house. He was sure that he should have made the call as soon as he had made the first observation, but he delayed, not wanting to alarm his neighbor unnecessarily. Using a prepaid cell phone, Ralph made the call, and the neighbor answered the phone. Briefly, Ralph explained what was going on and asked if the neighbor had given permission to anyone to use his property. The neighbor was alarmed and adamantly stated that he had not given anyone permission to use his house in his absence. He assured Ralph that he would call the police and have the situation investigated, thanking Ralph for the phone call.

Ralph, Todd, and Faye continued to closely observe the house across the street, watching for any other activity. In a few minutes, a police car drove up, parking in front of the neighbor's house. Two officers slowly stepped out of the car, pausing and giving Ralph's house their full attention. Of course, they could be seen through the one-way glass windows, but they could not see through the mirrored effect of the window glass. Ralph, Todd, and Faye were perplexed by the bizarre action of the police officers. Finally, the officers stepped up on the neighbor's porch, rapped on the door, and were permitted to enter the house.

After being out of sight briefly, the officers exited the house, heading for the patrol car. However, before entering the car and driving away, they studied Ralph's house several more minutes. All of this gave Ralph and his companions a creepy feeling. *What could be going on?*

As they turned away from the window, there was a new voice emitting from the TV. It was the voice of the president of the United States. He was condoning and confirming the policies of the recent speech by the Antichrist. All Americans were to understand that the new laws implemented by the Antichrist were now the unquestioned laws of the United States of America. He stressed that unity among the nations was essential to enduring these tormenting times, and the former speaker had the answers demanded for such climactic conditions. "The United States was not surrendering its identity but simply joining in the unity, which seemed so necessary," the president stated weakly.

In addition, he issued a weak warning to Russia and Iran against any aggressive actions toward Israel. He promised them speedy, effective actions from the United States in event of such maneuvers. The statements were so weakly stated that no one, including the leaders of Russia and Iran, were impressed or concerned. The president was weary of dealing with Israel and had no intentions of interfering with any military actions against them. Both the world and the Antichrist knew that. Almost everyone simply smiled or snickered at the warning statement issued by the president. They had heard him blow before. Thankfully, the president's speech was brief. At least verbally, he had fallen in line with the Antichrist.

"This absolutely sealed the doom of the United States, for God would not lie," Ralph lamented. "That was the reason one of the greatest nations of all time—and most blessed by God— was not even mentioned in the end time prophesies," Ralph concluded. The Russian/Islamic alliance was determined to wipe Big and Little Satan (the United Stated and Israel) off the map. This constantly contended action by the Iranian leaders now had more credence because for the first time in history they were allied with Russia.

Ralph Prepares to Teach Tormenting Events of the Great Tribulation

For the next two days, Ralph arose early, finished breakfast, then left the house in his truck to drive in seclusion, thinking and planning. He was always alert to any possibility of being followed. There was no evidence of such. A black vehicle would instantly get his undivided attention, regardless of its direction or destination. His driving took him to different towns, within the limits of a day's travel. It was good for him to get away from the frustrations of his local setting.

Todd and Faye were being diligent in their observations of any strange activities across the street. And each evening, they would brief him on anything that indicated importance. The occupants in his neighbor's house were remaining even without proper permission. Ralph was absolutely certain, it would eventually come to no good ending. He could just do his best, remain true to his faith, and courageously face his inevitable fate when it came.

Since time was of the essence and he had just over three weeks to finish the studies to share with other believers, he determined to get back to serious study in a day or so. His mind must be clear to delve into the plagues, wrath, and woes of God upcoming in the great tribulation. He thought foreknowledge was important to a victorious outcome.

Often he was deeply troubled because he was even caught up in this terrible time, recalling that it was all because he had missed the rapture. And that was because of an unsettled issue in his heart between him and God. Everything had been settled now, and he could meet the Lord with confidence in his heart. But there was the horrible fact of this tormenting tribulation, of which he had to be a part. How foolish and insensitive he had been to the faithfulness of the Holy Spirit prior to the rapture. Oh, how he wished he was gone.

Ralph spent two more days traveling the surrounding country. Occasionally, he spent time simply sitting on a park beach by the ocean, hoping that the soothing sounds of the waves would calm him and clear his troubled mind. Reluctantly, he would leave the beauty of the ocean waves and their rhythmic washing upon the beach.

He walked and wondered about upcoming events. There were many questions, but few answers readily available. The main consolation was that God had saved him, forgiving him of his failure to be ready for the rapture. In spite of all his efforts, that did not spare him the turmoil of this horrifying time of tribulation. All that he was encountering and enduring was not God's fault, but the result of his misguided choices and hurts he had harbored in earlier life.

Dusk was gathering as Ralph stepped into his truck and began the drive home. He was filled with anxiety and dread as he neared his house. What would Todd and Faye have to tell him about today's activities across the street? Turning the corner his headlights flashed on a frightening sight. The black Lincoln was parked in his neighbor's driveway. That was not a welcome home greeting as far as he was concerned.

Slowly, he turned into his own driveway, closely observing everything possible. It was a relief to hear the garage door going down without any adverse activity. At last, he was safely home and would enjoy the food and fellowship of the evening meal with Faye and Todd and catch up on the day's activities here.

Ralph was informed that the black Lincoln had arrived across the street about four o'clock, but no one had been seen since then.

The same couple had entered the house. Furthermore, Todd and Faye had monitored the TV news for anything noteworthy or new. Most of it had been the same propaganda that was pervading minds worldwide. There was more threatening saber rattling from Russia and Iran against Israel and the United States. And it really did seem to be more sinister and threatening, they relayed to Ralph. However, there had been no response to the recent demands by the Antichrist or to the weak threats of the United States president. Evidently, the Russian/Islamic leaders were unimpressed and planned to continue their aggressive course of action. Ralph thanked Todd and Faye for their diligence and informed them that he planned to be gone again the next day. Following that, he was determined to devote full time to final lesson preparations to be presented to the volunteer trainers.

Early the next morning, Ralph prepared a sack lunch and soft drinks for the day out. He took time to share breakfast with Faye and Todd before leaving. His intention was to spend the day at the beach, enjoying the sunshine and soothing effects of the ocean. Leaving, he observed nothing alarming across the street or in the neighborhood, for which he was thankful. He had taken a beach chair and a novel that he wanted to complete. Finding a secluded spot on the beach, he parked his truck, took off his sandals, and waded into the incoming tide, all the while observing everyone within sight. It just seemed to be others, unknown to him, enjoying the beach as he was. Walking in the shallow waves as they washed over his feet, he completely relaxed, putting his mind into neutral. There would be time to think and study tomorrow.

Returning to the truck, taking out the beach chair, he reached into the truck cab and retrieved the novel. Taking both to the edge of the washing waves, unfolding the chair, sitting where the waves could wash over his feet, he began to read and relax. Quickly, he became engrossed with the plot of the novel. All of this was precisely what he needed before plunging into the complicated studies ahead of him. Several times he paused to move his chair back from the deepening incoming tide. This gave him an unsuspecting opportunity to scan his surroundings. Nothing seemed to be amiss.

A little after noon, he returned to the truck for the sack lunch and a soft drink. Sitting alone in the sunshine, he watched several young people having the time of their lives romping in the surf. He imagined that some of them were enjoying a Florida beach for the first time. Possibly, they were oblivious to the awesome events of the great tribulation in which they were living. On the other hand, they might be trying to forget it by having fun on the beach. Often a lifeguard would blow his whistle and wave some of them back to shallower water. Their safety was his main concern while at the same time not wanting to spoil their adventuresome spirit. "Very soon no one would have any desire to visit the beach," Ralph mulled over regretfully.

Seeing nothing, nor anyone, to arouse his suspicion, Ralph completely unfolded the beach chair, lay back, closed his eyes, and relaxed. Sleep was not an option, but cautious relaxation was desperately needed and enjoyed. He was convinced that his truck had been observed so many times by those who might want to do him harm, so he stayed semialert as unrecognized vehicles drove slowly up and down the beach.

A little later, he raised the chair to a sitting position and finished the novel. The ending of the book was pleasing and much as Ralph had suspected. Western novels were a favorite of his, and he had an extensive collection of paper and hard back books plus e-books on his digital reader and smart phone.

Late in the afternoon, sunburned but serene, he loaded the beach chair into the truck, climbed in, drove slowly down the beach to the first exit, and headed home. As soon as he began to enter traffic, he instinctively began to scan the rear view mirrors to be sure he was not being tailed. Everything appeared to be in order, so he took a direct route home. Fortunately, his neighbor's driveway was empty of vehicles. This could be a good ending of a perfectly relaxing day. And it might be the last one for some time to come.

As soon as he opened the truck door, he smelled the aroma of food being prepared for supper. Faye was an excellent cook, and Ralph looked forward to a delicious meal as she knew that he had taken a light sack lunch with him. He was not disappointed in the meal. There was absolutely nothing of any significance to report to Ralph, by either Todd or Faye. The evening meal was enjoyed with positive conversation, which is as positive as it could be in such troublesome times. That was always in the back of their minds. After the meal, they relaxed together before retiring for the night.

Ralph was very thankful that he had opened his home to such an accommodating couple. They were an encouragement to him, and he hoped they shared the same feelings about him. All of them had been purchasing extra nonperishable food, water, other necessary supplies, charcoal, candles, and matches, storing them for future use, as needed. Todd had installed shelving in an obscure windowless room in the house. Ralph had also followed his advice to other believers, and now, a fresh water well with a hand pump stood near the back of his house. They were hopeful that all believers were doing the same thing, as Ralph had urged. The time was approaching when that would be the main source of food and supplies. Of course there was the possibility of a black market as had been the case when food and supplies were constrained in the past. And for a limited time, friends whom the believers had cultivated might be of assistance. Howbeit, these sources could not be depended upon for the long haul.

Before going to sleep, Ralph jotted down several notes that he wanted to be sure to explore in his study the next day.

Ralph awoke early, relaxed, ready to study and prepare the final lessons for the believers. He did not want them to be shocked or surprised by upcoming events, which could shake their faith.

Showering and dressing lightly, he slipped quietly into his study, not wanting to disturb Todd and Faye. First of all, he knelt in front of his desk, thanking the Lord for salvation, eternal life, and hope. Then he prayed earnestly for God's assistance and guidance as he delved into the deep, prophetic teachings of the Bible. He did not want to mislead anyone nor evade the woeful truth of the end times as he had done earlier in his ministry. He had claimed not to understand it too well back then, or that was his excuse, but now much to his chagrin, he was dealing with soul-shaking, stark reality. This entire matter he confessed openly to the Lord in prayer. For some time, he continued to pray, talking to the Lord and listening for God to speak through his insights and intuition. He concluded his prayer in faith that God would reward his requests. He remembered the Bible reminding everyone that often they did not have because they did not ask God (James 4:2).

Selecting his study Bible, commentaries, study books, and spreading them over his desk for ready reference, he had faith that God would guide him in this endeavor. He had just seated himself at his computer when there was a gentle knock on the door. Todd invited him to breakfast as Faye had prepared waffles, which were Ralph's favorite. Accompanying Todd to the kitchen, they shared the meal together.

Before going back to his study, Ralph asked Todd and Faye to pray with him for guidance as he studied and prepared the lessons. He wanted to be sure that he presented the Word of God as clearly as possible. Both of them assured him of their spiritual support.

Going back to his study, with a cup of coffee in his hand, he was ready to begin the mentally exhausting task, trusting God to help him.

First, he was going to deal with the events which the Bible stated would take place in the great tribulation. That would take him to the book of Daniel, prophesies of Ezekiel, the book of

Revelation, and possibly other books of the Bible. He recalled that they were not pleasant, from former casual reading, but they could not be evaded.

Ralph spent almost two hours reading and reviewing all the Scriptures relating to the end times. As he read, he jotted down notes, attempting to visualize the events of the great tribulation in some chronological order. Slowly, as he read and reread, prayerfully comparing Scriptural references, a sequence of events began to take shape in his mind.

With a legal pad before him, he began to outline the main events as he comprehended them. Several times he moved them around until it made sense to him. He was convinced that an overview of the primary phenomenon of the tribulation period was pivotal to understanding and being prepared to face the inevitable trauma.

Before finalizing the outline, putting it in lesson form to be taught and being able to be presented in a teachable manner, Ralph needed a break. Leaving all the study material spread over his desk, he left the room. He enjoyed a soft drink and chatting with Todd and Faye for a few minutes.

Outside, it was a beautiful, sunny day, so Ralph decided to take a stroll down the street, preparing his mind to continue the strenuous study. It worked. Also, he observed nothing taking place in the community to be of any serious concern. Caution was still crucial for all believers. Walking back to the house, he was prepared to press on with the preparation for the next lesson to be taught to trainers. The physical exercise had been good for him.

Almost every day, Ralph would walk in the community. Sometimes he would walk the half mile to a park in the housing development. That is where children used to play, and adults would relax or read, sitting on the park benches. Of course, now, there are no children to play. They were all gone. Ralph varied the directions he walked, as well as the time of day. He would frequently carry a battered shopping bag containing newspapers (turn

or magazines to read at the park. Often, he would stroll after dark, always being alert to the possibility of being followed.

Ralph noted, with delight, that there was a city bus stop across the street from the park. All of this walking was not being done simply for the exercise but was planned to be used in the future to continue his mission.

On several occasions, Ralph was aware that he was being watched and followed. One afternoon, he heard footsteps close behind him, but he kept on walking toward the park. Finally, halfway there, his follower stepped beside him, beginning chat and walk with him. Ralph recognized him as one of the men who was occupying his neighbor's house across the street. Finding an empty bench at the park, Ralph sat down, pulled out a newspaper and began to read, watchful of his uninvited companion who sat down on the other end of the bench. No further comments were made between them, and his companion took a paperback novel from his hip pocket and also began to read. After about half an hour, Ralph's uninvited guest excused himself and walked away toward his neighbor's house. *Now, what was that all about?* Ralph wondered disgustingly.

A time or two, Ralph had waited at the bus stop and taken the bus downtown, disembarked, found a bench, and sat there to read. During these times, he was always alert to his surroundings. He would wait for a different bus and bus driver, get on board riding back to the park bus stop, and then walk home. All of this was done to prevent a pattern, which could be observed and used against him by any ill-intended foe.

Twice Ralph had been followed by the black Lincoln. Although very wearisome to him, he tried to ignore the matter and kept on walking. On another occasion, the black Lincoln had driven back and forth, passing him from both directions. He was being observed, but his erratic actions had to be troubling them greatly. And he would keep it up, using it to his advantage later. His walking was a planned diversion tactic to confuse the enemies of believers.

It was lunch time, and following a brief lunch and chat with Todd and Faye, Ralph was back in his study, deep in prayerful thought and planning. He had just started to write when Todd rushed in and urged him to hurry to the TV where alarming news was being broadcast. Quickly following Todd into the family room and sitting down in his easy chair, he gave full attention to the news report.

The TV reporter was in a different mood. There was an independence and breakaway attitude from the canned news of recent days. Hard, cold facts were being proclaimed, without any apparent concern for what world leaders might presume.

Strange, world-shaking actions were being taken by the United States military. Reporters were sharing observations about what was taking place at the United States Pentagon. Many lighted windows at the Pentagon had shown evidence of activity all night. In addition, there had been a steady stream of limousines in and out of the Pentagon area. *Is something major shaping up militarily?* No one will give a news reporter the time of day. Whatever is taking place is highly secretive.

A reporter was discussing the likelihood of all this activity relating to the strong public and military resistance to the weak, inflammatory, inconsistent statements of the president a few days ago. People were wondering just who is leading this nation. Strangely, the president has not been contacted nor an attempt made by the media to interview him. *What is his involvement in these apparent emergency measures? What has triggered this confusing conduct of military muscle flexing?*

News reporters were quickly being dispatched to major military, naval, and air bases. They were trying to determine if there was unusual activity there. Since they have been barred from the bases themselves, it will become necessary to observe from the outside. That is quite unusual. In spite of the verbal secrecy, there was a steady stream of vehicles with soldiers in full military dress, pouring into every military base observed. Are the threats from Russia and Iran now being taken seriously? Or has there been a provocative movement by the Russian/Islamic forces?

Foreign correspondents have been scrambled to look into these issues. There is not only tension in the room where Ralph, Todd, and Faye were straining to catch every reported word, but there was tension in the world. It was showing on the faces and in the voices of the TV reporters. No one can leave the TV. And no official word of explanation is being given. *Could this simply be a practice maneuver to send a message to someone?*

Finally, Ralph wandered back to his study since the news reports have reached the stage of being repeated over and over again. It was early afternoon, and Ralph was attempting to outline, in an orderly listing, the major events of the great tribulation, which all living persons are facing. He noticed, from the Scriptural accounts, that there was not a consistent time frame indicated between events nor was there always a duration described.

Ralph paused to pray again before putting it all down on paper to be taught and distributed. He wanted it to be true to the Scripture and able to be clearly conveyed. It was important to Ralph that he is as forthright as John the revelator was in Revelation 4:1, "After these things I looked, and behold, a door *standing* open in heaven. And the first voice which I heard *was* like a trumpet speaking with me, saying, 'Come up here, and I will show you things which must take place after this.'" He humbly deduced that he was not authoring Scripture, but he desperately desired to "rightly divide" it (2 Timothy 2:15).

Ralph eventually determined to entitle the lesson, "Major World Shaking Events During the Great Tribulation." As stated before, this lesson would simply be an overview of the great tribulation. In subsequent lessons, the specific events would be dealt with in more detail. He was sure that the first fact facing mankind following the rapture was the tormenting realization that they had missed it, having been left in a world without mercy and under the wrathful tribulations of almighty God. That was the first shocking fact that had confronted him. He had to come to grips with the fact that Madeline was gone, and he had been left. Actually, that was an incomprehensible, tormenting tribulation within itself.

Secondly, the revelation and rise of the Antichrist will take place soon after the rapture, according to 2 Thessalonians 2:3–4, "Let no one deceive you by any means; for *that Day will not come* unless the falling away comes first, and the man of sin is revealed, the son of perdition, who opposes and exalts himself above all that is called God or that is worshiped, so that he sits as God in the temple of God, showing himself that he is God."

The day of the Lord referred to in verse 2 of that same chapter is alluding to the final phase of the return of Christ or the revelation. So the Antichrist will be revealed after the rapture but prior to the revelation when Jesus literally comes to this earth to reign for a thousand years with his saints.

The prophet Daniel has given a very unflattering description of the rise of the Antichrist in (Daniel 7:23–25), as previously quoted. And God revealed to John the revelator the rise of the Antichrist in very descriptive prophetic terms in (Revelation 13:1–8), also listed previously.

Regretfully, Ralph had to admit that this man of sin had been revealed and presently was establishing himself and his kingdom. He knows no limits as to how he accomplishes his world dictatorship. Conflict, power grabs, deception, intrigue, blatant lies, military action, and every other evil tactic, were favorite weapons he used to take over the world. It must be remembered that the devil is giving him all of his evil power to accomplish his evil mission. More will be discussed later.

While the Antichrist is establishing his evil kingdom, one of his first administrative acts was to successfully broker a peace treaty with and for Israel. This was something that six or seven United States presidents have attempted but failed to accomplish. The Antichrist, being a Muslim, was able to convince Israel's

Muslim neighbors that peace would be in their best interest. They were also urged to trust his final outcome of the matter.

Israel was presently enjoying peace, for which they have hungered since becoming a nation in 1948. And peace will last until the Russian/Islamic invasion due to their outrage with the unilateral action of the Antichrist. According to news reports, that invasion is in the making at the present time. The Russians and Iran, along with their allies, wanted it to be understood that the Antichrist does not speak for them, and they were going to prove it militarily. They intended to wipe Little Satan, which is Israel, and Big Satan, alluding to the United States, off the map. Ralph stares blankly out of the window, realizing that this attempt could become cataclysmic action any day.

Israel seemed to be drunken by the temporary peace they are enjoying, as their people and leaders cry, "Peace and safety." For some unseen reason, they ignored the imminent threat that will shock them into stark reality very soon. They were also ignoring the authenticity of the Word of God.

Have none of the leaders or people of Israel ever read 1 Thessalonians 5:3? "For when they say, 'Peace and safety!' then sudden destruction comes upon them, as labor pains upon a pregnant woman. And they shall not escape."

The Bible also declares that the Antichrist will break the treaty with Israel halfway through its promised duration, move in and take over:

Then he shall confirm a covenant with many for one week;
But in the middle of the week
He shall bring an end to sacrifice and offering.
And on the wing of abominations shall be one who makes desolate,
Even until the consummation, which is determined,
Is poured out on the desolate.

(Daniel 9:27)

As usual, Israel's peace will be short-lived. Without the promised intervention by God Himself, Israel would be wiped off the map. And the emphasis should be on the words "short-lived."

Ralph glanced at his wall clock and was shocked to see that it was a few minutes after five o'clock. He had been so engrossed in study, research, and Scriptural comparisons, along with putting it into understandable printed form on his computer that he had become oblivious to time. As he paused, he suddenly realized how mentally spent he was. It was time to stop for the day and prepare for the evening meal. The pleasing aroma of the food had already been drifting into his study. He was looking forward to a leisurely evening, as much as that was possible, knowing he was in the tribulation period. He concluded that tomorrow he would continue his study and preparation for teaching.

Faye had prepared another delicious meal for which Ralph was extremely thankful, remembering his own limited cooking ability. For a change, the conversation was light, even upbeat. All of them looked forward to an evening watching the news, reading, and relaxing. But in the tribulation period, plans could change promptly and ponderously.

Walking into the family room, Ralph glanced out the front window. There was the black Lincoln parked in his neighbor's driveway again and four people were conversing on the front porch. Heads turned periodically, and Ralph's house came under scrutiny. Since this action was nothing new, Ralph only watched the proceedings for a few minutes. He was not going to permit their presence spoil a relaxing evening that he desperately needed. If they wanted anything, they could cross the street and ask for it. Of course, Ralph hoped that would not happen.

Babylon the Great Identified
and the Assassination
of the Antichrist

The evening TV news was more of the same, a lot of propaganda from the Antichrist in Europe and more severe saber rattling by Russia and Iran. As usual, there was silence from Israel and the United States. They either did not care about the threats or put no credence in them. One reporter mentioned that US spy satellites had picked up more troop and military movements in Iran and Russia. For the first time, the satellites detected movement of large forces in Libya, Turkey, Syria, Iraq, and Jordan. This could be of important significance since these nations are en route to Israel from Russia and Iran. Also, Ezekiel lists these nations as part of the coalition that will invade Israel, along with smaller nations.

Strange as it might seem, there was no mention of the military movement earlier. Everyone was left to wonder what it was all about. Evidently, someone had gotten to the news media and silenced them by some method, Ralph surmised.

The time of the invasion will come when Israel senses security and peace:

> "Therefore, son of man, prophesy and say to Gog, 'Thus says the Lord God: "On that day when My people Israel dwell safely, will you not know *it?* Then you will come from your place out of the far north, you and many peoples with you, all of them riding on horses, a great company and a mighty army. You will come up against My people Israel

like a cloud, to cover the land. It will be in the latter days
that I will bring you against My land, so that the nations
may know Me, when I am hallowed in you, O Gog, before
their eyes." Thus says the Lord God.

(Ezekiel 38:14–17)

In light of the present peace treaty and Israel's complacency,
Ralph, Todd, and Faye discuss the immenency of the invasion
of Israel. Ralph was confident that when Israel was attacked,
the United States will be the target of a secret nuclear ICBM
attack. That will be to prevent United States's assistance to Israel.
Evidently, they had not picked up on the lack of concern and
cooperation of the United States with Israel. If so, a secret nuclear
attack upon the United States should have been of no concern.

Ralph was convinced that the United States was the national
Babylon the Great, which will fall in Revelation 18. Also,
Ralph believed that the mystery, Babylon the Great, described
in Revelation 17 is referring to the fall of a world powerful
religious order:

For God has put it into their hearts to fulfill His purpose,
to be of one mind, and to give their kingdom to the beast,
until the words of God are fulfilled. And the woman whom
you saw is that great city which reigns over the kings of the
earth.

More will be said about this later, for Ralph will insert it into
future lesson preparation.

When the TV was turned off, they discussed the potential
problems of having future training at Ralph's house with the
interfering foe occupying the house across the street. They may be
watched too closely to have the trainers go there. Ralph decided
to test the situation. Caution must be maintained for the safety
of every volunteer.

After going to his bedroom, Ralph prayed and puzzled over the predicament of what to do about the training location. When he is finally prepared to present the lessons, a site must be settled upon. Since it would be three or four weeks before he is adequately prepared to teach with clarity, there is time to figure it out.

In the middle of the night, Ralph was awakened with a possible plan crystallizing in his mind. "God can work with our minds asleep or awake," Ralph jubilantly but quietly stated to himself.

The plan was so simple that he wondered why he had not thought of it outright. He would do a test run at his house, calling select trainees, and have them come to his home a week from Tuesday. Using one of his prepaid cell phones, he would keep the matter a mystery for any foe that would be trying to listen in on all his planned activities. All trainees would be instructed to take the same precautions that were used before when coming to his house. They would be told not to expect training and not to mention anything about such for the entire evening. The meeting was purely for a test and fellowship.

Jim and Sue would not be invited, nor anyone else who had been present during a previous intrusion by the unidentified couple looking for a party. In case of an interruption by this couple at the test meeting, Ralph did not want anyone present who might be recognized. Thinking through this process several times, Ralph was satisfied that the resulting outcome would determine the direction he must take in future meeting places for training. With that problem settled, he soon fell asleep.

Over breakfast that morning, Ralph shared the idea with Todd and Faye. They were impressed and confident that the plan would give him the information he needed. In the meantime, Ralph would determine which trainers to contact. After brief phone calls to them, he continued his study and lesson preparation. He also continued his sporadic walks, carrying the old shopping bag part of the time for a confusing effect.

Breakfast being over, Ralph headed to his study, sipping a cup of coffee, as usual. He prayerfully continued the overview outline, which he had been working on the day before. A cursory review of where he left off helped him to concentrate as to where he should begin.

As Ralph studies Ezekiel, Daniel, and Revelation again, he concluded that the next early event in the great tribulation will be the attack upon Israel by the Russian/Islamic forces. They are enraged by the peace treaty signed unilaterally by the person known as the Antichrist. For years, Iran had been boasting that they would wipe Israel off the map. And now that they are confederated with Russia, they will never be content to permit Israel to continue to exist. Ezekiel 39 is one of the convincing Scriptures, speaking distinctly on that issue:

> "And you, son of man, prophesy against Gog, and say, 'Thus says the Lord God: "Behold, I *am* against you, O Gog, the prince of Rosh, Meshech, and Tubal; and I will turn you around and lead you on, bringing you up from the far north, and bring you against the mountains of Israel. Then I will knock the bow out of your left hand, and cause the arrows to fall out of your right hand. You shall fall upon the mountains of Israel, you and all your troops and the peoples who *are* with you; I will give you to birds of prey of every sort and *to* the beasts of the field to be devoured. You shall fall on the open field; for I have spoken," says the Lord God.
>
> (Ezekiel 39:1–4)

Additionally, Revelation refers to the terrible attack, which will affect the entire world:

> When He opened the second seal, I heard the second living creature saying, "Come and see." Another horse, fiery red, went out. And it was granted to the one who sat

on it to take peace from the earth, and that *people* should kill one another; and there was given to him a great sword.

(Revelation 6:3–4)

Most commentators agree that the phrase "fiery red" is a reference to the bloodshed inflicted as the results of a war. Furthermore, Ralph had an opinion that this conflict was described in more detail in Revelation 9:

> Then the sixth angel sounded: And I heard a voice from the four horns of the golden altar which is before God, saying to the sixth angel who had the trumpet, "Release the four angels who are bound at the great river Euphrates." So the four angels, who had been prepared for the hour and day and month and year, were released to kill a third of mankind. Now the number of the army of the horsemen *was* two hundred million; I heard the number of them. And thus I saw the horses in the vision: those who sat on them had breastplates of fiery red, hyacinth blue, and sulfur yellow; and the heads of the horses *were* like the heads of lions; and out of their mouths came fire, smoke, and brimstone. By these three *plagues* a third of mankind was killed—by the fire and the smoke and the brimstone which came out of their mouths. For their power is in their mouth and in their tails; for their tails *are* like serpents, having heads; and with them they do harm.

(Revelation 9:13–19)

Ralph, also, believed that simultaneously, with the attack upon Israel, the United States will suffer a surprise nuclear ICBM attack, alluded to in the above Scripture, since no nuclear weapons will be used against Israel. For some time, Iran has identified them as the Big Satan to be destroyed.

In a speech before the United Nations in February 2008, Ahmadinejad, president of Iran, defiantly declared that Iran, with the assistance of Allah and others, all world powers would be brought to their knees, and Muslims would rule the world. Many in the United States simply smirked at that threat. Ralph feared that it was finally about to become a reality.

These Scriptures and others will be expounded upon in more detail when the acts of God's wrath during the great tribulation are explored in later lessons.

Revelation 17 calls attention to the fall of mystery Babylon the Great, then strongly indicated that it is the fall of a worldwide religious order. This will make way for the rise of the false prophet and his damnable doctrine of devil-worship, along with adulation and awe of the Antichrist.

Another alarming event of the great tribulation is the rise of the false prophet, alluded to briefly above. It is not a pleasant picture:

> Then I saw another beast coming up out of the earth, and he had two horns like a lamb and spoke like a dragon. And he exercises all the authority of the first beast in his presence, and causes the earth and those who dwell in it to worship the first beast, whose deadly wound was healed. He performs great signs, so that he even makes fire come down from heaven on the earth in the sight of men. And he deceives those who dwell on the earth by those signs which he was granted to do in the sight of the beast, telling those who dwell on the earth to make an image to the beast who was wounded by the sword and lived. He was granted *power* to give breath to the image of the beast, that the image of the beast should both speak and cause as many as would not worship the image of the beast to be killed. He causes all, both small and great, rich and poor, free and slave, to receive a mark on their right hand or on their foreheads, and that no one may buy or sell except one who has the mark or the name of the beast, or the number of his name. Here is wisdom. Let him who has understanding calculate the number of the beast, for it is the number of a man: His number *is* 666.
>
> (Revelation 13:11–18)

Since this lesson was simply an overview, the terrible works and their tormenting effects upon believers will occupy a major part of a future lesson.

Just considering this much of the turmoil prophesied about the great tribulation caused Ralph to pause and pray for himself and all believers. They are being propelled progressively through these tormenting times. He was so overwhelmed that he must take a break from study and typing. It is not quite lunchtime, but he was going to leave his study and attempt to find some relaxation and mental rest in his favorite easy chair before lunch. Glancing across the street was not a relaxing sight, but he was in no frame of mind to seriously regard what he saw. "All of that will have to wait for later attention or action," he mumbled to himself as he slumped into his easy chair. If possible, his desire was to think about nothing relating to the great tribulation or his studies.

Following lunch, Ralph decided to tune in the noon TV news. Much to his chagrin, the Antichrist was delivering another blasphemous, worldwide speech of propaganda and hatred for God. Suddenly, a shot rang out, heard clearly on the TV. Abruptly, the Antichrist slumped lifelessly behind the podium where he was speaking.

There was a rush of activity in two directions. Many were rushing onto the platform from where the Antichrist had fallen. Evidently, one of them was a physician, for he seemed to take control, stretching out the limp, lifeless body of the Antichrist. Life-saving techniques were being applied constantly.

The wail of a siren was heard on the TV. In a matter of minutes, the Antichrist was rushed to an awaiting ambulance on a stretcher. He appeared to be lifeless. The ambulance rushed him to the nearest trauma center, which was fortunately part of a university hospital.

Ralph, Todd, and Faye were on their feet, standing very closely to the large flat screen TV mounted on the wall. They do not want to miss a single word or movement of activity. How could this be happening when all guns have been banned and supposedly confiscated and with hoards of bodyguards visible everywhere the Antichrist appears?

The other rush of activity was toward the assassin who has discarded his rifle and desperately attempting to escape. However, he was tackled and roughly dragged to the floor. He would have been killed then and there, but officers interfered since they first wanted to thoroughly interrogate him. Who was he, and why did he shoot the Antichrist?

A TV reporter has made his way to the hospital trauma center, seeking information about the fallen Antichrist. All that was revealed was that several of the best neurosurgeons in the country were working with him. It is evident that he is critically, if not fatally, wounded. An anxious mob was gathering at the hospital, and officers have been dispatched to control the crowd.

Finally, one of the surgeons who had been in the emergency room came out to give some kind of information to calm the expanding crowd. He told the anxious crowd and the world TV audience that the wound was grave. "Your leader is on life support, and skilled surgeons are working diligently with him. When further information is available you will be informed," the surgeon told them before immediately rushing back into the trauma center. All questions were ignored.

Really, there have been no signs of life since the Antichrist was rushed into the emergency room. Although the surgeons had begun immediate efforts to revive him, nothing had been accomplished. All of the life support equipment was clicking and humming, but there was no response from the man to which they are attached.

After the final known efforts were completed and still no signs of response, the head neurosurgeon had to declare the Antichrist dead. He had been brain dead from the beginning of all procedures. His lifeless body was covered with a white sheet and moved from under the glaring surgical lights.

Slowly, the head surgeon walked from the trauma center into the hallway leading to the exit, where an apprehensive crowd, TV cameras, and reporters awaited information about their leader.

The surgeon solemnly approached a battery of microphones and TV cameras in front of a mass of uneasy people. Clearing his throat, he said, "In spite of heroic efforts by a battery of skilled surgeons, they were unable to revive the Antichrist. I reluctantly have to inform you that he is officially dead."

Wails and screams of sorrow erupted from the crowd, almost drowning out questions being yelled by TV reporters. The surgeon informed them that there was nothing else he could share with them, for he did not have answers to their inquiries. Very slowly and deliberately, the surgeon turned, making his way back into the hospital emergency room. As could be expected, without their self-acclaimed charismatic leader, the world went into shock.

While the crowd was standing watch at the hospital, strange, unfathomable events were taking place in the trauma room where the lifeless body of the Antichrist had been left. For the last time, before leaving the room, one of the surgeons glanced at the sheet-covered body. He suddenly stopped in stride and screamed, "Did you see that?"

The other surgeons looked at him, wondering what had come over him. Speechless, he was pointing toward the covered body. A fellow surgeon rushed over to him, shaking him vigorously and demanding, "See what? Have the pressures of the evening gotten to be too much for him?" was going through the minds of the surgeons and nurses still in the room. At last, regaining use of his voice, he whispered frightfully, "The sheet moved."

Now, for sure, there were serious questions about his sanity. Those not staring at him were focused on the sheet-draped form lying on a narrow operating table.

Gasping, a nurse said, "His left hand just moved!" Then she fainted falling to the floor with a thud. Another surgeon had seen the same surprising movement. He rushed to the form on the table, stripped back the sheet away to reveal the head of the Antichrist, and was shocked to see his eyes were open and blinking! Now this seasoned surgeon was fighting to keep from fainting himself. Then the lips of the Antichrist began to move trying to form words. Miraculously, their star patient was recovering. He had been dead for over four hours. No one in that room had ever known of someone coming back to life after having been dead that long. However, he was alive and attempting to sit up.

The same surgeon who had pronounced the Antichrist dead rushed back outside where TV crews were disassembling equipment and preparing to leave. He was frantically waving his arms wanting to make an announcement. Available TV cameras were turned back on, and reporters ran toward the surgeon, wondering what this was all about.

With cameras rolling and a few stragglers from the crowd listening, the world was told that a miracle has just taken place. The Antichrist has revived and was recovering remarkably well. While people were trying to digest this phenomenon, many are wondering, *Who performed this miracle? God has all but deserted the world that he created.*

A TV reporter was permitted to take a camera and crew into the trauma room to record this world-shaking event. With the whole world having access to TV, viewers stared in disbelief as the Antichrist waved cheerfully to them. Many believers were as stunned as the rest of the world.

Leading neurosurgeons were telling the world that this cannot happen, but it has. They were confused but convinced that a miracle has taken place. None of them had believed in the miraculous working of God in earlier life, and they were not convinced that God had anything to do with this undeniable miracle. In fact, they did not even believe in God. To them, everything unusual that took place was simply luck or fate.

Without a doubt, this was a display of the power of Satan in resurrecting the Antichrist. It was a miracle performed by the devil. He accomplished this feat to mock the resurrection of Jesus Christ. The world has just witnessed one of its most astonishing moments. Surprise seemed to be the most common emotion prevalent in the world. The Antichrist will become more ruthless, demonic, and demanding. Without question, full allegiance can be expected, following this miraculous empowerment of Satan.

Ralph wondered why there was so much surprise in the world, even among believers. The Bible had foretold this event fully in Revelation 13. Bewildered, he watched the TV screen in shock even though he knew the Scriptural outcome:

> Now the beast which I saw was like a leopard, his feet were like *the feet of* a bear, and his mouth like the mouth of a lion. The dragon gave him his power, his throne, and great authority. And *I saw one* of his heads as It had been mortally wounded, and his deadly wound was healed. And all the world marveled and followed the beast. So they worshiped the dragon who gave authority to the beast; and they worshiped the beast, Saying, "Who *is* like the beast? Who is able to make war with him?"
>
> (Revelation 13:2–4)

What about the assassin? After being thrown to the ground and handcuffed, he was roughly thrown into a police van. With guns drawn, officers had to surround him to keep the crowd from killing him on the spot. The assault rifle used by the assassin was found where he pitched it before attempting an escape. It was evident from cursory observation that the attempted assassination was well planned. However, a thorough, lengthy, tedious interrogation would be conducted by specialists at police headquarters. Guilt had already been established, but the suspect would be interrogated as to background material and motivation. All of the procedures would be played out on TV to serve as an example to anyone else who might have similar thoughts.

The assassin was a European, from the same country as the Antichrist. He had stolen the rifle from a police vehicle while the officers were distracted by a serious disturbance. It had to have been stolen, for all weapons had been banned and confiscated. Of course that could not be 100 percent effective. "The word 'sword' used in Revelation 13:14 is simply a descriptive term to designate that a weapon would be used against the Antichrist," Ralph quickly explained to Todd and Faye. He did not want to interfere with the TV coverage of the events transfixing them, along with viewers from around the world.

Most troubling to believers was the confession of the assassin that he was a former believer but had turned away from trusting in God. He had become enraged by the tormenting events taking place in the world and with the dictatorial leadership of the Antichrist. Admission was wrangled out of him that he had been planning the attempt to assassinate the Antichrist for months, just waiting for an appropriate opportunity. He had been stalking the Antichrist all over Europe.

With TV cameras still running, when the interrogators were satisfied that they had all the information the assassin intended to give, he was executed. In fact, he was executed with the very rifle he had stolen from the police vehicle and used against the Antichrist. There was no hearing before a grand jury or a trial set. Those were only ambiguous memories of another day.

When the results of the interrogation were relayed to the Antichrist, he became enraged against all believers and declared worldwide war upon them. From that time onward, believers would be hunted, hounded, and rounded up. All who maintained a profession of faith in Christ would be executed upon detection. Ralph had to reveal another grave reality, most distressing to believers. Worship of the Antichrist would be demanded, without exception. And this diabolical deed was instituted by the false prophet but approved, with acclaim, by the Antichrist:

He performs great signs, so that he even makes fire come down from heaven on the earth in the sight of men. And he deceives those who dwell on the earth by those signs which he was granted to do in the sight of the beast, telling those who dwell on the earth to make an image to the beast who was wounded by the sword and lived. He was granted power to give breath to the image of the beast, that the image of the beast should both speak and cause as many as would not worship the image of the beast to be killed.

(Revelation 13:13–15)

This will have a dreadful effect upon believers who are spreading the gospel or having secret meetings for support and encouragement. Ralph remembered reading that "hunger and fear almost always trigger a stampede to security." And he predicted that this will happen again under the reign of the Antichrist, assisted by the false prophet. This issue will be explored more in another lesson.

The witnessing of believers being greatly hampered by the declaration of war upon them will result in another amazing event of the great tribulation. God will raise up two witnesses who will witness God's power to save. Their witness will be very convincing as it will be accompanied by awesome signs and wonders:

"And I will give *power* to my two witnesses, and they will prophesy one thousand two hundred and sixty days, clothed in sackcloth." These are the two olive trees and the two lampstands standing before the God of the earth. And if anyone wants to harm them, fire proceeds from their mouth and devours their enemies. And if anyone wants to harm them, he must be killed in this manner. These have power to shut heaven, so that no rain falls in the days of their prophecy; and they have power over waters to turn them to blood, and to strike the earth with all plagues, as often as they desire.

(Revelation 11:3–6)

Suffice it to say here that Ralph believed that the 144,000 Jews were converted due to the witness of these two special ministers of God.

Another momentous marvel of the great tribulation is that of God's angels taking over the responsibility of spreading the gospel. When his two witnesses were killed after their three and one half years of successful ministry, God's voice will not be silenced:

> Then I saw another angel flying in the midst of heaven, having the everlasting gospel to preach to those who dwell on the earth—to every nation, tribe, tongue, and people—saying with a loud voice, "Fear God and give glory to Him, for the hour of His judgment has come; and worship Him who made heaven and earth, the sea and springs of water." And another angel followed, saying, "Babylon is fallen, is fallen, that great city, because she has made all nations drink of the wine of the wrath of her fornication."
>
> Then a third angel followed them, saying with a loud voice, "If anyone worships the beast and his image, and receives *his* mark on his forehead or on his hand, he himself shall also drink of the wine of the wrath of God, which is poured out full strength into the cup of His indignation. He shall be tormented with fire and brimstone in the presence of the holy angels and in the presence of the Lamb. And the smoke of their torment ascends forever and ever; and they have no rest day or night, who worship the beast and his image, and whoever receives the mark of his name."
>
> Here is the patience of the saints; here *are* those who keep the commandments of God and the faith of Jesus.

(Revelation 14:6–12)

Prior to the ministry of the angels, there will be a spiritual warfare in the heavens:

> And war broke out in heaven: Michael and his angels fought with the dragon; and the dragon and his angels fought, but they did not prevail, nor was a place found for them in heaven any longer. So the great dragon was cast out, that serpent of old, called the Devil and Satan, who deceives the whole world; he was cast to the earth, and his angels were cast out with him.
>
> Then I heard a loud voice saying in heaven, "Now salvation, and strength, and the kingdom of our God, and the power of His Christ have come, for the accuser of our brethren, who accused them before our God day and night, has been cast down. And they overcame him by the blood of the Lamb and by the word of their testimony, and they did not love their lives to the death. Therefore rejoice, O heavens, and you who dwell in them! Woe to the inhabitants of the earth and the sea! For the devil has come down to you, having great wrath, because he knows that he has a short time.

Ralph determined that this was a spiritual warfare taking place during the great tribulation, not a rehearsing of the devil being cast out of God's heaven at an earlier time. Jesus said in Luke 10:18 "And He said to them, 'I saw Satan fall like lightning from heaven.'" Also, God revealed to the prophet Isaiah the fall of the devil, and that was over two thousand years prior to the great tribulation:

> How you are fallen from heaven,
> O Lucifer, son of the morning!
> *How* you are cut down to the ground,
> You who weakened the nations!
> For you have said in your heart:
> "I will ascend into heaven,
> I will exalt my throne above the stars of God;

I will also sit on the mount of the congregation
On the farthest sides of the north;
I will ascend above the heights of the clouds,
I will be like the Most High."
Yet you shall be brought down to Sheol,
To the lowest depths of the Pit.

(Isaiah 14:12–15)

Additionally, a historic statement is made in Revelation 12 concerning the fall of the devil and a third of the stars (angels) of heaven falling with him:

> And another sign appeared in heaven: behold, a great, fiery red dragon having seven heads and ten horns, and seven diadems on his heads. His tail drew a third of the stars of heaven and threw them to the earth.

(Revelation 12:3–4)

And it must be recalled that the devil was present to tempt Eve in the beautiful Garden of Eden, in which God had placed Adam and Eve (Gen. 3:1–6). And in Revelation 12:9, printed above, the devil is referred to as "that serpent of old, called the Devil and Satan, who deceives the whole world." That made it mighty clear that the conflict alluded to will take place during the great tribulation.

The Bible also credited the devil as being the "prince and power of the air" (Ephesians 2:1–3). This is a reference to the heavens, not God's heaven.

So the war that will break out between Michael, his angels, and the dragon (devil) and his angels will be a spiritual warfare during the great tribulation. Ralph affirmed this and was supported by other expert Bible commentators.

The purpose for clearing the heavens of the devil and his angels was to give the angel of God free access without delay. An angel of God was delayed twenty-one days in getting to Daniel with an answer to his request and prayer, by the forces of the devil in the heavens:

> And he said to me, "O Daniel, man greatly beloved, understand the words that I speak to you, and stand upright, for I have now been sent to you." While he was speaking this word to me, I stood trembling.
>
> Then he said to me, "Do not fear, Daniel, for from the first day that you set your heart to understand, and to humble yourself before your God, your words were heard; and I have come because of your words. But the prince of the kingdom of Persia withstood me twenty-one days; and behold, Michael, one of the chief princes, came to help me, for I had been left alone there with the kings of Persia. Now I have come to make you understand what will happen to your people in the latter days, for the vision *refers* to *many* days yet *to come*."
>
> (Daniel 10:11–14)

There will be no hindrances in the heavens by the devil or his angels, following the victorious war of Michael and his fellow angels. They will be cast to the earth, and that will be the limited location of their activity. God's angels will have complete access of the heavens to carry out the will and work of God. "This is another sign of God limiting the works of the devil, even in the great tribulation," Ralph is pleased to relate.

The apostle John was given the privilege of viewing the success of salvation being preached by believers having been saved, the two faithful witnesses, and the angels of God during the great tribulation:

> After these things I looked, and behold, a great multitude which no one could number, of all nations, tribes, peoples, and tongues, standing before the throne and before the Lamb, clothed with white robes, with palm branches in their hands, and crying out with a loud voice, saying,

"Salvation *belongs* to our God who sits on the throne, and to the Lamb!"…

Then one of the elders answered, saying to me, "Who are these arrayed in white robes, and where did they come from?"

And I said to him, "Sir, you know."

So he said to me, "These are the ones who come out of the great tribulation, and washed their robes and made them white in the blood of the Lamb. Therefore they are before the throne of God, and serve Him day and night in His temple. And He who sits on the throne will dwell among them. They shall neither hunger anymore nor thirst anymore; the sun shall not strike them, nor any heat; for the Lamb who is in the midst of the throne will shepherd them and lead them to living fountains of waters. And God will wipe away every tear from their eyes.

(Revelation 7:9–17)

Ralph made the following observation, "Many have proclaimed that there would be no post-rapture salivation. However, this Scripture alone declares that there will be. Then, whom shall we believe? Granted, most of the Bible teaches that mankind should take advantage of the privilege of being saved prior to the rapture and be ready to meet the Lord Jesus Christ in the air at his return. That is God's main plan and should be the first choice for mankind. And of course, that is the only way one may miss the troubling times of torment during the great tribulation. This truth needs to be seriously considered by everyone not confident of their readiness to meet the Lord, if he returned today."

Ralph stated in his printed lesson that the acts of God's wrath poured out on a wicked, ungodly people of this world will be taken up in future lessons.

Ralph's Conclusions about the Fall of Babylon the Great from Bible Teachings

Day after day, Ralph has prayed preparing lessons and himself while plotting how to cope with the dangers facing all believers. The time had come to test the experiment, attempting to determine if followers of the Antichrist were actually engaged in closely spying upon them. Since Ralph had at least two lessons completed and ready to be taught, he would precede with his plan next Tuesday evening.

Very carefully, Ralph selected four of the twelve couples he had been training. All of them were reliable and cooperative. He called them, using a prepaid cell phone, and explained the plan. They were to meet at his house the following Tuesday evening between 6:30 and 7:00. He advised them to either borrow or rent a car, if possible, as their vehicles may have been identified by potential spies. It is important that they park in different locations than they may have used before. Additionally, they should wear drab or black clothing since they would be arriving after dark.

On Tuesday, a few minutes after 6:30, the selected guests began arriving. Of course the porch light at Ralph's house was not on. Gently knocking with a prearranged number of taps on the door, they would be admitted into the house. By 7:00, all eight of the guests had arrived and were seated comfortably in the dimly lighted room. It was comforting and reassuring to be together again, and Ralph was delighted to see them. It is evident that they were deeply concerned about climactic events that were taking place in their world and lives. But after all, Ralph had warned them that these things would take place and that they must not permit them to shatter their faith in God.

Since it would be dangerous to sing out loud, the group simply mouthed the words of familiar hymns. That seemed strange at first, but the words flowing through their minds blessed them and encouraged them. Employing the silent method, they sang two or three favorite hymns to begin the evening of fellowship. All of them understood that they were conducting an experiment to determine if teaching could continue at Ralph's home.

About ten minutes after the final invited guests had arrived, there was the intrusion of a loud banging on the door. Quickly, Ralph rushed to the door, flipped on the porch light, and peeped thought the viewer in the door. Much to his dismay, he recognized the same couple who had interrupted other gatherings of believers. Signaling his guest to be quiet, he slowly opened the door and faced the uninvited guests. His face was visibly red and hot, but he displayed dignity and courage.

"Could we join the party?" the woman asked smugly. Instantly, the couple stepped around Ralph, entering the room before being invited inside. As Ralph glanced outside, he saw a chilling sight. The porch light was reflecting off a black Lincoln parked in front of his house.

As always, the uninvited couple accepted refreshments and entered into the ongoing casual conversations among the guests. In addition, they kept asking strange questions no one was willing to answer. They asked if there was any wine. Of course there was none. One of them responded, "What is a party without wine or whiskey?" Most of Ralph's invited guests simply stared at the invading couple, making few comments. The issue of alcoholic drink was dropped.

The rest of the evening passed with everyone appearing to have a pleasant time. However, there was tension due to the presence of the couple no one knew. Ralph did not know who they were, but he knew why they were there. The activities of believers were being closely observed and interrupted when possible.

Ralph's guests were very discrete in their comments and conversation. Nothing was hinted of training sessions taking place anywhere. When discussion turned to the disruptive events taking place in the world, the new couple blamed God and blamed believers for much of it. To avoid open conflict, no one challenged them but quickly changed the subject.

The uninvited couple was the first to leave. Evidently, the party was too tame for their taste and the fact that they were gathering no information concerning believers was disappointing. Ralph followed them to the door and opened it for them. He remained standing at the door watching them get into the black Lincoln and drive away. There was no need to take a chance of one of them remaining to eavesdrop on serious conversations that continued in the house.

Closing the door and turning off the porch light, confident that the couple was gone, Ralph returned to enter into the conversation with his guests. Quickly, Todd suggested that he slip out the back door, sitting unseen in the deep shadows, to be sure that no one slipped back to attempt to listen to comments made by those remaining in the house. He did this, but nothing happened.

Before everyone left, Ralph asked for volunteers for meeting places for the training sessions the following week. Almost immediately, three couples offered their homes as meeting places. They would meet Monday, Wednesday, and Friday evenings at different homes. Extreme caution should be exercised by everyone. Ralph would notify all those to be taught where to attend the sessions. All of this had risks, but the task was not for the faint of heart.

"Everyone must understand that their commitment was to work together arm in arm unafraid. The purpose of all this effort, and caution, is to listen, learn, and lead," Ralph reminded them.

Those trained by Ralph must make arrangements to meet in the different homes of those they are teaching. Meetings should not be in the same location twice in succession. With the safety of everyone in mind, this must be worked out as carefully as possible. Since most of the trainers have been identified by the enemy, all of them should use discretion when attending the meetings. No doubt their movements will be monitored closely. It must not be forgotten that war has been declared upon known believers by the Antichrist and his followers. Evidently, an attempt is being made to catch as many as possible gathered in one place to make arrests, severely persecute, or even assassinate.

After everyone left, Ralph discussed the matter with Todd and Faye. "We are being very closely observed," he commented to them. So Ralph began planning other meeting places to teach and encourage the believers.

The number of believers was now increasing as many of the lost were discovering that they could be saved. What was taking place in Ralph's location was taking place around the world as multitudes of people were realizing what a tragic mistake it had been not to have turned to God prior to the rapture. They could not escape the troubling turmoil of the great tribulation in their lives, but they could be saved and have peace in their hearts. The turmoil was not pleasant and would get worse, but the assurance of being right with God and ready to meet the inevitable with a strong faith diminished their sense of dread and other personal concerns.

If at all possible, Ralph felt that it was important to complete the lessons, if at all possible, helping believers draw strength from each other by gathering together. Keeping their confidence in God strong and their faith from faltering were a couple of Ralph's primary goals. He reminded Todd and Faye that if faith falters, one is flirting with disaster.

Since Ralph was sure that his every action would be closely observed, he had to devise methods of getting to the teaching sites. On Monday, he would walk to the park about an hour before dark and spend time reading a magazine, taken from the battered tote bag. And the tote bag contained more than magazines. It contained his teaching material to be distributed to the trainers, but who could know that? He would read until it was too dark to see the print, waiting for complete darkness. Then he would walk across the street and catch a bus to downtown where there were several car rental businesses. First making sure that he was not being followed, he would then rent a car and proceed to the teaching point. Taking a roundabout route, he was pleased to know he was not being tailed. The headlights of no vehicle appeared in his rearview mirrors as he drove to his destination. Parking two blocks away, he walked the remaining distance and gently knocked on the door with the predetermined number of taps. He was permitted to enter and ready to begin teaching. He was pleased that all of the four couples to train were already present and had no indication of having been followed. The lesson and discussion time went well and the trainees were ready to teach the materials the following week.

Ralph and the three other couples departed as cautiously as they had arrived. Ralph returned the rental car, walked to a bus stop, boarded a late-running bus to the park. He disembarked, carefully scanned the area, and walked home. He was pleased that it all appeared to be totally uneventful. Much to his relief, the black Lincoln had not been across the street since it left his house the evening the strange couple interrupted the test gathering.

Fortunately, the home of the couple scheduled to host the Wednesday training session was only a few blocks from a bus stop. Ralph waited until after dark and walked to the park, alert to any observers. Since there seemed to be none, he boarded the bus, operated by a different driver, and rode to the bus stop near his destination, where he got off and walked to the host home. Using the same identifying knock, he was welcomed into the home by all those who were waiting to be trained. Of course he was carrying the same battered tote bag, with a variety of printed material among that was the printed lesson material to be distributed. Everyone was cautiously optimistic, which was consoling to Ralph.

At the close of the session, Ralph departed, utilizing the same method used to arrive at the home. In a little less than an hour, he was safely home and had not detected any unusual activity by anyone who might be suspected of being a spy.

For the Friday training session, Ralph used a totally different method of transportation. The home for this meeting was farther away than the other two. He walked to the park again, carrying a brown paper bag, with a variety of printed material, just in case he was stopped and asked about its contents. His lesson materials were buried deep in the bottom of the bag. Arriving at the park, he took out a paperback novel and began to read but scanning his surroundings constantly for any suspicious activity. Nothing seemed to be amiss.

About an hour prior to the meeting time, using a prepaid cell phone, he called a cab to pick him up at the park. He had the cabdriver drop him off at a drugstore a few blocks from the home where the training session was to be held. After making a few minor purchases at the drugstore, he walked on to the gathering place.

This session was as successful as the two prior meetings. These trainers were just as committed to training next week as the previous eight couples had been. Ralph was encouraged at the prospects of the contents of chapter 15 being shared with many other believers. He was sure that questions would be raised for him to address when they met again in two weeks.

Ralph took Saturday and Sunday off from study and lesson preparation. He spent most of Saturday driving aimlessly through the Florida countryside in his truck. Stopping at a fast food restaurant for lunch, he listened to the people all around him lamenting the troublesome times coming upon them in this world. Someone said, "It seems as though God has forgotten about this world or is punishing it for some reason."

Another man angrily asked, "How could God let all this stuff happen to us?"

Silently, Ralph thought about those conversations. He had no inclination to enter into the angry accusations against God. As the talk continued, he wondered if they had forgotten so quickly how God had been banned from the schools of the United States. *Had they forgotten that any form of prayer or mention of God had been forbidden at all public gatherings, including graduation exercises of high schools and colleges? Why had the Ten Commandments been banned from all public buildings?*

"We do not like God's laws telling us what to do," was the prevailing attitude.

Were they ignoring the fact that Christian holidays had been outlawed from government and institutional observances? Had this bunch of God-haters forgotten that businesses had forbidden their employees to even say, "Merry Christmas," at Christmastime? How could they forget that a Christmas tree now had to be referred to as a holiday tree? How could this bunch forget that the president didn't even want the United States to be known as a Christian nation any longer? Ralph wanted to ask, "Why think of God now or blame him since he has been kicked out of all public life?" However, he did not. He quietly ate his hamburger and fries, sipping his cold drink.

He had to bite his tongue to keep from reminding all these agnostics that God was a gentleman, and being so, he was not forcing his goodness upon anyone, nor invading where he was not wanted. "Where was God?" God was gone, as he had been known to do before. *This was not a day of mercy and grace as prior to the rapture. This is the great tribulation, when God's wrath is being poured out on a God-forsaking world*, Ralph thought to himself.

One of the inevitable laws of God is being displayed. Galatians 6:7 states that law clearly and distinctly. "Do not be deceived,

God is not mocked; for whatever a man sows, that he will also reap." An ungodly world is reaping God's tormenting wrath because they rejected his love, mercy, grace, and, most of all, his Son, Jesus Christ.

Finishing his sandwich and soft drink, Ralph left the restaurant and the angry attacks upon God by people who had never had any time for him in their lives. Now they cannot escape the torments of the great tribulation. If he was not the cause, he was permitting the turmoil of this horrific time.

Late in the afternoon, Ralph returned home in time to share another delicious meal prepared by Faye. After supper, he shared time with Todd and Faye while taking in the evening news, such as it was. Most of it was propaganda disseminated by the Antichrist. There are more threats and saber rattling from Russia and Iran. They seem to be patiently wearing down the resistance and resolve of Israel and the United States. As usual, there was no response reported to the Russian/Islamic rhetoric. Is that really accurate, or are responses and actions not being reported?

Since there are no churches to attend on Sunday, Ralph planned to go to the beach tomorrow and spend much of the day reading and relaxing. Bibles having been banned, he had a clever plan for concealing a Bible that was just a little smaller than a paperback novel. Having two copies of a favorite western novel, he carefully removed the cover of one of them and secured the Bible inside the backing. That way he could read the Bible on the beach, without fear of detection. It could later be placed on his bookshelves with the other western novels, never being noticed without inspection of every book. Along with this concealed Bible, he had another novel he was reading. So reading, strolling along the beach in the lapping waves, silently praying, and relaxing in a beach chair at the edge of the water occupied most of his Sunday afternoon.

He did give some consideration to the studies he planned to complete the next day. During all of his activity and inactivity,

Ralph was constantly surveying everyone within sight of him. Was anyone giving him undue attention? The afternoon passed uneventfully, and as the sun was setting, he put everything into the truck and drove home, without being followed.

At the conclusion of a light evening meal, the three of them strolled into the family room, switching on the TV to catch any additional world-shaking news. Most of the reports were repeats of former events and propaganda. There were a couple news items that caught the serious attention of Ralph. First, Iran had issued a terse threat directed toward the United States.

The president of Iran was shown speaking, "The silence of Big Satan is totally unimpressive. Big Satan cannot evade the wrath and retribution of Iran allied with Russia. Just as Little Satan will be wiped from the map, so will Big Satan. All of the sanctions and hardships imposed upon the government and people of Iran will not go unnoticed. Big Satan will pay dearly for their leadership in these moves against Allah and his people. The world map is going to change in the immediate future. Let Big Satan take note of this. These are not idle words but truth backed up by determination, dedication, an adequate, anxious, desirous military power, and enough allies to disseminate the mighty United States. In addition to all this, we have the blessings of Allah, who is against all infidels, especially the United States leaders, who have mocked him in many ways. Allah and Iran cannot be ignored. Allah and his followers are to rule the world. We have been patiently working toward accomplishing Allah's will, and the final showdown is imminent. Let all who hear or ignore this decree be forewarned." The TV cameras remained fixed on the silent defiant face of Ahmadinejad for several seconds to let his message sink into the minds of all viewers.

Ralph was convinced that this message is more than a threat. He was hopeful that the leaders of the United States (Big Satan) were listening, really listening. If the threat was accomplished, and it could be, in light of the decision that the president of the United States had made to decrease military might and nuclear missiles, the United States was in grave jeopardy. It was an irresponsible decision, made by a commander in chief, which will help bring about the demise of a great nation. While the president was decreasing the military power of the United States, Russia and Iran were increasing all their military might, especially nuclear missiles. Also, Iran was moving ahead, unchecked, in their development of nuclear weapons. Now, who would they be used against? "That would explain why the former greatest nation in the world is not mentioned in any of the end-time prophecies of the Bible," Ralph lamented.

The second new item that captivated the concern of Ralph was what United States spy satellites had detected in the last few days. There was conclusive evidence of massive pontoon bridges being constructed across every north/south river and stream leading from Iran and Russia to the west. This was taking place in Iraq, Syria, and Lebanon. It was obvious that major military movement was planned to take place soon. Why else would these massive bridges be installed? In addition, the spy satellites were detecting increased activity at known, and previously unknown, nuclear missile sites. It appeared that an attack was being planned for the very near future.

Ralph wondered out loud, "Why are the military leaders and the president of the United States evidently still napping?" *And what is Israel doing about all this activity that is creating a clear military pathway to them? It is evident they are doing nothing. And what is the attitude of the Antichrist to all this saber rattling and military preparations? Is he oblivious to it all or does he have some sinister scheme?* Ralph, Todd, and Faye are deeply disturbed by the plethora of troubling news, but they reminded themselves that this is the time of great tribulation.

Monday morning, a feeling of urgency motivated Ralph to have the trainers continue their scheduled teaching. In spite of tragic world conditions, which seemed to be shaping up, he decided to dig into the study for future, final lessons yet to be taught to the trainers.

These scenarios of world events should not be surprising to believers who are Bible scholars. "Over twenty-five hundred years ago, God revealed to his prophet Ezekiel the very things which are taking place today," Ralph reflected. Here is a message from God to a defiant Russia:

> "After many days you will be visited. In the latter years you will come into the land of those brought back from the sword *and* gathered from many people on the mountains of Israel, which had long been desolate; they were brought out of the nations, and now all of them dwell safely. You will ascend, coming like a storm, covering the land like a cloud, you and all your troops and many peoples with you."
>
> Thus says the Lord God: "On that day it shall come to pass *that* thoughts will arise in your mind, and you will make an evil plan: You will say, 'I will go up against a land of unwalled villages; I will go to a peaceful people, who dwell safely, all of them dwelling without walls, and having neither bars nor gates'—to take plunder and to take booty, to stretch out your hand against the waste places *that are again* inhabited, and against a people gathered from the nations, who have acquired livestock and goods, who dwell in the midst of the land. Sheba, Dedan, the merchants of Tarshish, and all their young lions will say to you, 'Have you come to take plunder? Have you gathered your army to take booty, to carry away silver and gold, to take away livestock and goods, to take great plunder?'"
>
> "Therefore, son of man, prophesy and say to Gog, 'Thus says the Lord God: "On that day when My people Israel dwell safely, will you not know it? Then you will come from our place out of the far north, you and many peoples with you, all of them riding on like a cloud, to cover the land. It will be in the latter days that I will bring you against My land, horses, a great company and a mighty army. You will come up against My people Israel so that

the nations may know Me, when I am hallowed in you, O
Gog, before their eyes." Thus says the Lord God: "Are *you*
he of whom I have spoken in former days by My servants
the prophets of Israel, who prophesied for years in those
days that I would bring you against them?"

(Ezekiel 38:8–17)

Ralph was concerned that this prophecy will be fulfilled within
weeks or even days. The destruction of Israel will be horrific,
and the United States will cease to exist as a great nation. "The
fall of Babylon will come," Ralph sorrowfully concludes again.
And he agreed with other Bible scholars and students that the
United States was the national Babylon, which will come to a
tragic ending.

As Ralph studied the Bible prophecies concerning the fall of
Babylon the Great and the daughter of Babylon, he came to several
conclusions. First of all, the Scriptural prophecies are numerous,
and secondly, he concludes that they are references to one and the
same nation, not a single city. And thirdly, he is convinced that
the Scriptures do not refer to a revived, restored Babylon of Iraq.
Ralph is also strongly convinced that the Bible is not referring
to a religious institution. The main reason he rules these out is
because none of them fit the description of the fallen Babylon
given in Revelation 18. In addition, there is general consensus
among many Bible scholars supporting his conclusions.

Bible scholars have determined that there are over eighteen
thousand prophesies in the Old and New Testament. These
prophesies take up over 8,000 of the 31,124 verses of the Bible.
That means that over one-fourth of the Bible is prophecy. Many of
them have been fulfilled exactly as foretold, and other prophecies
are yet to take place. Rest assured that all of the prophecies will
be properly fulfilled by the end of time. One of the prophecies to
be fulfilled is the fall of Babylon, which Ralph strongly believes
is about to take place.

Ralph lists some of the Scriptures relating to the fall of Babylon for his students to consider:

O daughter of Babylon, who are to be destroyed.

(Psalms 137:8)

And Babylon, the glory of kingdoms,
The beauty of the Chaldeans' pride,
Will be as when God overthrew Sodom and Gomorrah.

(Isaiah 13:19)

Sit in silence, and go into darkness,
O daughter of the Chaldeans;
For you shall no longer be called
The Lady of Kingdoms.

(Isaiah 47:5)

A sound of battle *is* in the land,
And of great destruction.
How the hammer of the whole earth has been cut apart and broken!
How Babylon has become a desolation among the nations!

(Jeremiah 50:22–23)

"Behold, I *am* against you,
O most haughty one!" says the Lord God of hosts;
"For your day has come,
The time *that* I will punish you.
The most proud shall stumble and fall,
And no one will raise him up;
I will kindle a fire in his cities,
And it will devour all around him.

(Jeremiah 50:31–32)

Behold, a people shall come from the north,
And a great nation and many kings

Shall be raised up from the ends of the earth.
They shall hold the bow and the lance;
They *are* cruel and shall not show mercy.
Their voice shall roar like the sea;
They shall ride on horses,
Set in array, like a man for the battle,
Against you, O daughter of Babylon.

(Jeremiah 50:40–42)

And the land will tremble and sorrow;
For every purpose of the Lord shall be performed against Babylon,
To make the land of Babylon a desolation without inhabitant.
The mighty men of Babylon have ceased fighting,
They have remained in their strongholds;
Their might has failed,
They became *like* women;
They have burned her dwelling places,
The bars of her *gate* are broken.

(Jeremiah 51:29–30)

For thus says the Lord of hosts, the God of Israel:
"The daughter of Babylon *is* like a threshing floor
When it is time to thresh her;
Yet a little while
And the time of her harvest will come."

(Jeremiah 51:33)

As Babylon *has caused* the slain of Israel to fall,
So at Babylon the slain of all the earth shall fall.

(Jeremiah 51:49)

After these things I saw another angel coming down from heaven, having great authority, and the earth was illuminated with his glory. And he cried mightily with a loud voice, saying, "Babylon the great is fallen, is fallen, and has become a dwelling place of demons, a prison for every foul spirit, and a cage for every unclean and hated bird! For all the nations have drunk of the wine of the wrath of her fornication, the kings of the earth have committed fornication with her, and the merchants of the earth have become rich through the abundance of her luxury.

(Revelation 18:1–3)

Therefore her plagues will come in one day—death and mourning and famine. And she will be utterly burned with fire, for strong *is* the Lord God who judges her.

(Revelation 18:8)

Ralph pointed out that the Babylon of the end time is foretold of their destruction and the manner in which it will take place. It will be with fire and brimstone as with Sodom and Gomorrah. The end-time Babylon will be known as the hammer of the whole earth or a strong powerful nation. It is to the dismay of the United States that Russia has become their equal, as a hammer of the whole earth. And that hammer is about to be used in horror against the United States.

None of the horrible destructive devices were used against ancient Babylon, though they were destroyed. "These prophecies are reserved for the end-time Babylon," Ralph reminded his listeners. God gave the main reason that Babylon will be destroyed in Jeremiah 51:49. The judgment of God will fall upon Babylon, the United States, because they permitted or caused so many of Israel to be slain by ignoring their treaty with them and refusing to go to their aid in the Russian/Islamic invasion. This action, or inaction, by the United States is a curse against Israel, which God will not ignore.

Although the United States had blessed Israel from 1948 to 1989, the leadership of America began to curse Israel by demanding that they surrender some of their God-given lands.

Lately, the American administration ignored and defied Israel altogether. God had instructed Israel not to surrender any of the land given to Abraham and inherited by modern Israel in (Ezekiel 48:14), "And they shall not sell or exchange any of it; they may not alienate this best *part* of the land, for *it is* holy to the Lord."

Additionally, the daughter of Babylon, the United States's wickedness, immorality, violence, godlessness, and bloodshed had reached to heaven, and God recalled all of it (Revelation 18:5). Ralph asked his students, "What would be considered the number 1 source of bloodshed in America?" There was a quick response—murder. But Ralph had to kindly disagree in spite of the fact that over seven hundred thousand Americans had been murdered in the last thirty-eight years. However, during the same amount of time reliable estimates are that abortionists have killed over fifty million innocent unborn babies. And that is shedding innocent blood, which is condemned by God:

> Now, son of man, will you judge, will you judge the bloody city? Yes, show her all her abominations! Then say, "Thus says the Lord God: 'The city sheds blood in her own midst, that her time may come; and she makes idols within herself to defile herself. You have become guilty by the blood which you have shed, and have defiled yourself with the idols which you have made. You have caused your days to draw near, and have come to *the end of* your years; therefore I have made you a reproach to the nations, and a mockery to all countries. *Those* near and *those* far from you will mock you as infamous *and* full of tumult.'"
>
> (Ezekiel 22:2–5)

The United States led the world in the number of abortions committed. In addition, the abortionists pushed the murderous practice on other nations as well. Since January 22, 1973, when the supreme court struck down the law prohibiting abortion in every state, sixty other nations have followed their lead. But Ralph said, "Murder is murder whether committed inside or outside the womb." And God has taken note of all this bloodshed. In reality, the daughter of Babylon is bringing about their own destruction by disregarding God's directives, which is the judgment of God.

Ralph shared the reasons why he believed that the United States is the end-time daughter of Babylon or Babylon the Great, which he believed to be different from "Mystery, Babylon the Great" in Revelation 17. First, he saw them as perfectly fitting the description of "Babylon the Great" in Revelation 18. They are a rich, powerful, arrogant, godless, sinful, world-dominating, influential nation as described in Revelation 18:

> For her sins have reached to heaven, and God has remembered her iniquities. Render to her just as she rendered to you, and repay her double according to her works; in the cup which she has mixed, mix double for her. In the measure that she glorified herself and lived luxuriously, in the same measure give her torment and sorrow; for she says in her heart, 'I sit *as* queen, and am no widow, and will not see sorrow.
>
> (Revelation 18:5–7)

And in the second place, the mourning of merchants, other national leaders, shipping firms, and world financial institutions, as revealed in Revelation 18:9–19, could not be taking place over a fallen religious order or a restored city in Iraq. The United States is the only nation that presently fits this description. Again, it is noted that the United States has been referred to as the world's indispensable nation. The daughter of Babylon will have tremendous world significance until the time of their tragic fall, and it will fall.

Ralph also considers the United States as the Babylon, which will fall because of the constant threat and success of radical Islam against America. Al Qaeda has vowed to destroy America and showed definite signs of this determination. Ahmadinejad, the president of Iran, has boasted that Big Satan, the United States, and Little Satan, Israel, will be wiped off the world map. And since he was now allied with Russia, by treaty, this is a definite possibility. Actually, Muslims have vowed to conquer the world for Allah, who is a nonexistent false god. To be truthful, Allah is a false, fake god of the powerful, growing cult of Islam. Allah was, and is, a false moon god, which was the favorite god of Mohammad's family during the sixth century. At that time, there were 360 different gods in the Arabian world, one for every day of the year.

The idea for this successful Muslim cult was born in the deranged mind of a murderer by the name of Mohammad, born in Mecca in AD 570. He was reared by his grandfather since his father died before he was born and his mother died when he was six years old. Strangely, his father's name was Abed-Allah, in honor of the fake moon god.

Mohammad became a camel driver and, later, a merchant. Finally, he became a visionary political and religious leader in the Arab world although he could neither read nor write. As he promoted his false religion, it was only natural that he elevated and promoted the false moon god, Allah. It was his visions and, so-called, messages that Mohammad received from Allah that constitutes the Qu'ran. This is what Muslims consider the divine word of God. And many verses in the Qu'ran are about killing the infidels and those who resist Islam. In fact, Mohammad slaughtered thousands of people who resisted conversion to his false religion. He claimed that Allah commanded him to fight people until they became Muslims. And all Muslim scholars agreed to this. Muslims are bent upon world domination. They are committed to imposing Islam on every nation on earth.

Radical Muslims have a severe hatred for Israel and the United States, whom they call Little Satan and Big Satan, vowing to wipe both countries off of the map. There are over 1.5 billion

Muslims in the world today and over 1.4 million of these reside in the United States. They openly boast that one day they will gain political and religious control of the entire world, and Ralph believed this will take place under the rule of the Antichrist during the great tribulation.

Also, Ralph believed two other matters must be mentioned. First, those shouting, "Death to America," should be taken seriously. Secondly, contrary to what some religious leaders propagate, God and Allah are not synonymous.

Another reason Ralph saw the United States as the end-time Babylon, which is doomed to fall, is that the enemies of America now have enough nuclear weapons to completely destroy America. That was made possible since Iran has signed a treaty with Russia and was allied with them. And they will use them. They really intended to bring death to America and will. Russia has 8,800 nukes, while the United States has 5,535, unless the president has secretly had more destroyed. Destruction of America was paramount in the minds and plans of Muslim Jihadists, and they will use any method possible to accomplish their goal.

Ralph discussed with the groups what it would take to destroy America. They came to some conclusions that were staggering. It would mean taking out Washington, DC, the center of government; New York City, the financial center of America; Los Angeles; and Hollywood, the cultural pollution center. In addition, huge oil refineries would be bombed, along with electrical generators at major dams and the commerce centers in Chicago, Seattle, Houston, Atlanta, Miami, Boston, etcetera. All shipping ports would be among the first to be taken out. No major cities in the United States would be ignored and left intact.

In the discussions, they tried to imagine what it would be like with no national seat of government, no congress, as ineffective as they were at times, no supreme court, no White House, and no treasury. Further, they considered what it would be like with no Federal Reserve, no World Bank, no US Mint, no stock exchange, no Pentagon to direct the armed forces, no broadcasting or cable TV networks functioning, and no trading of world goods. Finally, all of them seriously concluded that they wished they were gone, for it appeared that these horrific, unbelievable conditions were about to become a reality.

A final concluding reason that Ralph believed that the United States was the Babylon the Great, which would soon fall, is that there is no mention of the greatest nation upon the earth in end-time prophecies. That is evident to him. They will be gone and, apparently, soon.

The rest of the day and the next day, Ralph attempted to concentrate on preparing the lessons for the following week. He was finding it difficult to stay focused because of fast-moving world events.

Wednesday afternoon, Todd rushed into Ralph's study with remarkable news. "The neighbors across the street are moving out," he almost shouted. Immediately, Ralph was on his feet rushing to the front window to observe the good news. They really were moving out. The black Lincoln was being hurriedly loaded with personal belongings by four people. In the process, they hardly gave a glance toward Ralph's house, which was very unusual. Once again, Ralph was thankful for the one-way glass windows. He can watch without being seen.

Soon the black Lincoln roared down the street with four troublesome people as passengers. *Now, what could that all be about,* the unseen observers thankfully wondered. Ralph was so overjoyed and thankful that he found it difficult to resume his studies and typing at the computer. Finally, he concluded his efforts, cheerfully taking the rest of the day off to celebrate the departure of the spies. For some unknown reason, there was no urgency to complete the studies to be presented the following week. However, late that afternoon, Ralph went back to his study to complete the document he had been working on for the next training presentation.

Three End-Time Wars and Russian/Islamic Attack of Israel and the USA

Halfway around the world, major military activity was taking place. As already detected by United States spy satellites, a mammoth Russian force was massed on their southwestern border. Tanks, along with all manner of military equipment have been photographed and relayed to the military leaders of Israel and the United States. At the same time, thousands of Iranian troops and military equipment were poised on the western border of Iran. There was anxiety and restlessness among the troops as they await completion of the pontoon bridges en route to their yet unrevealed destination. Only their leaders know for sure, but many of the troops suspect that it was Israel.

Along with the massive troops from Russia and Iran, thousands and thousands of troops and military machinery will be included from Iraq, Libya, Turkey, Syria, and most of the Muslim or pro-Muslim nations. All of the named nations are Muslim and are listed in Ezekiel 38. That is why the invading armies are referred to as Russian/Islamic.

The Bible proclaimed that the Russian/Islamic invasion of Israel would take place when Israel was seemingly at peace and enjoying safety, not involved in conflict with other nations. The Antichrist and the European Union had been able to secure a peace treaty for seven years (Daniel 9:27). This is the only period of peace Israel has enjoyed since becoming a nation in 1948. And it is about to come to an end.

Multiplied thousands of troops are just awaiting the command to move forward in an effort to wipe Israel off the map. *Why is Israel not taking preemptive action as they have done before? Do they trust the Antichrist and the European Union, along with their ally, the United States, to protect them? Of course, none of that is going to happen.*

There will be a simultaneous movement of troops toward Israel. They will not attack Israel with nuclear missiles as Ezekiel explained the goal:

> To take plunder and to take booty, to stretch out your hand against the waste places *that are again* inhabited, and against a people gathered from the nations, who have acquired livestock and goods, who dwell in the midst of the land. Sheba, Dedan, the merchants of Tarshish, and all their young lions will say to you, 'Have you come to take plunder? Have you gathered your army to take booty, to carry away silver and gold, to take away livestock and goods, to take great plunder?
>
> (Ezekiel 13:12–13)

Iran has hated Israel for many years because they were given land to form a nation. It is the intent of the Russian/Islamic army to take over Israel and give the land to the surrounding Muslim nations. The Russian/Islamic armies will assemble in Syria and Lebanon along the northern and eastern borders of Israel to make the devastating attack. They not only wanted to destroy the people of Israel but also to take away their bounty and riches.

The nuclear weapons will be used against Big Satan, the United States. The invasion of Israel and the nuclear attack upon the United States will take place simultaneously to avoid intervention by the United States. However, the president of the United States has no plans to intervene although such a treaty does exist. It is very possible that the Russian/Islamic force was the red horse mentioned in Revelation 6:

When He opened the second seal, I heard the second living creature saying, "Come and see." Another horse, fiery red, went out. And it was granted to the one who sat on it to take peace from the earth, and that *people* should kill one another; and there was given to him a great sword.

(Revelation 6:3–4)

The term "red" was used to indicate the bloodshed that will be so widespread. Literally, millions will die in this conflict.

Europe and other Western nations will be spared because of their major Muslim populations. Supposedly, secret radio frequencies and codes have been coordinated between the troops surrounding Israel and command centers in Russia. When the first mortar rounds were lobbed into Israel, command will be given for the launch of ICBMs, in mass, toward the United States. All major cities, especially port cities and governmental centers, known ICBM sites, and major military bases have been preset in nuclear armed missiles. No troop invasion of the United States was planned by the Russian/Islamic armies. That will be unnecessary. Within seconds after the official invasion of Israel, hundreds of these missiles will be launched to wipe Big Satan off the map.

Finally, word has gotten through to Israel of the intention of the massed troops. Immediately, all reserve forces are activated, and defensive positions are taken along their northern and eastern borders. All their aircraft pilots are called into action, and every attack jet and bomber are loaded with live ammunition, ready to be in the air within minutes. In addition, the nation is warned of the possibility of an imminent attack causing activation of all shelters and defensive positions.

Peacetime is over, and possible mass destruction is inevitable. All the Israeli forces facing the Russian/Islamic armies will be so outnumbered that no comparison can be projected, but they will fight to the death, defending their nation. They have finally awakened, but is it too late?

Repeated, urgent Israeli communications requesting assistance from to the United States go unanswered. The United States president is reminded of the existing treaties, but that communication is intentionally ignored. In disrespect, the Israeli ambassador is refused a conference with either the state department or the president. Additionally, appeals to the European Union and the Antichrist falls on deaf ears. Israel is on their own, facing the most threatening conflict of their history.

Early on a sunny morning, tank, truck, and all manner of military equipment motors come to life. The forward command has been given. In just a few minutes, there is the rumbling roar of military machinery on the move.

Within seconds, spy satellites relay this message to the United States and Israeli military command. Israeli troops and aircraft are in readiness, but they do not make a preemptive counter attack. They will await an actual attack by the enemy before they respond, as detrimental and ineffective as it may be. Within days, the Russian/Islamic armies will be in position against Israel. What will be the outcome of this one-sided war?

Is the United States president and military command still asleep? Why has their intelligence community not picked up on the intensions of Russia and Iran? Do they ignorantly believe that only Israel will be attacked? And why has the recent message of Ahmadinejad to the world, specifically naming the United States as a target to be wiped off the map, evidently been ignored? There are questions upon questions, but what is being done?

In the face of such staggering world developments, Ralph has called off all future training sessions. All believers were called upon to pray, staying close to God, in these uncertain, threatening times. Believers were panicky along with the rest of the world. How many of them will survive the rumored attack upon the United States? All of their lives have been lived with the possibility of nuclear war, but now it may be imminent for spy satellites have photographed hundreds of Russian ICBMs poised on their pads ready for launch. This information is in the hands of the United States military command, but what are they doing about it?

Along with the telephone calls temporarily canceling all training sessions, Ralph urged all believers to read Revelation 9:1–21. A description of what is about to take place is prophesied in that chapter, and they need to be aware of it, taking appropriate actions. Special attention should be given to Revelation 9:13–19:

> Then the sixth angel sounded: And I heard a voice from the four horns of the golden altar which is before God, saying to the sixth angel who had the trumpet, "Release the four angels who are bound at the great river Euphrates." So the four angels, who had been prepared for the hour and day and month and year, were released to kill a third of mankind. Now the number of the army of the horsemen *was* two hundred million; I heard the number of them. And thus I saw the horses in the vision: those who sat on them had breastplates of fiery red, hyacinth blue, and sulfur yellow; and the heads of the horses *were* like the heads of lions; and out of their mouths came fire, smoke, and brimstone. By these three *plagues* a third of mankind was killed—by the fire and the smoke and the brimstone which came out of their mouths. For their power is in their mouth and in their tails; for their tails *are* like serpents, having heads; and with them they do harm.

Ralph noted with intense interest how exactly God foretold of this conflict. The massive army was described along with a description of the major weaponry used against the daughter of Babylon. All one needs to recall was viewing a peaceful missile launch from Cape Kennedy. And Ralph had viewed many of these peaceful launches from the beaches or close proximity. Millions have seen the launches on TV. The power was in the tail or thrusting rockets. If it was a weapon of war, there would be awesome power in the head as a nuclear bomb would be affixed to the launched missile. It is the vapor trail of the rocket that reminds one of a snake trailing and drifting in the sky. Additionally, God described the destructive power of the nuclear bombs. People were consumed by the fire, brimstone, and the smoke, which was fallout from the initial blast. Shockingly, God declared that one-third of mankind will be killed by these horrible weapons of war. These facts caused Ralph to wonder how many of them might meet the Lord in the very near future.

Ralph concluded that this Scripture passage in Revelation was definitely referring to the imminent threat. His reasoning and conclusions were based upon the fact that three major end-time wars were identified in the Bible. Two of them will take place in the great tribulation, and the third one will be at the end when Satan convinces the pagan world to attack Christ and his kingdom. This war will take place at the ending of the thousand-year reign of Christ with his saints after Satan is released for a season.

The first war mentioned is the attack upon Israel in the end times when they are at peace. This is the conflict staring the world in the face now and referred to in Scriptures earlier. It is the only war that could possibly be with nuclear weapons, as described in Revelation 9. And this war will be led by Russia and Iran.

The second war is led by the Antichrist when Jesus comes to this earth to reign for a thousand years, with his saints and angels. The whole world will be engaged in that war against Christ. However, Christ will destroy that massive army by the word of his mouth. Both the Antichrist and the false prophet will be captured and cast bodily into hell, to be punished for ever, as foretold by God's Word:

> Now I saw heaven opened, and behold, a white horse. And He who sat on him *was* called Faithful and True, and in righteousness He judges and makes war. His eyes *were* like a flame of fire, and on His head *were* many crowns. He had a name written that no one knew except Himself. He

was clothed with a robe dipped in blood, and His name is called The Word of God. And the armies in heaven, clothed in fine linen, white and clean, followed Him on white horses. Now out of His mouth goes a sharp sword, that with it He should strike the nations. And He Himself will rule them with a rod of iron. He Himself treads the winepress of the fierceness and wrath of Almighty God. And He has on *His* robe and on His thigh a name written:

KING OF KINGS AND
LORD OF LORDS.

Then I saw an angel standing in the sun; and he cried with a loud voice, saying to all the birds that fly in the midst of heaven, "Come and gather together for the supper of the great God, that you may eat the flesh of kings, the flesh of captains, the flesh of mighty men, the flesh of horses and of those who sit on them, and the flesh of all *people,* free and slave, both small and great."

And I saw the beast, the kings of the earth, and their armies, gathered together to make war against Him who sat on the horse and against His army. Then the beast was captured, and with him the false prophet who worked signs in his presence, by which he deceived those who received the mark of the beast and those who worshiped his image. These two were cast alive into the lake of fire burning with brimstone. And the rest were killed with the sword which proceeded from the mouth of Him who sat on the horse.

And all the birds were filled with their flesh.

(Revelation 19:11–21)

No nuclear bombs are needed in that war, which will be led by the Antichrist. And fulfilling the prophecy of God to Daniel, the Antichrist is done away with, but not by human means:

Through his cunning
He shall cause deceit to prosper under his rule;

And he shall exalt *himself* in his heart.
He shall destroy many in *their* prosperity.
He shall even rise against the Prince of princes;
But he shall be broken without human means.

(Daniel 8:25)

The third, and final war, on this earth is described in Revelation 20:7–12. That conflict will be led by Satan himself, to his doom, for he will be cast into hell where the Antichrist and the false prophet are. In fact, hell was created by God for the devil and his fallen angels (Matthew 25:41). So Satan will finally arrive at his eternal home in the horrors of hell. And no nuclear weapons, as described in Revelation 9, are mentioned or needed in that battle:

> Now when the thousand years have expired, Satan will be released from his prison and will go out to deceive the nations which are in the four corners of the earth, Gog and Magog, to gather them together to battle, whose number *is* as the sand of the sea. They went up on the breadth of the earth and surrounded the camp of the saints and the beloved city. And fire came down from God out of heaven and devoured them. The devil, who deceived them, was cast into the lake of fire and brimstone where the beast and the false prophet *are*. And they will be tormented day and night forever and ever.
>
> (Revelation 20:7–10)

So Ralph prepared himself and prayed for his fellow believers as they faced the horrors of a soon-coming conflict. After all, this was the great tribulation, and easy days and events were not promised or to be expected. Confused and concerned by all of this, Todd rushed into Ralph's study, almost demanding that he come and view the disturbing TV news, which is being given.

For the first time since the Cold War, a warning of a nuclear war was being read, and reread, by a solemn-faced TV reporter.

The warning was coming from the president and the chairman of the joint chief of staff of the United States military. American citizens were informed that a massive army was now on the move toward Israel and threatening to wipe Israel and the United States off the map. These threats are now being taken seriously! All Americans should make plans to find the best possible shelters and secure basic food and water supplies to last for several days. To stress the importance of this warning, the reporter continued with this solemn statement: "The United States Intelligence Agency has confirmed that hundreds of known Russian ICBMs are presently poised on their launch pads, ready to be launched. And there is no question as to their destination. Also, the supposedly secret information between the Russian troops and launch commands has been intercepted by intelligence agents. When the first shots are fired against Israel, hundreds of nuclear tipped missiles will be launched against the United States." Much of the world's people have feared a nuclear holocaust for years, and now that may be only days away.

By midafternoon the next day, almost every food store shelf was empty of nonperishable food items and all containers of water. Truckloads of food supplies are en route to anxious awaiting customers. Distribution centers are now being emptied of food supplies and water. It is becoming evident that some citizens have put off this matter too long. When the convoy of trucks cease running, the food supplies will be depleted, much to the dismay of many. Panic was setting in among American citizens, and awful acts of theft and frustration were prevalent.

The seriously, somberly speaking TV announcer stated that there may be some encouraging word for Americans. Without declaring all out war against Russia, Iran, and their allies, which the president of the United States was unwilling to do for unknown reasons, Americans had to await the outcome. Americans were assured that adequate, extensive, retaliatory strike preparations have been accomplished. Probably the main reason the president was not willing to take preemptive action was because he has decreased the military power of the United States below that which existed prior to World War II. Defeat was inevitable by attack or delay.

The United States, which has been referred to as the world's indispensable nation is about to encounter indescribable destruction. At the same time, the United States will unleash incomprehensible retaliatory strikes against Russia and Iran. "What can be encouraging about the prospects of at least three major nations of the world being devastated within two or three hours, or less?" Ralph muttered mournfully.

"Encouraging words" continue by the TV news commentator. "Since the unusual military activity of a few weeks ago, the United States military has been quietly and undetectably preparing massive retaliatory strikes. Military leaders have not been ignoring the threats and actions by the Russian/Islamic officials as suspected by many Americans, and others, in the world. The Pentagon officials have become convinced that Russia and Iran have planned to secretly strike the United States simultaneously with their attack upon Israel. And this strong suspicion had been backed up by intelligence reports supplied to them."

There has not been a major call up of military reserves because the population of the main military bases has been purposefully decreased to only essential personnel. This has been done quietly and discreetly because United States military leaders are certain of nuclear attack upon these bases. Adequate underground bunkers and protection have been provided for those required to remain on bases. A conventional attack by troops and support military machinery was not in the offing for the United States. A nuclear attack has been planned in detail, which makes a conventional attack unnecessary.

All nuclear launching submarines have been secretly maneuvering to previously assigned attack positions, and there was no intelligence information indicating detection of their movement by Russia or Iran. All naval fleets were in attack position, their maneuvering having been explained as a practice exercise. In addition, nuclear bomb-carrying bombers have been flown, a few at a time, to positions closer to Russia and Iran, with maximum loads of live nuclear bombs. Flights of a few at a time were to avoid arousing alarm in the minds of the enemy or to raise undue questions by the news media.

Refueling tanker aircraft were constantly in the air at necessary refueling points for bombers around the world. Refueling will be necessary for the return to their bases. Questions as to why these tanker aircraft were continually airborne were again explained, again, as practice maneuvers.

Two of the most important actions taken by the United States were activating the reduced ICBM arsenal and the moving of patriot antimissile batteries. Increased, frantic activity surrounding known United States ICBM sites had been detected. Having been raised from their protective underground silos, missiles were presently poised on their pads ready for instant launch. That is why all news media had been barred from anywhere near these sites and banned from reporting any unusual activity.

Probably, most importantly, all available patriot antimissile batteries have been moved to protective positions and were fully manned for instant launches. Surrounding major cities, both coast lines, Canada (by their permission), Alaska, and numerous batteries of patriots in Europe were ready for instant launch. It is known, from experience by Israel's recent actions, that all incoming missiles in a massive attack cannot be taken out by the patriots. But United States military experts are hopeful that at least half, or more, may be destroyed far out over the oceans.

The Pentagon was encouraged by the fact that they have very high altitude spy satellites in constant orbit around the world, viewing and reporting the most minute launch activity by Russia and Iran. When a missile launch takes place anywhere in the world, the United States military knows it instantly, and the launched vehicle is tracked every second. When Russia and Iran launch their attack upon the United States (Big Satan), these satellites will relay information to the patriots as to position, altitude, speed, direction traveling, possible destination, and the appropriate patriot antimissile missiles will be launched for interception and destruction. "Doom's day is upon us," Ralph said to Todd and Faye.

It was announced that there will be a testing of all alarm systems in every city in the United States the next day at 2:00 p.m. With the blaring sirens, everyone was to take protective action, as if it were an actual attack. These practice sessions will take place at different times of the day and night for the next few days. Everyone should take the matter very seriously and act appropriately. Again, this was the first time for such action for decades since the Cold War. This news was causing major panic in the minds of many Americans. After the few days of practice alarms, the sirens went silent until there was an actual emergency alarm. When that alarm was sounded, all American citizens should move quickly to the nearest protection center.

Evacuation routes were to be planned and properly announced in every major city in the United States, and citizens were expected to give full cooperation. It may be a matter of life or death. Furthermore, citizens were warned of nuclear fallout from initial blasts and the dangers of radiation sickness. All precautions were to be taken for survival. There was a common topic of discussion as to which might be worse, instant death or slower death from radiation sickness. Ralph and his friends considered this same question.

Another news reporter broke in and informed TV viewers around the world that the Russian/Islamic forces were speedily advancing toward Israel. Frantically, Israel was preparing to meet this awesome force that was so intent on wiping them off of the map. Since all pleas for assistance have been ignored or refused, Israel faced this overwhelming enemy alone. But they have done that before and survived. There was always the hope or possibility of unforeseen assistance. Every able bodied Israeli was armed and in position to fight to the death, protecting their God-given nation. Row after row of tanks and mortar launchers were also expertly manned and maneuvered to welcome the advancing army. They might be overrun, but they were determined to inflict heavy casualties upon their enemies.

Israeli attack aircraft were constantly airborne, patrolling the northern and eastern borders of Israel. They were careful not to stray into Libyan or Syrian airspace. They were awaiting the first shots fired into Israel or the first tank to rumble into their territory. When that moment arrives, they will unleash a fiery attack upon the Russian/Islamic armies.

Late Wednesday afternoon, true to previous predictions, the first line of Russian/Islamic tanks and military armament arrived and began maneuvering into attack positions on the north and east of Israel's borders. By Thursday evening, a massive force was seemingly awaiting the command to advance into Israel. Tensions were tremendously high on both sides of the borders. Over twenty-five hundred years ago, God revealed to Daniel the very thing which is playing out before the eyes of the world via TV:

> "Therefore, son of man, prophesy and say to Gog," Thus says the Lord God: "On that day when My people Israel dwell safely, will you not know *it?* Then you will come from your place out of the far north, you and many peoples with you, all of them riding on horses, a great company and a mighty army. You will come up against My people Israel like a cloud, to cover the land. It will be in the latter days that I will bring you against My land, so that the nations may know Me, when I am hallowed in you, O Gog, before their eyes."
>
> (Daniel 38:14–16)

Early Saturday morning, which is the Jewish Sabbath, the first mortar rounds were fired into the Israeli forces, and tanks and mortar rounds were unleashed by both sides. As Russian/Islamic tanks maneuvered crossing the borders of Israel, they were met with murderous fire from Israeli tanks and attack aircraft. Instantly, the Israeli roaming attack fighters and bomber aircraft turned toward the advancing Russian/Islamic armies, firing and bombing very accurately. Their skillful maneuvering enabled them to avoid many enemy surface-to-air missiles. Repeated firing runs were stunning the enemy who thought the invasion would be simple. In fact, the advancing army was checked at the border for some time, and the casualties on both sides were astounding.

Of course, when the first shots were fired into Israeli forces, Russian and Iranian nuclear missiles were launched at the United States. Immediately, attack alarm sirens were screaming in almost every city in the United States. The wailing sirens were so numerous and loud that they could be heard clear up to heaven, but there was no mercy from God. The United States had turned their back upon Israel's plea for assistance, in a sense cursing them, and God has turned his back upon the United States, as he said he would in Genesis 12:3:

> I will bless those who bless you,
> And I will curse him who curses you;
> And in you all the families of the earth shall be blessed.

That was God's promise to Abraham and his descendants, the Jewish nation. And if one checked history, that was precisely the way it had been throughout the ages. Now it was taking place again, against a great nation that God brought into existence, but which turned against God, forgetting or ignoring their heritage. "They drifted so far away from God and his Word that today, they are compared to wicked Babylon," Ralph bemoans.

American citizens realized that they only have a few minutes to get to a shelter. *And will it give protection?* they wondered.

Long lines of vehicles attempting to evacuate major cities were caught by nuclear blasts. There was too little time to escape from nuclear attack by slow-moving evacuation attempts.

Ralph and his friends discussed what action they should take, and they had only minutes to decide. They decided to stay put in Ralph's house. They had adequate food stored to last for months, and the well will supply water indefinitely. On top of that, they lived in a smaller city on the east coast of Florida, over 250 miles north of Miami. However, they were within 100 miles of Cape Kennedy and Patrick Air Force Base. These could be targeted by Russian missiles, but they decided to take the risk.

Ralph and his friends were confident that if they should die instantly in a nuclear blast, their souls would immediately be with the great multitude in heaven who died in the faith during the great tribulation (Revelation 7:13–14).

Fortunately, a northwest wind was blowing rather strongly, and that would carry nuclear fallout away from their position. Although they were prepared to die and meet the Lord they love, all three of them spent the next hour on their knees praying for protection, if that is God's will. Most of all, they prayed for the millions who will meet their eternal fate in the next hour or so. In the background, they heard the unfolding events, as shown on TV, but it suddenly went silent. TV coverage had been knocked out or blacked out.

Ralph realized that Babylon was in the process of falling. One of the greatest, most blessed nations of all time was falling. *Why?* As a whole, leadership and a large majority of the citizens of the United States have forgotten the God who brought them into existence and blessed them. And the Bible has a solemn warning to such nations, "The wicked shall be turned into hell, *And* all the nations that forget God" (Psalms 9:17). Any casual study of history will confirm that prophetic promise of God.

Almost simultaneously with the launch of Russian ICBMs, hundreds of United States nuclear missiles were launched. The high altitude spy satellites picked up the ignition of Russian/ Islamic missiles, instantly alerting the United States military leaders. In a matter of seconds, hundreds of patriot antimissile missiles were also launched and were streaking skyward, having locked onto incoming ballistic missiles. They were not able to intercept all the massive Russian ballistic missiles, but many were destroyed by the patriots before reaching their destination or causing damage.

Nuclear holocaust was now taking place, and national Babylon was about to fall, as predicted by God's Word in Revelation 18. And Russia was being punished by fire, true to God's promise in Ezekiel 39:6. Preprogrammed United States nuclear missiles were exploding on target of every major Russian city and military compound. Millions died instantly in fiery nuclear blasts, and millions more will die slowly from radiation sickness in the United States, Russia, Iran, and among the allies of the Russian/ Islamic army. Major cities in the United States and Russia all but disappear in these fiery nuclear blasts. In fact, God's word stated clearly that one-third of the world population will die in this conflict (Revelation 9:17–18).

A second launch campaign by Russian missiles was ineffective as most launch sites were annihilated by United States missiles. All of this massive retaliatory action by the United States was taking place from ground based ICBMs, submarines, ships, and aircraft, in strategic positions. There were no second attacks, for within one hour, these nations were all but obliterated. That was the reason a nuclear holocaust had been so dreaded and dodged until this day. Iran and the nations joining Russia in their invasion of Israel suffered the same judgment of God. The United States bombers concentrated on Iran and their Islamic allies.

The halting of the Russian/Islamic armies by Israel's army was temporary, for they were greatly outnumbered. Israel's forces were pushed back with a humongous slaughter on both sides.

The methodical Israeli retreat was reluctantly slow, inflicting heavy causalities upon the enemy.

It became evident that Israel may be overrun by the invading hoards. Is this the ending of Israel as a nation? Are the threats and boasts of Ahmadinejad, the Iranian president, to wipe Israel off the map going to become a reality? God relayed this message to the prophet Zechariah that two-thirds of the Israelis will die in the tragic invasion by the Russian/Islamic armies:

"And it shall come to pass in all the land,"
Says the Lord,
"*That* two-thirds in it shall be cut off *and* die,
But *one*–third shall be left in it:
I will bring the *one*–third through the fire,
Will refine them as silver is refined,
And test them as gold is tested.
They will call on My name,
And I will answer them.
I will say, 'This *is* My people';
And each one will say, 'The Lord *is* my God.'"

(Zechariah 13:8–9)

Many of the one-third of the Jews who survived the Russian/Islamic onslaught turned to God, accepting Christ as Messiah and Lord. God called them his people, and they referred to the Lord as my God. What a price Israel had paid to finally come to this conclusion.

Just when it looked as though Israel would be wiped off the world map, assistance arrived. It was not from the United States, for they are no longer a viable world power, nor from the European Union and the Antichrist, for he is too preoccupied in establishing himself as the world ruler. The assistance came from God as he promised over twenty-five hundred years prior to this horrific conflict:

"And it will come to pass at the same time, when Gog comes against the land of Israel," says the Lord God, "*that* My fury will show in My face. For in My jealousy *and* in the fire of My wrath I have spoken: 'Surely in that day there shall be a great earthquake in the land of Israel, so that the fish of the sea, the birds of the heavens, the beasts of the field, all creeping things that creep on the earth, and all men who *are* on the face of the earth shall shake at My presence. The mountains shall be thrown down, the steep places shall fall, and every wall shall fall to the ground.' I will call for a sword against Gog throughout all My mountains," says the Lord God. "Every man's sword will be against his brother. And I will bring him to judgment with pestilence and bloodshed; I will rain down on him, on his troops, and on the many peoples who *are* with him, flooding rain, great hailstones, fire, and brimstone."

(Ezekiel 38:18–22)

Intervention by God was the only thing that could spare Israel from being wiped off the map. God's arsenal of weapons will be a massive convulsive earthquake; panic and confusion among the invading troops, who began killing each other; contagious disease, making it impossible for them to continue their warfare against Israel; and calamities from the heavens, flooding rain, great hailstones, fire, and brimstone. God continued by telling mankind how effective his weapons will be:

"And you, son of man, prophesy against Gog, and say, 'Thus says the Lord God: "Behold, I *am* against you, O Gog, the prince of Rosh, Meshech, and Tubal; and I will turn you around and lead you on, bringing you up from the far north, and bring you against the mountains of Israel. Then I will knock the bow out of your left hand, and cause the arrows to fall out of your right hand. You shall fall upon the mountains of Israel, you and all your troops and the peoples who *are* with you; I will give you to birds of prey of every sort and *to* the beasts of the field to be devoured. You shall fall on the open field; for I have spoken," says the Lord God. "And I will send fire on Magog and on those who live in security in the coastlands. Then they shall know that I *am* the Lord. So I will make My holy name known in the midst of My people Israel, and I will not *let them* profane My holy name anymore. Then the nations shall know that *I am* the Lord, the Holy One in Israel. Surely it is coming, and it shall be done," says the Lord God. "This *is* the day of which I have spoken.

"Then those who dwell in the cities of Israel will go out and set on fire and burn the weapons, both the shields and bucklers, the bows and arrows, the javelins and spears; and they will make fires with them for seven years. They will not take wood from the field nor cut down *any* from the forests, because they will make fires with the weapons; and they will plunder those who plundered them, and pillage those who pillaged them," says the Lord God... "And as for you, son of man, thus says the Lord God, 'Speak to every sort of bird and to every beast of the field:

"Assemble yourselves and come;
Gather together from all sides to My sacrificial meal
Which I am sacrificing for you,
A great sacrificial meal on the mountains of Israel,
That you may eat flesh and drink blood.
You shall eat the flesh of the mighty,
Drink the blood of the princes of the earth,
Of rams and lambs,
Of goats and bulls,
All of them fatlings of Bashan.
You shall eat fat till you are full,
And drink blood till you are drunk,
At My sacrificial meal
Which I am sacrificing for you.
You shall be filled at My table
With horses and riders,

With mighty men
And with all the men of war," says the Lord God.

(Ezekiel 39:1–10, 17–20)

The Antichrist was amazed and awed and could not understand the survival of Israel. "How could this happen when they were so outnumbered and outmaneuvered?" he asked those around him. "I will take care of that in the future," he promised.

Actually, it is just as well that the Russian/Islamic armies perished on the mountains and plains of Israel, for their homeland had been decimated by the fire and brimstone of the retaliatory strikes by the United States's nuclear arsenal. Now, there was nothing for a proud, haughty Russia ruler to smile and grin so smugly about. God himself brought them to their knees.

And there were no more tirades by the tyrant of Iran. He had made his last mocking threat against Big Satan and Little Satan. The shambles of his country were a constant symbol that God is superior to his false god, Allah.

The startled, shaken, shattered United States was in shambles, as much as Russia or Iran. Regretfully, the United States became so wicked, violent, murderous, having murdered over fifty million babies by Godless abortion, God rejecting, immoral, popularizing and pushing homosexuality and abortion on other nations, persecuting Christians, loving pleasures more than God, adulterous, practicing unimaginable immorality, and marriage becoming a trite meaningless matter, like in the days of Noah, that they remind God of the wickedness of Babylon. In reality, morality had declined to the level of the decaying Roman empire of long ago.

The Antichrist was pleased with the destruction of Russia and the United States, which were the two most powerful nations in the world at that time. It simply meant that he would not have to deal with them in his takeover as the one man who rules the world. Also, it explained why the United States was not mentioned anywhere in end time prophecies of the Bible. The United States was out of all contention or consideration in these early months of the great tribulation. That greatly simplified the worldwide takeover by the Antichrist.

Ralph thought, *If God had spared the United States, he might need to apologize to Sodom and Gomorrah, who were destroyed by fire for their gross immorality.* However, the major miscalculation of the United States leadership was turning their back upon Israel at the time of their greatest need for assistance.

The great United States may have been referred to as the world's indispensable nation, but in one hour, they have fallen as God predicted in Revelation 18:17–18:

> "For in one hour such great riches came to nothing." Every shipmaster, all who travel by ship, sailors, and as many as trade on the sea, stood at a distance and cried out when they saw the smoke of her burning, saying, "What *is* like this great city?"

It had been true that what happened to, or in, the United States affected the rest of the world. In spite of sinister efforts of so many in the United States to erase God from any influence in any area of public life, he let it be known that was an impossibility. God's Word reminded mankind that God took note and remembered to settle the score. Of course, few had bothered to read his Word, considering it archaic and without any meaningful authority. So how would they comprehend what was happening? Consider the Word directly from heaven to John, the revelator, and to all mankind:

> And I heard another voice from heaven saying, "Come out of her, my people, lest you share in her sins, and lest you receive of her plagues. For her sins have reached to heaven, and God has remembered her iniquities. Render to her just as she rendered to you, and repay her double according

to her works; in the cup which she has mixed, mix double for her."

(Revelation 18:4–6)

Ralph considered this a direct message to national Babylon, the United States, having now been fulfilled by horrific devastation.

When the missiles and antimissile missiles stop streaking the skies and their sonic booms were silent, a shaken, shattered world was trying to come to life. Millions were dead, with no trace of their bodies remaining. Millions more were suffering from burns and dismemberments, as a result of being near a nuclear blast area.

Pictures of the devastation and suffering shown from the nuclear attack upon Japan, ending World War II, flashed into Ralph's mind. No doubt the same thing was happening in the affected parts of the stricken world. But it must be remembered that those unbelievable pictures came from just two cities. Multiply that by thousands, and one would get some reality of conditions in nations, not just two cities. It was not a pleasant thought or picture. But this was the great tribulation, and suffering was a terrible trend of that time.

Despite all the death, dying, and anguish, people did not turn to God. The Word of God gave the conclusion of the indescribable nuclear conflict of nations:

> But the rest of mankind, who were not killed by these plagues, did not repent of the works of their hands, that they should not worship demons, and idols of gold, silver, brass, stone, and wood, which can neither see nor hear nor walk. And they did not repent of their murders or their sorceries or their sexual immorality or their thefts.

(Revelation 9:20–21)

It was apparent that Ralph and his friends made a wise decision to stay put where they were on the east coast of Florida. Evidently the patriot antimissile missiles had protected the area of Cape Kennedy and Patrick Air Force Base from incoming Russian missiles. It had been rumored that those two areas were saturated with patriot antimissile batteries with skilled operators.

Miami, Florida, had not been as fortunate. Being a major shipping port, much of the city, along with the port was gone. Untold thousands were dead and almost as many are suffering unbearably. Fortunately, the strong northwest winds were blowing nuclear fallout out to sea, away from Ralph's location. They survived the onslaught, along with the believers and general population of the area.

Smaller towns and villages were more fortunate than major cities, many of which were obliterated by Russian nuclear missiles. What lies ahead for the survivors? Will they be able to cope with the unfathomable catastrophe and resulting immediate needs? Almost the entire necessary infrastructure of the nation had been destroyed or rendered incapable of use. Will there be any system of survival for the living?

Mourning for Babylon the Great and Fall of Mystery, Babylon the Great

As the living cautiously came out of shelters and houses, they found a very different world. There were major problems because of lack of electricity, leaving no source of communication other than local word of mouth. There was no news of what had happened in the rest of the world, and travel was a major problem since there was no electricity to power fuel pumps. Hopefully, temporary measures may materialize in a few days.

Crews began working on recovery of electricity as soon as fuel for vehicles was available. That was vitally important as so much about the way of living depended upon access to electricity. Also, news and communication instructions were critical to survival. Of course, thousands did not have electricity permanently since power centers had been destroyed in the attack.

In the meantime, everyone must do the best they can. Hopefully, most had purchased enough food and water to sustain life. Police protection was limited because of lack of vehicle fuel. Everyone was on the alert and personally protected their interests. After all, should people expect lives of comfort and contentment? Or must they be constantly reminded that they are living in the great tribulation when only trouble and turmoil are to be expected, even promised?

No doubt the world was in grievous misery and mourning because of personal dilemma and deceased nations. Greed, hatred, and godlessness has plunged the world into this state of grief.

Many smaller nations and major businesses were mourning the fall of the United States. They had depended upon the United States because it was the richest trading nation in the world. God had predicted that grieving:

> And the merchants of the earth will weep and mourn over her, for no one buys their merchandise anymore: merchandise of gold and silver, precious stones and pearls, fine linen and purple, silk and scarlet, every kind of citron wood, every kind of object of ivory, every kind of object of most precious wood, bronze, iron, and marble; and cinnamon and incense, fragrant oil and frankincense, wine and oil, fine flour and wheat, cattle and sheep, horses and chariots, and bodies and souls of men. The fruit that your soul longed for has gone from you, and all the things which are rich and splendid have gone from you, and you shall find them no more at all. The merchants of these things, who became rich by her, will stand at a distance for fear of her torment, weeping and wailing, and saying, 'Alas, alas, that great city that was clothed in fine linen, purple, and scarlet, and adorned with gold and precious stones and pearls! For in one hour such great riches came to nothing.' Every shipmaster, all who travel by ship, sailors, and as many as trade on the sea, stood at a distance and cried out when they saw the smoke of her burning, saying, "What *is* like this great city?"
>
> (Revelation 18:11–18)

Maybe it was a good thing that TV screens were blank so that news of all the misery in the world was not blaring and adding to the misery of the living. The reality of all that has happened sank in soon enough. It has not yet dawned upon many that the nuclear holocaust was going to quickly cause a food shortage and eventually a famine upon the earth. There was no ending to the conditions over which to mourn.

After several days spent mostly in silence in the home of Ralph Waterman because of the grievous national and world conditions, finally, the three of them began to loosen up and converse more. The recent attack, and resulting events following, have shocked them into silent grieving. Ralph began to deliberate and discuss how to get in touch with the other believers and continue teaching, preparing them for the rest of the great tribulation. Knowing the addresses of all of the trainers, he could use his bicycle as a means of transportation to communicate with them.

He prayerfully pored over what he should teach in the next lesson. For some strange reason, he could not get out of his mind the importance of dealing with the reliability of the Bible as the Word of God. No doubt, some of the believers might be shaken by the tragic events of recent days. They needed to realize that these events were not accidental, but God had foretold all of them in his Word. And since these were only the beginning days of the great tribulation, believers should be prepared to accept God's Word as reliable.

The lesson Ralph had prepared to teach a month ago but had to be canceled because of adverse world conditions was now history, not prophecy, as he would have presented it. Faith in what the Bible teaches concerning the end times must be strongly emphasized. And since there was no electricity, all his teaching notes had to be in longhand on legal pads. The computer was useless until electricity was restored. It was also necessary for his listeners to take careful notes to be passed on to the believers they were to train. Ralph would supply everything necessary for the trainers because of the uncertainty of the times.

The next day, he took a test ride on his bicycle, trying to determine if he was still under any scrutiny. Todd and Faye were not convinced that Ralph should attempt this due to former actions against him and the unpredictable conditions of the present. Nonetheless, Ralph felt that his actions were necessary to continue his work in encouraging and informing believers, enabling them to witness to others. Following a breakfast of toast, toasted in the oven of a gas stove, which fortunately still worked, and coffee, percolated on a stove burner, Ralph took off on his bicycle, peddling toward the park.

The community was extremely quiet, as if in mourning, and it probably was. He rode a little over five miles through the community, always observant of any undue attention given to him. There was none. Evidently, any foe of his or of believers were too self-consumed with perplexing personal problems to give any consideration to a bicycle rider. It seemed to Ralph that official opposition to believers was not being practiced as diligently as it was before the holocaust. If that was true, he wanted to take advantage of the reprieve, teaching and encouraging weak believers as much as possible. Maybe he could work more freely since open persecution of believers had come to an end in the shattered United States. Ralph was certain that it would only be temporary. Also, nothing had been said about the Antichrist since Americans were attempting to make a semblance of recovery from unbelievable chaos. Of course, limited communication was contributing to this silence. This did not mean that the Antichrist was permanently out of the picture.

For the next few days, Ralph took bicycle tours at different times of the day and in diverse directions. All of this was important for at least two reasons. First, he needed the physical exercise to condition him for longer trips on his bicycle, for his normal mode of transportation had been his truck. Secondly, he must be sure of not being followed before going to the home of one of the believers now in training.

Since Ralph had not observed anyone giving him undue attention or attempting to follow him, he felt free to follow his plan of contacting other believers, especially the trainers. Monday morning of the following week, he peddled the bicycle to the home of Jim and Sue. They were surprised but grateful to see him. After personal greetings and a brief discussion of the possible conditions people were facing in a fractured world, Ralph revealed his purpose for being there. Reaching other believers and encouraging them in the faith were paramount in the mind of Ralph. Jim and Sue were excited with the plan presented by Ralph and promised their full cooperation. They were ready to begin studying, training, and witnessing.

Since it would take several days for Ralph to ride his bike to the homes of the other eleven trainers, a training date was set for Monday, 7:00 p.m., two weeks from that day. The meeting would be at the Ralph's home, and all former precautions must be observed. There did not seem to be anyone watching what was going on at his house, but caution was still advisable. It was possible that believers would have more freedom and come under less scrutiny and persecution following the nuclear holocaust. But how long would it last? The Antichrist was still in control, possibly more so, with the fall of the United States and Russia. Ralph was determined to take advantage of the temporary relief from the resistance and ruthlessness of followers of the Antichrist against Christianity.

Ralph spent the rest of the week on his bicycle traveling to the homes of the other eleven trainers. All of them were excited about seeing him and eager to begin the studies so they could train the believers who were to become their responsibility. Every couple promised to be present at Ralph's home the following Monday evening, understanding that they must still put to practice the precautions previously taken when arriving and departing.

In between trips, Ralph studied and prepared the lesson plan to be presented throughout the following week. Study in the evenings was laborious due to the fact that the only light was from candles. However, Ralph pressed on with vigilance, for he was on a mission. Almost daily, Todd or Faye expressed concern that Ralph was overworking himself on the limited diet forced upon them. Faye was doing her best to prepare adequate meals, but present conditions made it very difficult. However, Ralph never complained, thankful for what they had, and was complementary of Faye's consistent efforts.

Monday's training session took place without any intrusion or apparent interest from anyone outside the invited group. No one had been followed or questioned about their destination or activity. Due to that, another week of training was planned for three weeks later since walking or using a bicycle was the only means of travel. That seemed necessary to give the trainers time to contact the believers they were training. Excitement was high in spite of the adverse conditions in which they were forced to live. That was a constant reminder that they were living in the great tribulation, and conditions might get worse.

At times, it was difficult for them to imagine the suffering going on since they had been miraculously spared a direct hit by a nuclear blast nor were they feeling the apparent effects of nuclear fallout. All believers in other parts of the world had not been as fortunate. Every session, the groups prayed for their fellow believers who were experiencing unimaginable suffering. Ralph had helped them understand that some of them might not survive future persecutions against believers but that they could leave this tormented world not just as victims but victors. The important issue was to maintain a strong faith in and faithfulness to God.

Would electricity ever be restored, giving them an opportunity to learn what was going on in their world, outside their local community? It might not be encouraging news, but good or bad, it was eagerly sought. Only rumors were being spread at the present, and they might be reliable or they might not be. Reliable news was desired. Rumors were being shared because neighbors had begun talking together again, and word was spreading across community lines.

In fact, there was a rumor that repairs were being made to the nearest electric power plant and that electricity will be back on in the community where Ralph lived in a few days. Two weeks later, during a light noon meal, the electric lights flickered several times and started glowing. At the same time, there were the familiar sounds of conversation coming from the family room. The TV was back on. Rejoicing was heard from the neighbor's homes, and Ralph, Todd, and Faye joined in. What a relief.

"Now that electricity is back on in our area, maybe gasoline will be available soon," Ralph said hopefully. *That will remain to be seen. When automobile fuel is available again, it will probably be limited or rationed, and very soon, believers will be unable to purchase it anyway.*

Taking their remaining lunches with them, they rushed into the family room to catch up on what might be taking place in their tormented world. It was not pleasant as limited areas were being photographed. Often they have to close their eyes or bow their heads, for the scenes were too gruesome to watch. No wonder world leaders put off a nuclear holocaust for many years. The dying wish they had died in the initial blasts. Soon Faye left the room in tears, having encountered more than she could endure. In a few minutes, Ralph switched off the TV to avoid seeing more gruesome scenes and accompanied by interruptions of propaganda from the Antichrist. It was apparent that he was seizing more and more control of nations, or they were simply surrendering to his ruthless leadership.

Quickly, Ralph rushed to his study, switched on his computer, and began typing the material for the next teaching session. Now that he has successfully dealt with the reliability of the Scriptures in the last lesson, he was moving on with the outline of events which will continue to take place in the great tribulation. He wanted to alert these weak believers to faith-shaking events they can expect and urge them to be prepared. Some situations will demand strong resisting faith, and some may result in martyrdom.

Having dealt with the fall of the national Babylon, which is now history, Ralph moved on to another falling institution in Revelation 17. The Mystery, Babylon of Revelation 17 is apparently different from the Babylon of chapter 18. The term "Babylon" was simply identifying a nation or institution that is godless and as wicked as ancient Babylon. As pointed out before, Babylon of Revelation 18 was a rich, godless, immoral, influential nation that was the source of worldwide trade. None of that fit into the program or influence of a religious institution.

The word "Babylon" was not to be confused with and/or limited to a given city. Actually, nations were often identified in news reports and other correspondence by simply the name of their capitol. France is often inferred to by Paris, and Moscow is oftentimes used to identify Russia as London calls attention to Great Britain, and Washington, DC, denotes the United States. Babylon is used to describe the decadent, godless condition of a nation or institution.

Ralph considered Revelation 17 to be describing a degraded, godless religious institution identified as "Mystery, Babylon the Great." "Be sure to read it carefully," Ralph highlights in his notes:

> Then one of the seven angels who had the seven bowls came and talked with me, saying to me, "Come, I will show you the judgment of the great harlot who sits on many waters, with whom the kings of the earth committed fornication, and the inhabitants of the earth were made drunk with the wine of her fornication."
>
> So he carried me away in the Spirit into the wilderness. And I saw a woman sitting on a scarlet beast *which was* full of names of blasphemy, having seven heads and ten horns. The woman was arrayed in purple and scarlet, and adorned with gold and precious stones and pearls, having in her hand a golden cup full of abominations and the filthiness of her fornication. And on her forehead a name *was* written:

MYSTERY, BABYLON THE GREAT, THE MOTHER OF HARLOTS AND OF THE ABOMINATIONS OF THE EARTH.

I saw the woman, drunk with the blood of the saints and with the blood of the martyrs of Jesus. And when I saw her, I marveled with great amazement.

But the angel said to me, "Why did you marvel? I will tell you the mystery of the woman and of the beast that carries her, which has the seven heads and the ten horns. The beast that you saw was, and is not, and will ascend out of the bottomless pit and go to perdition. And those who dwell on the earth will marvel, whose names are not written in the Book of Life from the foundation of the world, when they see the beast that was, and is not, and yet is.

"Here *is* the mind which has wisdom: The seven heads are seven mountains on which the woman sits. There are also seven kings. Five have fallen, one is, *and* the other has not yet come. And when he comes, he must continue a short time. The beast that was, and is not, is himself also the eighth, and is of the seven, and is going to perdition.

"The ten horns which you saw are ten kings who have received no kingdom as yet, but they receive authority for one hour as kings with the beast. These are of one mind, and they will give their power and authority to the beast. These will make war with the Lamb, and the Lamb will overcome them, for He is Lord of lords and King of kings; and those *who are* with Him *are* called, chosen, and faithful."

Then he said to me, "The waters which you saw, where the harlot sits, are peoples, multitudes, nations, and tongues. And the ten horns which you saw on the beast, these will hate the harlot, make her desolate and naked, eat her flesh and burn her with fire. For God has put it into their hearts to fulfill His purpose, to be of one mind, and to give their kingdom to the beast, until the words of God are fulfilled. And the woman whom you saw is that great city which reigns over the kings of the earth."

(Revelation 17:1–18)

Ralph identified one of the key verses that strongly indicate that this Babylon was a religious institution. Revelation 17:18 was enlightening, "And the woman whom you saw is that great city which reigns over the kings of the earth." This has been taking place for centuries by a worldwide religious institution. Religious matters and many governmental issues were decreed by the leader of a powerful worldwide religious institution. The decrees of this leader were the law, for he was considered to be infallible. World leaders were subject to his power and authority out of fear and intimidation. In fact, it would still be practiced if it was not for independence and the popularity of democracy. In some parts of the world, this practice was still taking place.

Another enlightening verse, pointing to a religious institution is Revelation 17:6, which states, "I saw the woman, drunk with the blood of the saints and with the blood of the martyrs of Jesus. And when I saw her, I marveled with great amazement."

From years past, there was a religious institution that had bloody hands—that is, the blood of true Christian martyrs who dared to disagree with their teachings and doctrines. In fact, Martin Luther was invited to his execution, but he chose not to go, and was protected by the German government. Martin Luther was insistent that the Bible taught salvation by faith, not by works or obedience to a manmade religion, contrary to the Scriptures.

The extensiveness of the religious Babylon was indicated in Revelation 17:15, "Then he said to me, 'The waters which you saw, where the harlot sits, are peoples, multitudes, nations, and tongues.'" It was a worldwide religious institution, numbering in the billions. Until the rapid rise of Muslimism, it was the largest religious institution in the world. Also, the national Babylon never ruled over the vast array of multitudes or nations pointed out by this verse. The religious influence was more far-reaching than the business impact of Babylon the Great, or the United States.

It was interesting that the religious Babylon was destroyed by what Ralph strongly believes to be the ten main nations of the European Union, led by the Antichrist. The Antichrist did not tolerate any institution that has religious inclinations. The fall of the religious Babylon gave place for the rise of devil and Antichrist worship, without any major organized religious objections.

Included in this lesson plan, or the next one, Ralph decided to deal with the important issue of the rise of the false prophet found in Revelation 13:11–18:

> Then I saw another beast coming up out of the earth, and he had two horns like a lamb and spoke like a dragon. And he exercises all the authority of the first beast in his presence, and causes the earth and those who dwell in it to worship the first beast, whose deadly wound was healed. He performs great signs, so that he even makes fire come down from heaven on the earth in the sight of men. And he deceives those who dwell on the earth by those signs which he was granted to do in the sight of the beast, telling those who dwell on the earth to make an image to the beast who was wounded by the sword and lived. He was granted *power* to give breath to the image of the beast, that the image of the beast should both speak and cause as many as would not worship the image of the beast to be killed. He causes all, both small and great, rich and poor, free and slave, to receive a mark on their right hand or on their foreheads, and that no one may buy or sell except one who has the mark or the name of the beast, or the number of his name.
>
> Here is wisdom. Let him who has understanding calculate the number of the beast, for it is the number of a man: His number *is* 666.

Ralph noted that the appearance of the false prophet completed a trinity of evil upon the earth in the great tribulation. The trinity of evil was composed of Satan, the Antichrist, and the false prophet. These three complemented one another and cooperated in efforts to discredit God and finally attempt to destroy Christ and his kingdom.

Ralph highlighted the accomplishments attributed to the false prophet. First, he will have all the power and authority of the Antichrist and will attempt to deify the Antichrist by demanding worship of him. That act itself will put believers in direct conflict with him. True believers worship God and him only. Secondly, he will be empowered by Satan to perform great signs and miracles, thus deceiving many people on earth. In the third place, he will cause an image of the Antichrist to be erected with the power to speak and cause all who do not worship the image and the Antichrist to be killed.

The final diabolic deed of the false prophet will be to institute the mark of the beast. Ralph believed that the mark of the beast will be a visible pledge of allegiance to the Antichrist, Satan, and the false prophet. The instituting of the mark of the beast will have intimidating consequences for believers. Anyone not having the mark of the beast will be unable to buy or sell anything.

Believers who were not killed because of refusing to worship the image of the Antichrist will face unimaginable hardship, leading to possible starvation and death. Under these adverse conditions, there will be strong temptation to accept the conditions of the false prophet to obtain food. Hunger and adversity were two conditions that caused people to take compromising actions. "It will take a strong faith to endure those conditions," Ralph cautioned the believers. "Are you strong enough to stand under these circumstances, which will be thrust upon you?" Ralph paused and asked. "What would you do?"

God admitted that world conditions will become so cataclysmic for believers that death will be a blessing:

I heard a voice from heaven saying to me, "Write: 'Blessed *are* the dead who die in the Lord from now on.'" "Yes," says the Spirit, "that they may rest from their labors, and their works follow them.

(Revelation 14:13)

The blessing will only be a reality for those who are right with God and prepared to die in the Lord. One must understand that the great tribulation is not going be a pleasant time for anyone who is still alive. The truly blessed are those who were ready and called to the marriage supper of the lamb as revealed in Revelation 19:9:

> Then he said to me, "Write: 'Blessed *are* those who are called to the marriage supper of the Lamb!'" And he said to me, "These are the true sayings of God."

Ralph recalled a person telling him, "If I put off salvation prior to the rapture, it would be no big deal, for I will get saved after Jesus returns, and everything would be okay." It must be stated sadly that everything will not be okay. According to Jesus, that will be a time of tribulation like it has never been in all of history (Matthew 24:21). It will be a time of God's wrath and judgment upon all who rejected his great salvation through his Son Jesus Christ. Who could possibly, intelligently, choose to put off getting saved until such times of turmoil and tribulation?

Giving time for discussion, Ralph believed that the material in this chapter was enough to cover in the next lesson. He decided to begin working on the material for future lessons as he waited two more weeks for this presentation and discussion.

The USA Surrenders to the Antichrist and the Torments of the Great Tribulation

T he two weeks of waiting and preparation passed swiftly as Ralph prayed and planned the materials that he considered important to be taught. During that time, he had taken numerous bicycle rides to survey the areas and be assured of no adverse activity. A few vehicles were being seen on the streets, so some gasoline must be available somewhere. It was most encouraging that no one seemed to give any undue attention to Ralph.

Feeling secure and free from any apparent scrutiny, he felt it was safe to have the training sessions at his house, as scheduled. Monday arrived and so did all of the invited trainers. They were thrilled to be together again, ready to prepare themselves to help those they were training. There were no problems or interruptions of any kind and none of the trainers had been aware of undue observation on the way. The same conditions held for the sessions on Wednesday and Friday. *What a relief to be out from under the gun*, everyone thought. Ralph was hopeful that the secure conditions would prevail until the completion of the training. But that might be too much to expect in these uncertain times. He would take advantage of the good times and remain vigilant, ready for instant change.

At the conclusion of the sessions, Faye served refreshments, and plans were made to meet again three weeks from that date. Ralph informed the groups that he felt he could complete the training in two or three more sessions. However, they would stay in contact with one another for spiritual support.

Ralph continued the same routine for the next three weeks. Vigilance was uppermost in his mind, lest he become too relaxed during these times when persecutions were nonexistent. He knew the prophetic Scriptures too well to expect these good trouble-free days to be permanent.

Each evening, he spent time watching the TV news. The main news items were scenes of a devastated United States attempting to deal with the disaster. There were times when Ralph was almost sickened by the scenes. "How sad it is to see such greatness become nothing short of gloom," Ralph somberly commented.

For days, the newscasts were almost unbearable. One evening, Faye commented, "Wouldn't it be a blessing to receive some kind of good news?"

Ralph looked at the troubled expression on Faye's face and reminded her, "Faye, this is the great tribulation, and good news is very rare. In fact, it is almost nonexistent. About the only good news is that when this troublesome life is over, we will go to a place where turmoil, trouble, and tears will be missing. It is important that we remain true to God, who graciously saved us, and one day soon will welcome us to join the great multitude, which likewise has been saved during the great tribulation. What a shame it has been to have missed the rapture and been left to endure the turmoil of the tribulation, but with a shout of victory, we can leave this troublesome world." At the thoughts of final victory, Faye wiped away tears of joy in spite of all the adversity.

A special report broke in on the TV programming in progress. There was quiet anticipation in the home of Ralph Waterman as well as in every location where TV programming was being viewed. A reporter was standing on the outskirts of a devastated Washington, DC, in radiation protective clothing, for safety. He reported that several government officials, housed in deep underground bunkers, have survived the holocaust, which leveled most of Washington, DC. These bunkers were well stocked with food, water, supplies, and electrical generators with adequate fuel to operate them for as long as needed. Most government officials perished en route to their families when the fatal alarms sounded.

The few remaining officials have made a decisive decision since there was no possibility of operating from a central government any longer. They have notified the Antichrist, by underground emergency radio equipment, that they have committed all governing responsibility of the United States to him, as of this date. It was not a difficult decision since many of them had already secretly become followers of the Antichrist. His laws had become those of the United States. All Americans were notified that everyone is now subject to the Antichrist and his rule.

There were no more haughty speeches from the president. As a matter of fact, he has not been seen or heard from since the nuclear attack upon the United States. If seen, he would be forced to drop his haughty, uplifted chin and hanging his head in shame. His power and popularity are gone forever. Too late, the president has seen that all world conflicts were not solved by fancy rhetoric and negotiations. Ralph lamented the possible fate of the president.

The Antichrist has assured Americans that assistance of all kinds will be flown from Europe as soon as adequate aircraft runways can be cleared or constructed. Doctors and medical supplies will be on the first incoming aircraft. In addition, the Antichrist has personally appointed loyal supporters to be flown to America, taking over all governing activities. When they arrived, they will appoint assistants to help carry out the wishes of the Antichrist.

Every location where there are survivors, the Antichrist's appointed leaders will be governing, or dictating. All surviving American citizens were expected to give complete commitment to these rulers. Any dissenting activity will be dealt with decisively. Every order of the new leaders is to be followed without question or objection. Anything said in opposition to the Antichrist or his appointed leaders will be a grave crime, punishable by death.

Also, everyone is obligated to report such action to officials. And knowledge, without reporting, makes one as guilty as the offender. Ralph asked Todd and Faye, "Do you question what that decisive action will be?"

Staring out a front window, Ralph commented blankly, "We are now the subjects of the Antichrist, with no recourse. The great United States has not only fallen, we are another nation under the control of the Antichrist. Soon it will be most of the entire world. Believers will soon be facing unimaginable persecutions, torture, and martyrdom."

What Ralph will do about continuing the training and encouraging believers has taken a terrible turn. Ralph decided that he must act quickly and decisively. The days of temporary leniency are coming to an end.

Early the next morning, Ralph was in his study, feverishly attempting to complete his lesson preparations. The following week, there are to be sessions at his house on Monday, Wednesday, and Friday. He was not about to cancel them due to fear. There was more information that these new believers need to equip them for their remaining days of the great tribulation. He will make every effort to do his best for them.

Ralph felt that it was important to inform his students of the judgments of God to be revealed by the seven seals, trumpets, and bowls of his wrath. To encounter these unexpectedly could shake their faith. They needed to be aware of the events and pray for assistance from God to endure the persecutions arriving from some of them.

Believers must never forget that they were victims of the great tribulation by their personal choices—that is, they made a choice to put off God's great salvation too long and ignored the signs of the Lord's return in the rapture. It is just by the graciousness of God that they had been saved following the rapture. Now Ralph desperately wanted them to be able to maintain a strong faith and not falter in the midst of the judgments of God upon the ungodly. Also, he was aware that some of them, including himself, may encounter the ultimate test of renouncing their faith or face death. He was praying and attempting to prepare these new converts and himself for that hour, which may overtake them. Knowing these things will diminish the surprise and soften the shock measurably.

Ralph was in the process of gathering reference books, commentaries, and everything available in his study to simplify the presentation of the seals, trumpets, and bowls of the wrath of God to be faced by a godless, worldly people, when Todd tapped on the door, reminding him that breakfast was ready. Reluctantly, he left the unfinished studies and joined Todd and Faye for breakfast. He was uncommonly quiet since his mind was preoccupied with the study materials and presentation that needed to be completed as soon as possible. Todd and Faye commented upon his unusual silence, wondering if there was something wrong with him. He assured them that there was nothing wrong but that his mind was on the subjects to be delved into today.

As soon as breakfast was over, he excused himself and headed back to his study and the important presentations to be finished. He sensed the encroaching pressure of the Antichrist and his appointed leaders. It was evident that he and all known believers were hated by the Antichrist and would be under constant scrutiny very soon. Time was of tremendous essence to Ralph and his mission. He was certain that he had been identified as a believer prior to the holocaust, and that information would still be on record. And persons spying upon him could come forward again at any time. These possibilities were a driving force, compelling him to complete the presentations yet to be passed on to the selected trainers.

Ralph did not leave his study for lunch, and Faye brought him a sandwich and soft drink, which he nibbled and sipped on, continuing to study and type. He only took a brief break for supper, working late into the night. By noon the following day, he had completed a rough draft of what he felt should be shared to prepare other believers facing the inevitable. What God inspired to be recorded in his Word was really without recourse.

Reconsidering, editing, and attempting to make the Word of God alive to his listeners was a time consuming endeavor. "However, the end result was worth the effort," Ralph concluded. For the rest of the day, evening, and all of the following day, Ralph put the finishing touches on the document to be presented in the training sessions for the following week.

First, he dealt with the seven seals referred to in Revelation chapters 5–8:

> And I saw in the right *hand* of Him who sat on the throne a scroll written inside and on the back, sealed with seven seals. Then I saw a strong angel proclaiming with a loud voice, "Who is worthy to open the scroll and to loose its seals?" And no one in heaven or on the earth or under the earth was able to open the scroll, or to look at it.
>
> So I wept much, because no one was found worthy to open and read the scroll, or to look at it. But one of the elders said to me, "Do not weep. Behold, the Lion of the tribe of Judah, the Root of David, has prevailed to open the scroll and to loose its seven seals."
>
> And I looked, and behold, in the midst of the throne and of the four living creatures, and in the midst of the elders, stood a Lamb as though it had been slain, having seven horns and seven eyes, which are the seven Spirits of God sent out into all the earth. Then He came and took the scroll out of the right hand of Him who sat on the throne.
>
> Now when He had taken the scroll, the four living creatures and the twenty-four elders fell down before the Lamb, each having a harp, and golden bowls full of incense, which are the prayers of the saints. And they sang a new song, saying:

"You are worthy to take the scroll,
And to open its seals;
For You were slain,
And have redeemed us to God by Your blood
Out of every tribe and tongue and people and nation,
And have made us kings and priests to our God;
And we shall reign on the earth."

(Revelation 5:1–10)

The truth of this passage is self-evident. It is Christ himself who was qualified to open the seven seals. When he came as redeemer, he was rejected, crucified, and buried. But he arose and returned to heaven as advocate seated at the right hand of God Almighty. Now he is seen in heaven as the one worthy to execute judgment and justice upon the world that jilted him.

Now I saw when the Lamb opened one of the seals; and I heard one of the four living creatures saying with a voice like thunder, "Come and see." And I looked, and behold, a white horse. He who sat on it had a bow; and a crown was given to him, and he went out conquering and to conquer.

(Revelation 6:1–2)

Some Bible scholars interpreted this as being Christ on the "white horse." However, more commentators claimed otherwise. It seemed that someone other than God gave the rider a crown. In addition, his conquering seemed to be bloodless, yet effective. The white horse may be used to indicate goodness, which may be a false goodness. And the peace offered was not lasting. Along with Ralph, some see this as the, seemingly innocent, rise of the Antichrist. That is consistent with the beginning rise of the Antichrist with deception, duping nations to follow him.

Christ will certainly come riding on a white horse and will conquer the entire world and set up his earthly kingdom, but that will be later in the great tribulation (Revelation 19:11–12).

When He opened the second seal, I heard the second living creature saying, "Come and see." Another horse, fiery red, went out. And it was granted to the one who sat on it to take peace from the earth, and that *people* should kill one another; and there was given to him a great sword.

(Revelation 6:3–4)

The "red horse" indicates massive bloodshed. As discussed earlier, this is very possibly referring to the Russian/Islamic invasion of Israel and the United States. The nuclear attack upon the United States and their reactionary attack, along with two-thirds of the Israelis being killed, will account for a third of the world's population being destroyed (Revelation 9:18). Also, the attacking Russian/Islamic armies will become confused and begin killing each other (Ezekiel 38:21).

When He opened the third seal, I heard the third living creature say, "Come and see." So I looked, and behold, a black horse, and he who sat on it had a pair of scales in his hand. And I heard a voice in the midst of the four living creatures saying, "A quart of wheat for a denarius, and three quarts of barley for a denarius; and do not harm the oil and the wine.

(Revelation 6:5–6)

Great worldwide famine is promised by the opening of the third seal by Christ. Much of the famine will result from the nuclear holocaust since the United States was a major source of food. Plus, there will be no rain during the prophesying of the two prophets (Revelation 11:6).

Hunger and death will be widespread upon the earth.

When He opened the fourth seal, I heard the voice of the fourth living creature saying, "Come and see." So I looked, and behold, a pale horse. And the name of him who sat on it was Death, and Hades followed with him. And power was given to them over a fourth of the earth, to kill with sword, with hunger, with death, and by the beasts of the earth.

(Revelation 6:7–8)

The great tribulation will be a time of massive dying. Ralph stressed that one-fourth of the world's population will die from wars, hunger, and killed by hungry wild beasts, which will be affected by the famine. "Those who fear death should have been prepared to meet Christ in the rapture," Ralph explained, "for death will be prevalent in the great tribulation."

When He opened the fifth seal, I saw under the altar the souls of those who had been slain for the word of God and for the testimony which they held. And they cried with a loud voice, saying, "How long, O Lord, holy and true, until You judge and avenge our blood on those who dwell on the earth?" Then a white robe was given to each of them; and it was said to them that they should rest a little while longer, until both *the number of* their fellow servants and their brethren, who would be killed as they *were,* was completed.

(Revelation 6:9–11)

The scene changes with the opening of the fifth seal. Actually, John "The Revelator" is shown a scene in heaven. Those who have been saved during the great tribulation wonder how much longer they must await complete justice for the injustices done to them on earth. They are reminded that others, who have been saved, will join them soon, for they also will be killed for their faith in God. This again points out that there will be people saved during the great tribulation, but what a price they will pay for their faith. It would have been much more blessed to have gone in the rapture.

I looked when He opened the sixth seal, and behold, there was a great earthquake; and the sun became black as sackcloth of hair, and the moon became like blood. And the stars of heaven fell to the earth, as a fig tree drops its late figs when it is shaken by a mighty wind. Then the sky receded as a scroll when it is rolled up, and every mountain and island was moved out of its place. And the kings of the earth, the great men, the rich men, the commanders, the mighty men, every slave and every free man, hid themselves in the caves and in the rocks of the mountains, and said to the mountains and rocks, "Fall on us and hide us from the face of Him who sits on the throne and from the wrath of the Lamb! For the great day of His wrath has come, and who is able to stand?

(Revelation 6:12–17)

God gave John a vision of the final judgment. Over and over, there have been evidences of God's judgment upon sinful mankind. However, there has never been anything to compare to the awesomeness of the final judgment. "And it must be stressed that it will be the final one," Ralph emphasized. "Will all of you be able to stand at the judgment with confidence in your heart?" he intended to ask. And the only ones able to stand will be those who are right with God. All of the others will find no hiding place and be turned into hell.

When He opened the seventh seal, there was silence in heaven for about half an hour. And I saw the seven angels who stand before God, and to them were given seven trumpets. Then another angel, having a golden censer, came and stood at the altar. He was given much incense that he should offer *it* with the prayers of all the saints upon the golden altar which was before the throne. And the smoke of the incense, with the prayers of the saints, ascended before God from the angel's hand. Then the angel took the censer, filled it with fire from the altar, and threw *it* to the earth. And there were noises, thunderings, lightnings, and an earthquake.

So the seven angels who had the seven trumpets prepared themselves to sound.

(Revelation 8:1–6)

Christ's opening of the seventh seal was preparing for the seven angels with the seven trumpets to sound. In addition, there were troublesome eruptions in the atmosphere with severe storms, plus a world-shaking earthquake. Ralph concluded that, "Godless mankind is getting a taste of the wrath of God in this time of tribulation." Mankind had denied God's existence, but now it is impossible to deny his wrath.

Ralph found it necessary to take a break before reviewing the consequences of the seven trumpet blasts. He left his study and drank a soft drink with Todd and Faye before getting on his bicycle and taking a half-hour tour of the community. There were no new faces, and nothing was amiss as far as he could ascertain.

Returning to his study, Ralph continued to edit the document to be presented the following week. The prophecy of the seven trumpet blasts was recorded in Revelation 8–11. Each trumpet blast brought more tribulation and torment to mankind struggling to live in the great tribulation:

The first angel sounded: And hail and fire followed, mingled with blood, and they were thrown to the earth. And a third of the trees were burned up, and all green grass was burned up.

(Revelation 8:7)

Following the trumpet blast of the first angel, a scorched earth is left, with a third of all trees withering, and all green grass having turned a sickening brown. This, no doubt, will add to the famine.

Then the second angel sounded: And *something* like a great mountain burning with fire was thrown into the sea, and a third of the sea became blood. And a third of the living creatures in the sea died, and a third of the ships were destroyed.

(Revelation 8:8–9)

As incredible as it may seem, a third of the seas will lose their attraction by becoming blood. Many of the beautiful, alluring beaches will be polluted with the dead bodies of fish and creatures of the seas. In addition, a third of the nation's ships will be destroyed. And this action will add to famine, as well, since many fish markets will be empty.

> Then the third angel sounded: And a great star fell from heaven, burning like a torch, and it fell on a third of the rivers and on the springs of water. The name of the star is Wormwood. A third of the waters became wormwood, and many men died from the water, because it was made bitter.

(Revelation 8:10–11)

Water pollution will be worldwide, causing massive deaths. And it is doubtful that scientists will be able to develop filters to purify this defiled water. Ralph underlined the fact that everyone must understand that this is a tormenting act of God.

> Then the fourth angel sounded: And a third of the sun was struck, a third of the moon, and a third of the stars, so that a third of them were darkened. A third of the day did not shine, and likewise the night.
>
> And I looked, and I heard an angel flying through the midst of heaven, saying with a loud voice, "Woe, woe, woe to the inhabitants of the earth, because of the remaining blasts of the trumpet of the three angels who are about to sound!

(Revelation 8:12–13)

The fourth trumpet blast will affect the heavens, and mankind will stumble through semidarkness in the daytime and inky blackness at night. Then, an angel warns mankind of the horrors of the remaining three trumpet blasts. "But mankind is probably wondering how conditions could get any worse," Ralph adds.

> Then the fifth angel sounded: And I saw a star fallen from heaven to the earth. To him was given the key to the bottomless pit. And he opened the bottomless pit, and smoke arose out of the pit like the smoke of a great furnace. So the sun and the air were darkened because of the smoke of the pit. Then out of the smoke locusts came upon the earth. And to them was given power, as the scorpions of the earth have power. They were commanded not to harm the grass of the earth, or any green thing, or any tree, but only those men who do not have the seal of God on their foreheads. And they were not given *authority* to kill them, but to torment them *for* five months. Their torment *was* like the torment of a scorpion when it strikes a man. In those days men will seek death and will not find it; they will desire to die, and death will flee from them.
>
> (Revelation 9:1–6)

No wonder the angel warned mankind of further torments. For five months, mankind will be tortured by the sting of demonic creatures from the abyss. The misery and suffering will be so unbearable that people will seek death rather than the torture of the demonic creatures. Nevertheless, death will elude them for five months. Strangely, the demonic creatures do not attack the people of God. When this fact comes to the attention of the Antichrist, he is more enraged against believers, even blaming them for the torturous creatures.

> Then the sixth angel sounded: And I heard a voice from the four horns of the golden altar which is before God, saying to the sixth angel who had the trumpet, "Release the

four angels who are bound at the great river Euphrates."
So the four angels, who had been prepared for the hour
and day and month and year, were released to kill a third
of mankind. Now the number of the army of the horsemen
was two hundred million; I heard the number of them.
And thus I saw the horses in the vision: those who sat
on them had breastplates of fiery red, hyacinth blue, and
sulfur yellow; and the heads of the horses *were* like the
heads of lions; and out of their mouths came fire, smoke,
and brimstone. By these three *plagues* a third of mankind
was killed—by the fire and the smoke and the brimstone
which came out of their mouths. For their power is in their
mouth and in their tails; for their tails *are* like serpents,
having heads; and with them they do harm.

But the rest of mankind, who were not killed by these
plagues, did not repent of the works of their hands, that
they should not worship demons, and idols of gold, silver,
brass, stone, and wood, which can neither see nor hear nor
walk. And they did not repent of their murders or their
sorceries or their sexual immorality or their thefts.

(Revelation 9:13–21)

Ralph believed that this description of a nuclear holocaust is
the Russian/Islamic attack against Israel and the United States
in an attempt to wipe them off of the map. And this passage of
Revelation has been dealt with earlier.

Then the seventh angel sounded: And there were loud
voices in heaven, saying, "The kingdoms of this world
have become *the kingdoms* of our Lord and of His Christ,
and He shall reign forever and ever!" And the twenty-four
elders who sat before God on their thrones fell on their
faces and worshiped God, saying:

"We give You thanks, O Lord God Almighty,
The One who is and who was and who is to come,
Because You have taken Your great power and reigned.

The nations were angry, and Your wrath has come,
And the time of the dead, that they should be judged,
And that You should reward Your servants the prophets
and the saints,
And those who fear Your name, small and great,
And should destroy those who destroy the earth."

Then the temple of God was opened in heaven, and the ark of His covenant was seen in His temple. And there were lightnings, noises, thunderings, an earthquake, and great hail.

(Revelation 11:15–19)

The seventh angel's trumpet blast announces that Christ's earthly kingdom is coming and that he will reign forever. With the tremendous announcement, the elements convulse with lightening, thundering, a great hail storm, and an earthquake. "The earth was shaking itself in anticipation of the reign of Christ as King of kings and Lord of lords," Ralph commented joyously.

By the middle of the seven years of great tribulation, the Antichrist will have amassed so much control of the nations that he can do as he wills. As stated earlier, he will broker a peace treaty with Israel, but that did not protect Israel from the Russian/Islamic invasion. In the middle of the great tribulation, the Antichrist will accomplish what Russia and Iran were unable to achieve. He will march into Israel, take over, and set up his office in the Jerusalem temple. At the same time, he will abolish all Jewish worship of God. It is known as the abomination of desolation (Mark 13:14).

The whole prophetic process is described in (Daniel 9:27) as quoted again:

Then he shall confirm a covenant with many for one week;
But in the middle of the week
He shall bring an end to sacrifice and offering.
And on the wing of abominations shall be one who makes
desolate,

Even until the consummation, which is determined,
Is poured out on the desolate.

In addition, the desecration of the temple and rule of the Antichrist from Jerusalem are explained in 2 Thessalonians 2:

> Now, brethren, concerning the coming of our Lord Jesus Christ and our gathering together to Him, we ask you, not to be soon shaken in mind or troubled, either by spirit or by word or by letter, as if from us, as though the day of Christ had come. Let no one deceive you by any means; for *that Day will not come* unless the falling away comes first, and the man of sin is revealed, the son of perdition, who opposes and exalts himself above all that is called God or that is worshiped, so that he sits as God in the temple of God, showing himself that he is God.
>
> (2 Thessalonians 2:1–4)

Ralph explained that this coming of Jesus Christ refers to his appearing in the Revelation, not the rapture since the Antichrist will make his move against Israel, violating his peace treaty, during the great tribulation.

A host of the one-third of the Jews, who survive the Russian/Islamic invasion, will turn to God, accepting Christ as Messiah. But all that open worship will come to an end when the Antichrist takes over in Jerusalem. Under the rule of the Antichrist, worship will be reserved for him alone. All other worship will be banned.

It will become the sole purpose of the Antichrist to annihilate every Jew, but God will never permit that. Ralph reminded his students again that neither the Antichrist, nor the devil has unlimited powers. It is true that they will have awesome power but will be permitted to do only what God allows.

Following this brief deviation from the seals, trumpet blasts, and bowls to explain the Antichrist's violation of his peace treaty with Israel, Ralph returned to the Bible's description of the final bowls of God's wrath. Revelation 15 and 16 tells mankind what else they can expect in the final days of the great tribulation:

> Then I saw another sign in heaven, great and marvelous: seven angels having the seven last plagues, for in them the wrath of God is complete.
> And I saw *something* like a sea of glass mingled with fire, and those who have the victory over the beast, over his image and over his mark *and* over the number of his name, standing on the sea of glass, having harps of God. They sing the song of Moses, the servant of God, and the song of the Lamb… And out of the temple came the seven angels having the seven plagues, clothed in pure bright linen, and having their chests girded with golden bands. Then one of the four living creatures gave to the seven angels seven golden bowls full of the wrath of God who lives forever and ever.
>
> (Revelation 15:1–3, 6–7)

Ralph reminded his hearers that it is likely that many of them will not live to see these horrific events. The Antichrist's declaration of war against all believers will have eliminated many of them. But some believers will survive to see the severe final wrath of God against rebellious, godless mankind and the kingdom of the Antichrist.

> Then I heard a loud voice from the temple saying to the seven angels, "Go and pour out the bowls of the wrath of God on the earth."
> So the first went and poured out his bowl upon the earth, and a foul and loathsome sore came upon the men who had the mark of the beast and those who worshiped his image.
>
> (Revelation 16:1–2)

"Nothing like this has ever befallen mankind," Ralph commented. "Actually, it would be impossible to describe the suffering from the sores." One Bible commentator described the sores as "loathsome and malignant ulcers." And there will be no manmade cure, for this is the wrath of God. Another thing which enrages the Antichrist and his followers is that the awesome sores are only affecting those who have received the mark of the beast. Believers, being exempt from this wrathful act of God, will incur the indignation and ire of the Antichrist and his suffering servants.

> Then the second angel poured out his bowl on the sea, and it became blood as of a dead *man;* and every living creature in the sea died.
>
> (Revelation 16:3)

It must be recalled that one third of the seas had already been turned into blood by the second trumpet blast. Now, the final wrath of God turns all salt water into blood, killing every living creature in the seas. Every beautiful sandy beach will be contaminated with coagulated blood, along with dead decaying bodies of fish and all creatures of the seas. No sea creature will be able to live in the former saltwater for the bloody seas are like the blood of dead people.

Beach going will be a thing of the past! No one will stand gazing at the beautiful breakers washing upon the beaches. Every rising wave will be foaming blood. There will be no surfers catching the challenging breakers anywhere. "Can you imagine the stench filling the atmosphere from the decaying dead bodies of every sea creature?" Ralph asked.

> Then the third angel poured out his bowl on the rivers and springs of water, and they became blood. And I heard the angel of the waters saying:

"You are righteous, O Lord,
The One who is and who was and who is to be,
Because You have judged these things.
For they have shed the blood of saints and prophets,
And You have given them blood to drink.
For it is their just due.

(Revelation 16:4–6)

To awaken one morning and find blood gushing from a faucet, staining the sink into which it spills will be sickening, and startling, to say the least. God will punish mankind by turning all freshwater into blood. Every river, spring, well, lake, pond, and puddle will be bloody. The craving for moisture can be satisfied only with blood. *How will coffee taste when brewed with blood?* Ralph wondered, shuddering. The base of every beverage will of necessity be blood. People will avoid the unthinkable drink until every cell in their body cries out for moisture; then it will be only blood to satisfy their craving thirst. And the angel of the waters declares that mankind deserves this for they have shed innocent blood. No wonder Jesus said that it would be tribulation like never has been.

> Then the fourth angel poured out his bowl on the sun, and power was given to him to scorch men with fire. And men were scorched with great heat, and they blasphemed the name of God who has power over these plagues; and they did not repent and give Him glory.
>
> (Revelation 16:8–9)

Adding to the suffering from the sores, the stench from the bloody seas, craving thirst to be satisfied by only blood, will be the blazing, blistering heat of a God-stricken sun. No doubt there will be massive sun storm eruptions sending radiation and scorching heat through the universe, reaching the earth. The suffering will be so intense that people will shake their fists at

God, blaspheming his name, with no thought of repenting of their wicked ways. Unconceivable suffering will be the unavoidable trend of the day during the great tribulation. "And it could have been avoided!" Ralph regretfully bemoaned.

> Then the fifth angel poured out his bowl on the throne of the beast, and his kingdom became full of darkness; and they gnawed their tongues because of the pain. They blasphemed the God of heaven because of their pains and their sores, and did not repent of their deeds.
>
> (Revelation 16:10–11)

Darkness always adds to the suffering of sores or sickness. God knew this will plunge the kingdom of the Antichrist into tongue gnawing darkness. How God will do this is not explained, but promised. Hatred for God will be increased because of the unbearable suffering and darkness. As usual, mankind wanted to blame God, taking no responsibility for the adverse acts of God's judgment. They wanted to ignore the inevitable law of sowing and reaping, which is no new attitude of sinful mankind.

> Then the sixth angel poured out his bowl on the great river Euphrates, and its water was dried up, so that the way of the kings from the east might be prepared. And I saw three unclean spirits like frogs *coming* out of the mouth of the dragon, out of the mouth of the beast, and out of the mouth of the false prophet. For they are spirits of demons, performing signs, *which* go out to the kings of the earth and of the whole world, to gather them to the battle of that great day of God Almighty…
>
> And they gathered them together to the place called in Hebrew, Armageddon.
>
> (Revelation 16:12–16)

The drying up of the river Euphrates will be making preparation for the final conflict of the great tribulation. It will enable the rulers from the east to have unhindered access to Israel and the battle of Armageddon. The purpose of the battle of Armageddon will be to totally annihilate the Jews and defeat Christ and his heavenly army when he comes in the Revelation.

> Now I saw heaven opened, and behold, a white horse. And He who sat on him *was* called Faithful and True, and in righteousness He judges and makes war. His eyes *were* like a flame of fire, and on His head *were* many crowns. He had a name written that no one knew except Himself. He *was* clothed with a robe dipped in blood, and His name is called The Word of God. And the armies in heaven, clothed in fine linen, white and clean, followed Him on white horses. Now out of His mouth goes a sharp sword, that with it He should strike the nations. And He Himself will rule them with a rod of iron. He Himself treads the winepress of the fierceness and wrath of Almighty God. And He has on *His* robe and on His thigh a name written:
>
> KING OF KINGS AND
> LORD OF LORDS.
>
> (Revelation 19:11–16)

When Christ returns in the Revelation, he will literally come to this earth, with the armies of heaven, the resurrected saints of all ages, and the assisting angels of heaven. At that time, there will be a resurrection of the bodies of all who were saved and died during the great tribulation. In addition, angels will gather his saints from the ends of the earth, according to Jesus:

> Then they will see the Son of Man coming in the clouds with great power and glory. And then He will send His angels, and gather together His elect from the four winds, from the farthest part of earth to the farthest part of heaven.
>
> (Mark 13:26–27)

And I saw thrones, and they sat on them, and judgment was committed to them. Then *I saw* the souls of those who had been beheaded for their witness to Jesus and for the word of God, who had not worshiped the beast or his image, and had not received *his* mark on their foreheads or on their hands. And they lived and reigned with Christ for a thousand years. But the rest of the dead did not live again until the thousand years were finished.

(Revelation 20:4–5)

The devil, the Antichrist, and the demonic spirits will convince the godless world leaders and their armies that now is the time to wipe the Jews off the map and overthrow Christ and his followers and angelic forces. To their demise, the world leaders will be duped to their doom at the battle of Armageddon. How foolish for the rulers of the world to fall for such folly of the devil, who had set out to destroy Christ from the time of his birth.

"Christ will not come in the Revelation to be defeated but to set up his earthly kingdom and reign with his resurrected saints and angels for a thousand years. And he will not be defeated by the thousands of thousands arrayed against him on the plains of Megiddo and the surrounding areas of Israel," Ralph explained joyously.

In the battle of Armageddon, the Antichrist will be the leader, but the armies of the entire world will be involved, having been deceived and gathered by the devil and his demonic spirits:

And I saw the beast, the kings of the earth, and their armies, gathered together to make war against Him who sat on the horse and against His army. Then the beast was captured, and with him the false prophet who worked signs in his presence, by which he deceived those who received the mark of the beast and those who worshiped his image. These two were cast alive into the lake of fire burning with brimstone. And the rest were killed with the sword which proceeded from the mouth of Him who sat on the horse. And all the birds were filled with their flesh.

(Revelation 19:19–21)

The seventh, final bowl of the wrath of God will consummate the time of the great tribulation, with the most awesome earthquake that has ever taken place, mighty storms with hail stones weighing about a hundred pounds, crashing upon armies of the Antichrist. Christ will purge the earth, conquer and destroy the armies of the world, which will greatly enhance his reign of peace and tranquility:

> Then the seventh angel poured out his bowl into the air, and a loud voice came out of the temple of heaven, from the throne, saying, "It is done!" And there were noises and thunderings and lightnings; and there was a great earthquake, such a mighty and great earthquake as had not occurred since men were on the earth. Now the great city was divided into three parts, and the cities of the nations fell. And great Babylon was remembered before God, to give her the cup of the wine of the fierceness of His wrath. Then every island fled away, and the mountains were not found. And great hail from heaven fell upon men, *each hailstone* about the weight of a talent. Men blasphemed God because of the plague of the hail, since that plague was exceedingly great.
>
> (Revelation 16:17–21)

When the battle of Armageddon comes to an ending, Christ is victorious! The Antichrist and the false prophet are cast bodily into hell, a place of fire and brimstone. As a final act of Christ against evil deception, the armies of the world will be destroyed at his command. And their dead bodies will be left to lie where they drop to be consumed by the fowl of the air, which are called to this feast. And the devil is finally caught and bound for a thousand years:

Then I saw an angel coming down from heaven, having the key to the bottomless pit and a great chain in his hand. He laid hold of the dragon, that serpent of old, who is *the* Devil and Satan, and bound him for a thousand years; and he cast him into the bottomless pit, and shut him up, and set a seal on him, so that he should deceive the nations no more till the thousand years were finished. But after these things he must be released for a little while.

(Revelation 20:1–3)

Exhausted late at night, Ralph concluded the document to be shared with his trainers. In spite of his tiredness, his heart and spirit were thrilled as he anticipated enjoying final victory with Christ and participation in the thousand-year reign with him in a world of peace. And to think that there will be no devil to torment or tempt mortal mankind for the thousand years.

He looked forward to presenting this material the following week. Allowing for questions and discussion, Ralph foresees the possibility of this material necessitating two sessions for adequate presentation. "Hopefully, I will have the time to complete the lessons," he said to himself.

He left his study, ate a small snack alone, and retired for a night of much needed rest. Ralph has one final lesson of triumph and victory to complete, and he will start on that the next day. For some strange reason, he still senses an urgency and uncertainty about completing the lessons for the needy believers.

Training of Believers Halted by Agents of the Antichrist and Ralph Arrested

Monday evening at seven o'clock, the four couples who were to be present for training were on time at the home of Ralph and anxious for the lesson Ralph had prepared. They had ridden their bicycles, parked them, and locked them safely some distance from Ralph's house, then walked the rest of the way. All of them knew that four bicycles parked at Ralph's house could raise suspicion in anyone watching. None of those present had noticed anyone paying undue attention to them as they traveled to their destination.

The training went well with much discussion and many profitable questions asked. As Ralph had suspected, it would take two sessions to cover the material he had prepared. That second session would take place in three weeks since those trained needed time to notify and teach the lesson to those who were on their responsibility list. As usual, Faye served refreshments at the conclusion of the session, and everyone left in high spirits without any incidents.

Training sessions Wednesday and Friday were also without interruptions. As with the Monday session, it would be necessary to finish the material in two sessions. And that posed no problems for anyone.

When they returned to Ralph's house in three weeks, they would be very cautious as the grip of the Antichrist's appointed representatives seemed to be more evident now. Plus, the TV news repeatedly reported that the representatives of the Antichrist were becoming better organized in the United States. Listeners were cautioned to be in observance of all rules and policies of the Antichrist.

During the three weeks preceding the next training session, which would conclude the acts of God through the seal, trumpet blasts, and wrathful bowls, Ralph was busy preparing the final lesson material. It was much more uplifting and promised final victory for the kingdom of Christ and his followers. As Ralph prayed, studied, and prepared the document, he was blessed and looked forward to the presentation. But most of all, he looked forward to being a participant in the final kingdom of God. What a blessing that would be!

Often during those three weeks, especially once the lesson material was completed and printed for distribution, Ralph took long bicycle rides throughout his community and beyond. There were many new faces, which he carefully observed. He also noticed several strangers watching his activities more closely. In addition, more motorized vehicles were in evidence. A few times the same vehicles were observed passing his house very slowly. It seemed strange to Ralph that all these vehicles had darkly tinted glass so he could not see anyone inside. *Am I being spied upon again?* was a serious question in his mind. What should he do about the classes that were now just a few days away? After considering the matter and discussing it with Todd and Faye, he decided to proceed as planned. Confident that those attending would use extreme caution in arriving, he left it in the hands of God.

Monday evening arrived, as did all those anxious to complete the great tribulation lesson stressing the acts and judgments of God. The evening was uneventful, and the lesson material was completed. Before everyone left, they decided to meet for the final teaching session three weeks from that evening.

After Ralph was alone with his live-in friends, they discussed the possibility that perhaps they had undue concern about being spied upon. Of course, that was a remote possibility, but Ralph sensed a strange alarm about something. Despite his sense of alarm, the Wednesday class would meet as planned. He was too near the completion of the training to permit an uneasy feeling to disrupt the program.

The Wednesday evening training session had just completed, and Faye and Todd were serving light refreshments when shuffling feet were heard on the porch, followed by pounding on the door. Quickly, all teaching material was put away, and Ralph's teaching material was rushed to his study and placed in a packing box. After more loud pounding on the door, Ralph opened the door to be greeted by that same strange couple who had interrupted meetings in the past. They had also survived the holocaust and were back to their old tricks. As before, they rudely pushed past Ralph and were among his guests with strange expressions upon their faces.

"We're back to join the party," they said, glaring at Ralph. "Let me introduce ourselves," the man said. "I am Verlin, and this is my companion Sylvia. We are agents of the Antichrist, and we know that you are not having a party but are meeting to study the forbidden Bible. Ralph, we know that you are a former pastor and the leader of these teaching sessions. You have been under observation for a lengthy time, and we know the names and addresses of all of your followers. We are here to search your house to determine how much banned material you are hiding. We will begin by searching your office to see how many forbidden Bibles you have refused to surrender, as demanded."

As Verlin and Sylvia move toward Ralph's study, they are stopped in stride as Ralph and Todd quickly block the doorway. Instantly, the other four men ringed them in, refusing them access to any of Ralph's house. As one of the men took Ralph's position blocking the doorway to his study, Ralph opened the front door and ordered Verlin and Sylvia out of his house. Pausing for a moment, Verlin and Sylvia realized that they were outnumbered and possibly in danger. So they headed for the open door held by Ralph. "Of course, you know that you will not get away with this defiant action," Verlin derided. "We will be back with agents, who will do as they well wish, while we laugh on your faces," he warned. With that, they stepped through the open door, after pausing to give Ralph a final defiant glare.

When Verlin and Sylvia were out of sight, Ralph urged his guests to leave immediately and take random routes home on their bicycles. Some of them scurried out the front door, others out the back door and were gone into the darkness of the night.

Todd and Faye were urged to hurriedly leave and hide under the furniture on a neighbor's porch behind Ralph's house as those neighbors were gone. Quickly, they complied and found very safe hiding places, as Ralph had suggested. However, this escape did not assure any of them a safe future asylum.

Ralph was left alone to await the agents, accompanied by Verlin and Sylvia, whom they had assured him would come immediately. During the waiting time, he securely hid much of the valuable study documents, commentaries, and Bibles. He placed the final lesson documents in a hiding place known by Todd and Faye. Ralph deemed that it was vitally important that the final lesson document get into the hands of the new believers even if he could never teach the lesson. He looked around his study, surveying the books and files, trying to determine if there was anything else he should safely hide in other parts of the house. He had destroyed everything on his computer. He was satisfied with his steps to secure as much as possible anything that could be used as evidence against him when he was arrested.

Having completed his hiding project, Ralph retired to the family room, sat down in his favorite easy chair, switched on the TV for the noise, and awaited the arrival of the threatened agents. Since he did not care about what was being shown on TV, he read a novel to occupy his mind and find some enjoyment.

Ralph was not scared, but he did sense tension and dread of the unknown and his uncertain future. Of course, he knew what his final future would be, but it was the in-between that caused him concern. His spirit was uplifted as he contemplated the fact that he might be just hours away from his heavenly home. He had endured enough of the great tribulation, and it would be a blessing to leave it, if that was God's will.

It was past midnight, and no agents had arrived. *Could it be that Verlin and Sylvia were bluffing?* the thought flashed through his mind. At a little after one o'clock, Ralph went to where Todd and Faye were hiding and invited them to return to his house. Since they were cramped, cold, and sleepy, they did not need much coaxing to go with Ralph. About 2:30, they all retired to catch a little sleep. The remainder of the night was uneventful, and they rested well. Upon awakening, they had no idea what the day would bring forth, but there was a sense of foreboding in all of them.

After supper that day, from food they had stored prior to the holocaust, Ralph, Todd, and Faye sauntered into the family room and turned on the TV to catch any new news updates. There was still tension and frequent glances out a window as they watched for the promised agents to arrest Ralph and possibly others. There was a troubling news item given by a reporter.

"The Antichrist had ordered all his agents to search for secret groups of believers meeting for Bible studies and proselytizing, winning numerous others to their faith. It was stressed again that all Bibles were to be surrendered or destroyed by burning. Any observed violation would be treated as a major crime against the Antichrist, punishable by martyrdom. And these forbidden activities had been brought to the attention of the Antichrist. It must be stopped at any cost."

Ralph sensed a chill shake his entire body. Tomorrow's meeting at his house must be cancelled immediately. He reached for a prepaid cell phone and made the calls to the four couples expected to meet. They had heard the same TV report and were relieved by the cancellation.

This was a new frustrating time for all believers. Would any of Ralph's group survive? Would any believers in the rest of the world survive? The believers Ralph felt responsible for were only a fraction of those in the rest of the world, posing as an imagined threat to the Antichrist. "They must be eradicated," the Antichrist mumbled to those around him as he watched the same TV report.

A little after nine o'clock, Ralph and his friends heard several vehicle doors slam in front of his house. But there had been no vehicle lights to observe through cracks in the blinds. Ralph rushed to the door looking through the peep device. To his dismay, four armed agents, along with Verlin and Sylvia, were approaching the front porch steps. And a van was parked by the curb in front of his house. Evidently, they had approached with their vehicle lights out to affect surprise.

Silently, he instructed Todd and Faye to quietly and quickly exit by the rear door and rush to a hiding place. There was no advantage in them being arrested along with him. And there was the final lesson document for them to get to other believers. They complied promptly, turning off all lights as they exited.

There were heavy steps on the porch, and a gun butt was used to hammer on the door by one of the armed agents. Ralph did not answer the door instantly, standing in the dark of the room. Suddenly, there was a crash as the agents kicked in the door. A blinding light searched the room, fixing the glare in Ralph's face. Two of the other agents rushed to either side of Ralph, pinning his arms behind him. Verlin was asked to turn on the lights. And sure enough, he and his companion Sylvia were smugly smiling at him, just as they had promised to do the evening before. Handcuffs were quickly and roughly snapped tightly on Ralph's wrists. And the two agents held him tightly as though he would attempt an escape.

"You are under arrest for flagrant violation of the demands of the Antichrist," one of the agents shouted at him.

"Where are the others?" one of the other agents demanded.

Ralph responded as kindly as he could, "I am the only one here, sir."

A snarling agent said, "We will just have a look to see for ourselves." So all the lights in every room were turned on, and the agents went about their search.

As the two agents making the search reentered the room, one of them demanded, "Where are they, or where did they go?"

Ralph said kindly, "I do not know, sir."

An agent informed Ralph, "That is no problem, for we know the name and address of all of your followers, and they will be arrested like you within the next few days. Agents have secretly followed all of the people attending your illegal meetings, so we know where to pick them up. The Antichrist wants the earth purged of pompous people like you. And purge it we will!"

Satisfied that only Ralph was present, they roughly pushed him past the broken down door toward the parked van. A rear door of the van was opened, and Ralph was violently pushed into it, and an armed agent sat on either side of him. Throughout the entire process of Ralph's crude arrest, he demonstrated peace and perfect spiritual poise, in spite of the scary situation. His enemies and arresting officers noted this and could not comprehend it. In the eyes of a deranged world, Ralph would die in disgrace and dishonor, but not in the eyes of God. He determined to die in the faith, not a victim, but a victor over death. He would be able to say, "Oh, death, where is your victory?"

The van drove off into the night, and its destination was never determined. That was the last that was ever heard of Ralph Waterman. His mission had been cut a little short by his arrest, but the final encouraging lesson was safely hidden where Todd and Faye could find it and then get it to key believers.

All who knew Ralph were certain that he maintained his faith to the end, refusing to recant his faith in Jesus Christ as Lord and Savior. He was willing to pay the ultimate price to die for his faith in his loving Lord. His friends and followers were sure that he was gone.

When the executioner's sword flashed, decapitating Ralph, as this was the favorite method of execution by the Muslims and followers of the Antichrist, his soul joined the great white-robed throng to be with his Lord forever. Ralph had tragically missed the rapture, but having been saved by faith in the Lord, he died triumphantly. He was rescued from the remaining torturing torments of the great tribulation. He died thankful that he had attempted to ably teach and encourage many new believers, helping them prepare for a victorious death. His mission had been completed.

Sometime after midnight, Todd and Faye silently slipped back into Ralph's house. They had huddled in the shadows for some time to be sure the house was not being observed. Finding a flashlight, Faye went to the stove, opening the bottom drawer, removing several pans, and, from a large baking pan, took out the final lesson prepared by Ralph. With the documents was the phone number of Jim and Sue, along with a prepaid cell phone with which to call them. The instructions were to call them, letting them know that Todd would be leaving on his bicycle in a few minutes to take the valuable documents to them. They were not to turn on any lights in their house, and Todd would give the coded knock at the door when he arrived. Faye hid her bicycle in the bushes of a neighbor's house so there would be no evidence of any activity at the home of Ralph Waterman.

She would silently wait and pray for a safe trip and delivery of valuable items to Jim and Sue. As instructed, she kept two copies of the final lesson prepared by Ralph for her and Todd. Anxiously, she awaited the return of Todd, which would take at least two hours. Almost to the minute, Todd returned in two hours. Slipping into the house, he joined Faye, leaving the front door crashed in, so any observer would not know of their return to the house. They slept fitfully on the floor the rest of the night, hoping for daylight, but then what would they do? Where could they go?

Todd and Faye awoke a little before sunrise and carefully stayed away from the fallen front door. No drapes were moved nor did anything change from its position from the night before. Ralph was gone, and they would have to figure out their future on their own. This posed a dreaded dilemma. They did not realize how much they had leaned upon Ralph for help and guidance. Quietly eating a makeshift breakfast in the shadows, they prayed and were puzzled about what to do. There did not seem to be any easy answers.

They cringed as the van, which had hauled Ralph away, crept by the house. Thankfully, it went on down the street. Todd and Faye realized that they had to figure out something soon.

Realizing that they had one of Ralph's prepaid cell phones and the phone number of Jim and Sue, they decided to call them. They would ask to meet them at the park at one o'clock that day, if at all possible. Jim and Sue were extremely close to Ralph, and they might be able to help them figure out the situation. The phone call was made, and arrangements were made for the meeting.

Extreme caution must be maintained as the home of Jim and Sue might be under scrutiny. When they arrived at the park, they would ignore each other for some time, riding in the park and beyond before stopping to talk. They would always be watching for possible spies or anyone considering them closely. As the time for the meeting approached, all of them were anxious and tense.

At exactly one o'clock, four bicyclists passed by, hardly noticing one another and several trips were made around the park, even out into the surrounding community. Finally, Jim and Sue stopped to rest on a park bench. After several more minutes of riding, Todd and Faye parked their bicycles and sat down beside them, treating them as total strangers for some time. As no one else was visible, they began to talk to each other. Todd came to the point quickly before anyone else might observe them. "Jim,

John F. Hay Sr.

where should Faye and I go, and what should we do?" he asked, staring off into the distance. Jim and Sue conversed with each other, cautiously watching for intruders. In a few minutes, they seemed to have a solution.

Looking at no one in particular, Jim said, "Todd, you and Faye could come to our house for a few days as we have extra rooms. You should do that late tonight but arriving one at a time and coming by different roundabout routes as our house may be under scrutiny. And do not bring anything with you. We are all about the same size, so you and Faye can wear our clothing. That way, it would not look as though you were moving into our house. Would that be acceptable to you and Faye?" Jim continued, "And while you are there, we can figure out what is best for you and Faye. The time together would give us an opportunity to study the final lesson prepared by Ralph and thoroughly discuss any of the material that needs to be clarified.

Remaining quiet, Todd and Faye simply looked at each other for a minute or two. Then their faces took on a look of relief and surprise. Todd spoke to Jim, still looking at Faye, as though talking to her, "Jim and Sue, that is an overwhelmingly generous offer to Faye and me. We would not want to be an imposition upon you, and possibly, we can soon come up with a more permanent plan. Both of us are deeply appreciative of your offer and sacrifice for us. We will arrive at your house late tonight, following your instructions carefully." After a few more minutes of silent resting, the bikers rode off in different directions, still appearing to be strangers. In the dark of that night, the trip to Jim and Sue's took place without incident,

Following breakfast the next morning, the four of them sat down in the living room to seriously consider what the immediate future might be for Todd and Faye. In fact, the future of all of them was discussed, in light of the recent announcements of the Antichrist, and the pressure of his followers. Nothing really jelled during the discussions that morning. Finally, they let the subject

266

drop and talked about other things. Of course, the name of Ralph Waterman often entered into their conversations. They were all indebted to him for helping them be saved and strengthening their faith in God. Very often one of them would go to a window to scan the area for any strangers or parked vehicles in sight of their house.

Later in the afternoon, Jim came up with an idea that just might work. Calling them all together, he shared the following thoughts with them. "After spending at least a week with us, Todd and Faye should wander back to Ralph's house. If the door is still kicked in, they should find tools in Ralph's garage and begin to repair the damage. If they are questioned by anyone, including official officers, they should inform them that as homeless people and noticing that this house was evidently vacant, they would claim it as a temporary home." This plan seemed very plausible to everyone.

"Jim, you have come up with a solution that has good possibilities," Todd said happily.

After spending a few days over a week with Jim and Sue, Todd and Faye rode their bicycles back to Ralph's house. Sure enough, the front door was still broken in, and there was no evidence of anyone having been there. Parking their bicycles by the front steps, they cautiously entered the house. First of all, they examined the food storage room. Fortunately, everything was exactly as they had left it nor did it appear that anything else had been removed from the house. The only thing missing was Ralph, and he was gone for good.

Finding tools in the garage, they began to repair the door, planning to put it back on its hinges. It would not be perfect but would provide adequate protection from stray animals or any curious persons who just happened to be wandering by. As they were repairing the door, a vehicle came down the street slowly, pulled to the curb, and parked in front of the house. Todd and Faye did not stop their work nor did they appear to notice the vehicle although their hearts were almost pounding out of their chests. What now?

Hearing footsteps on the walkway, Todd and Faye finally paused from their efforts and looked up. Two armed agents were approaching slowly. Stepping upon the porch and observing Todd and Faye at work, they asked, "What do you two think you are doing?"

Laying aside his hammer, Todd said matter-of-factly, "We are repairing this door so we can have a place to live. We are homeless people and have noticed that no one seems to live here any longer, so we are preparing to have a temporary home."

One of the agents asked rather sternly, "Do you have permission to do what you are planning to do?"

"No," Todd responded. "We have never seen anyone to ask about permission."

"Would you move out if asked to do so, without causing any difficulty?" the other agent asked. To this question, Todd and Faye both answered yes very affirmatively.

The agents stepped a little distance away and whispered something to each other. Coming back to Todd and Faye, they asked them to stand together so they could take a photograph of them, and the couple complied with their request. Checking the digital photograph for clarity, the agents turned and walked away without any further comments.

Todd and Faye stood in shock and amazement as they watched the agents drive away. "Evidently, they are new officers," Todd commented, "for they did not notice that we do not wear the mark of the beast nor did they ask to see evidence of a pledge of allegiance to the Antichrist." *What a relief, and how amazing.*

A little while later, Jim and Sue rode by on their bicycles without stopping; they simply gave Todd and Faye a thumbs up on the progress they were making. When the door was repaired and replaced on its hinges, Todd and Faye had a temporary home, and that was all they were going to need.

The Great Tribulation Ends With the Coming of Christ in the Revelation to Reign a Thousand Years, the Final Judgment, the New Heaven and New Earth

Prior to this event and while Todd and Faye were the guests of Jim and Sue, they had studied the final lesson Ralph had prepared to be presented to believers. It was all about the final ending of time on this earth and the glorious victory of Christ and his saints. The lesson was uplifting, making these believers more determined to keep their faith unwavering to whatever ending they might face.

According to Ralph's final lesson, the following events and conditions would take place, according to the Bible, the Word of God:

> First of all, the great tribulation will end with the coming of Jesus Christ in the Revelation. That is when Jesus literally returns to this earth with his resurrected saints and the angelic hosts of heaven. His coming will dethrone the Antichrist, false prophet and Satan, along with the destruction of the rebellious armies of the world, who follow the Antichrist in the battle of Armageddon. This will be the final action of the Antichrist.

Ralph had reprinted several Scriptures he had previously used, stressing other points:

Now I saw heaven opened, and behold, a white horse. And He who sat on him *was* called Faithful and True, and in righteousness He judges and makes war. His eyes *were* like a flame of fire, and on His head *were* many crowns. He had a name written that no one knew except Himself. He *was* clothed with a robe dipped in blood, and His name is called The Word of God. And the armies in heaven, clothed in fine linen, white and clean, followed Him on white horses. Now out of His mouth goes a sharp sword, that with it He should strike the nations. And He Himself will rule them with a rod of iron. He Himself treads the winepress of the fierceness and wrath of Almighty God. And He has on *His* robe and on His thigh a name written:

KING OF KINGS AND
LORD OF LORDS.

Then I saw an angel standing in the sun; and he cried with a loud voice, saying to all the birds that fly in the midst of heaven, "Come and gather together for the supper of the great God, that you may eat the flesh of kings, the flesh of captains, the flesh of mighty men, the flesh of horses and of those who sit on them, and the flesh of all *people,* free and slave, both small and great."

And I saw the beast, the kings of the earth, and their armies, gathered together to make war against Him who sat on the horse and against His army. Then the beast was captured, and with him the false prophet who worked signs in his presence, by which he deceived those who received the mark of the beast and those who worshiped his image. These two were cast alive into the lake of fire burning with brimstone. And the rest were killed with the sword which proceeded from the mouth of Him who sat on the horse. And all the birds were filled with their flesh.

(Revelation 19:11–21)

Jesus himself predicted his coming to earth in the Revelation when all mankind will see him. For only the prepared and ready will see him when he returns in the rapture:

> Immediately after the tribulation of those days the sun will be darkened, and the moon will not give its light; the stars will fall from heaven, and the powers of the heavens will be shaken. Then the sign of the Son of Man will appear in heaven, and then all the tribes of the earth will mourn, and they will see the Son of Man coming on the clouds of heaven with power and great glory.
>
> (Matthew 24:29–30)

The Bible lets it be known in 1 Thessalonians that when Jesus returns to this earth in the Revelation, the resurrected saints will come with him:

> But I do not want you to be ignorant, brethren, concerning those who have fallen asleep, lest you sorrow as others who have no hope. For if we believe that Jesus died and rose again, even so God will bring with Him those who sleep in Jesus.
>
> For this we say to you by the word of the Lord, that we who are alive *and* remain until the coming of the Lord will by no means precede those who are asleep. For the Lord Himself will descend from heaven with a shout, with the voice of an archangel, and with the trumpet of God. And the dead in Christ will rise first. Then we who are alive *and* remain shall be caught up together with them in the clouds to meet the Lord in the air. And thus we shall always be with the Lord.
>
> (1 Thessalonians 4:13–17)

Two items are important in this 1 Thessalonians Scripture. First, the souls of the righteous will come with Jesus when he returns in the rapture to be rejoined with their resurrected bodies.

Secondly, all those having met the Lord in the air in the rapture will always be with the Lord. So that means when Jesus returns to this earth in the Revelation, all his resurrected, glorified saints will come back to earth and reign with him for a thousand years:

> And I saw thrones, and they sat on them, and judgment was committed to them. Then *I saw* the souls of those who had been beheaded for their witness to Jesus and for the word of God, who had not worshiped the beast or his image, and had not received *his* mark on their foreheads or on their hands. And they lived and reigned with Christ for a thousand years. But the rest of the dead did not live again until the thousand years were finished.
>
> (Revelation 20:4–5)

Also, consider that Ralph had put Revelation 5:9–10 in his notes.

> And they sang a new song, saying:
> "You are worthy to take the scroll,
> And to open its seals;
> For You were slain,
> And have redeemed us to God by Your blood
> Out of every tribe and tongue and people and nation,
> And have made us kings and priests to our God;
> And we shall reign on the earth.

No doubt that rebuilding and restoration of a greatly damaged earth will begin during the great tribulation and will continue to completion during the early years of the thousand-year reign of Christ. Every city, town, and village will have a glorified saint as leader. All governors, mayors, city managers, tribal chiefs, any government leaders, etcetera will be glorified saints. Christ and his followers will rule the earth for those thousand years in perfect peace.

All mankind who survives the great tribulation will be subject to Christ and his rule of righteousness. It will be a worldwide theocracy under Jesus Christ, the King of kings and Lord of lords. For a thousand years, there will be no rebellion or resistance because there will be world peace and tranquility.

World peace will be a reality because the devil will no longer be roaming the earth seeking to stir up trouble, and devouring people by his cunning devices:

> Then I saw an angel coming down from heaven, having the key to the bottomless pit and a great chain in his hand. He laid hold of the dragon, that serpent of old, who is *the* Devil and Satan, and bound him for a thousand years; and he cast him into the bottomless pit, and shut him up, and set a seal on him, so that he should deceive the nations no more till the thousand years were finished. But after these things he must be released for a little while.
>
> (Revelation 20:1–3)

When the devil is released for a little while at the end of the thousand-year reign of Christ, he will have no power or permission to tempt, test, or treat the glorified saints of Christ with contempt or touch them in any way. He will only be permitted to stir up strife and confusion with mortal mankind, who have lived in subjection to Christ until that time. He will convince worldly mankind that Christ can be overthrown, and he can become the world's ruler, but that will never happen:

> Now when the thousand years have expired, Satan will be released from his prison and will go out to deceive the nations which are in the four corners of the earth, Gog and Magog, to gather them together to battle, whose number *is* as the sand of the sea. They went up on the breadth of the earth and surrounded the camp of the saints and the beloved city. And fire came down from God out of heaven and devoured them. The devil, who deceived them, was

cast into the lake of fire and brimstone where the beast and the false prophet *are*. And they will be tormented day and night forever and ever.

(Revelation 20:7–10)

The Scripture passage above needs no explanation, for it is clearly self-explanatory. The devil is coming to his final ending, along with all who choose to fall for his deceptive devices, which are his age-old tactics. There have been constant wars and rumors of wars since the fall of mankind, but the final war of all wars will take place when Satan gathers a numberless host to overthrow Christ and his kingdom. The outcome of that war is plainly prophesied by the Word of God as stated above.

After the final earthly war, the "great white throne" judgment will be set up by God, and all mankind will be judged, facing their final destiny:

Then I saw a great white throne and Him who sat on it, from whose face the earth and the heaven fled away. And there was found no place for them. And I saw the dead, small and great, standing before God, and books were opened. And another book was opened, which is *the Book* of Life. And the dead were judged according to their works, by the things which were written in the books. The sea gave up the dead who were in it, and Death and Hades delivered up the dead who were in them. And they were judged, each one according to his works. Then Death and Hades were cast into the lake of fire. This is the second death. And anyone not found written in the Book of Life was cast into the lake of fire.

(Revelation 20:11–14)

The Bible has much to say about the final judgment, for everyone will be present and have their final sentence pronounced. The Word of God proclaims this truth in Hebrews 9:27, "And as it is appointed for men to die once, but after this the judgment."

Jesus described the final judgment in simple terms so everyone could comprehend it:

> When the Son of Man comes in His glory, and all the holy angels with Him, then He will sit on the throne of His glory. All the nations will be gathered before Him, and He will separate them one from another, as a shepherd divides *his* sheep from the goats. And He will set the sheep on His right hand, but the goats on the left. Then the King will say to those on His right hand, 'Come, you blessed of My Father, inherit the kingdom prepared for you from the foundation of the world: for I was hungry and you gave Me food; I was thirsty and you gave Me drink; I was a stranger and you took Me in; I *was* naked and you clothed Me; I was sick and you visited Me; I was in prison and you came to Me.'
>
> "Then the righteous will answer Him, saying, 'Lord, when did we see You hungry and feed *You,* or thirsty and give *You* drink? When did we see You a stranger and take *You* in, or naked and clothe *You?* Or when did we see You sick, or in prison, and come to You?' And the King will answer and say to them, 'Assuredly, I say to you, inasmuch as you did *it* to one of the least of these My brethren, you did *it* to Me.'
>
> "Then He will also say to those on the left hand, 'Depart from Me, you cursed, into the everlasting fire prepared for the devil and his angels: for I was hungry and you gave Me no food; I was thirsty and you gave Me no drink; I was a stranger and you did not take Me in, naked and you did not clothe Me, sick and in prison and you did not visit Me.'
>
> "Then they also will answer Him, saying, 'Lord, when did we see You hungry or thirsty or a stranger or naked or sick or in prison, and did not minister to You?' Then He will answer them, saying, 'Assuredly, I say to you, inasmuch as you did not do *it* to one of the least of these, you did

not do *it* to Me.' And these will go away into everlasting punishment, but the righteous into eternal life.

(Matthew 25:31–46)

But we know that the judgment of God is according to truth against those who practice such things. And do you think this, O man, you who judge those practicing such things, and doing the same, that you will escape the judgment of God? Or do you despise the riches of His goodness, forbearance, and longsuffering, not knowing that the goodness of God leads you to repentance? But in accordance with your hardness and your impenitent heart you are treasuring up for yourself wrath in the day of wrath and revelation of the righteous judgment of God, who "will render to each one according to his deeds": eternal life to those who by patient continuance in doing good seek for glory, honor, and immortality; but to those who are self-seeking and do not obey the truth, but obey unrighteousness—indignation and wrath, tribulation and anguish, on every soul of man who does evil, of the Jew first and also of the Greek; but glory, honor, and peace to everyone who works what is good, to the Jew first and also to the Greek. For there is no partiality with God.

(Romans 2:2–11)

Then the Lord knows how to deliver the godly out of temptations and to reserve the unjust under punishment for the Day of Judgment.

(2 Peter 2:9)

The final judgment will be the last event taking place upon this present earth, according to the Word of God:

But the heavens and the earth *which* are now preserved by the same word, are reserved for fire until the day of judgment and perdition of ungodly men. But, beloved, do not forget this one thing, that with the Lord one day *is* as a thousand years, and a thousand years as one day. The Lord is not slack concerning *His* promise, as some count slackness, but is longsuffering toward us, not willing that any should perish but that all should come to repentance.

But the day of the Lord will come as a thief in the night, in which the heavens will pass away with a great noise, and the elements will melt with fervent heat; both the earth and the works that are in it will be burned up. Therefore, since all these things will be dissolved, what manner *of persons* ought you to be in holy conduct and godliness, looking for and hastening the coming of the day of God, because of which the heavens will be dissolved, being on fire, and the elements will melt with fervent heat? Nevertheless we, according to His promise, look for new heavens and a new earth in which righteousness dwells.

2 Peter 3:7–13

Since this world will be destroyed by the fire of God, he will create a new heaven and a new earth. The new earth will be different from this earth but perfectly fitted for the righteous, which have been resurrected, and glorified, just as Jesus had a glorious body following his resurrection. In fact, the Bible declares that the righteous will be like him:

> Beloved, now we are children of God; and it has not yet been revealed what we shall be, but we know that when He is revealed, we shall be like Him, for we shall see Him as He is.

(1 John 3:2)

Just before the final destruction of this earth, there will be a great moving day. The glorified saints of all ages, who have reigned with Christ for a thousand years on this earth and who have heard him say at the final judgment, "Well *done,* good and faithful servant; you have been faithful over a few things, I will make you ruler over many things. Enter into the joy of your lord" (Matthew 25:23), will be moved to the glorious new earth. The angelic hosts will be included in this gigantic move.

John "The Revelator" was permitted to see the new heaven and earth to confirm the prophetic Word of God:

> Now I saw a new heaven and a new earth, for the first heaven and the first earth had passed away. Also there was no more sea. Then I, John, saw the holy city, New Jerusalem, coming down out of heaven from God, prepared as a bride adorned for her husband. And I heard a loud voice from heaven saying, "Behold, the tabernacle of God *is* with men, and He will dwell with them, and they shall be His people. God Himself will be with them *and be* their God. And God will wipe away every tear from their eyes; there shall be no more death, nor sorrow, nor crying. There shall be no more pain, for the former things have passed away."
>
> Then He who sat on the throne said, "Behold, I make all things new." And He said to me, "Write, for these words are true and faithful."
>
> And He said to me, "It is done! I am the Alpha and the Omega, the Beginning and the End. I will give of the fountain of the water of life freely to him who thirsts. He who overcomes shall inherit all things, and I will be his God and he shall be My son. But the cowardly, unbelieving, abominable, murderers, sexually immoral, sorcerers, idolaters, and all liars shall have their part in the lake which burns with fire and brimstone, which is the second death.
>
> (Revelation 21:1–8)

Ralph wanted to stress some of the wonders and blessings of the new earth. It will be new, not a worked over present earth. The Word of God proclaimed that many things that were prevalent on this earth will be missing on the new earth. There will be no more tears of pain or sorrow, for God himself will wipe these away and out of each memory. Death will be a forgotten dilemma, and there will be no more sorrow or crying. Also, there will be no more debilitating pain. Sin and sinners will not inhabit the new earth nor will Satan ever invade it as he did in the Garden of Eden on this earth.

God revealed to the prophet Isaiah that he was going to create new heavens and a new earth in Isaiah 65:17: "For behold, I create new heavens and a new earth; And the former shall not be remembered or come to mind."

Ralph considered the thought that the new earth might be similar to the original Garden of Eden in which God placed Adam and Eve. But God barred them from that paradise because of rebellion and sin against him. The new earth will be perfectly fitted for an eternity where God will dwell with his children and angels. Every child of God can look forward to this new earth and heaven, which will be a haven for resurrected bodies and souls. It will literally be what this earth would have been like without Satan and sinfulness, only better.

God also revealed to John "The Revelator" the new Jerusalem, which would come down to the new earth as its capital city:

> Then one of the seven angels who had the seven bowls filled with the seven last plagues came to me and talked with me, saying, "Come, I will show you the bride, the Lamb's wife." And he carried me away in the Spirit to a great and high mountain, and showed me the great city, the holy Jerusalem, descending out of heaven from God, having the glory of God. Her light *was* like a most precious stone, like a jasper stone, clear as crystal. Also she had a great and high wall with twelve gates, and twelve angels at the gates, and names written on them, which are *the names* of the twelve tribes of the children of Israel: three gates on the east, three gates on the north, three gates on the south, and three gates on the west.
>
> Now the wall of the city had twelve foundations, and on them were the names of the twelve apostles of the

Lamb. And he who talked with me had a gold reed to measure the city, its gates, and its wall. The city is laid out as a square; its length is as great as its breadth. And he measured the city with the reed: twelve thousand furlongs. Its length, breadth, and height are equal. Then he measured its wall: one hundred *and* forty-four cubits, *according* to the measure of a man, that is, of an angel. The construction of its wall was *of* jasper; and the city *was* pure gold, like clear glass. The foundations of the wall of the city *were* adorned with all kinds of precious stones: the first foundation *was* jasper, the second sapphire, the third chalcedony, the fourth emerald, the fifth sardonyx, the sixth sardius, the seventh chrysolite, the eighth beryl, the ninth topaz, the tenth chrysoprase, the eleventh jacinth, and the twelfth amethyst. The twelve gates *were* twelve pearls: each individual gate was of one pearl. And the street of the city *was* pure gold, like transparent glass.

But I saw no temple in it, for the Lord God Almighty and the Lamb are its temple. The city had no need of the sun or of the moon to shine in it, for the glory of God illuminated it. The Lamb *is* its light. And the nations of those who are saved shall walk in its light, and the kings of the earth bring their glory and honor into it. Its gates shall not be shut at all by day (there shall be no night there). And they shall bring the glory and the honor of the nations into it. But there shall by no means enter it anything that defiles, or causes an abomination or a lie, but only those who are written in the Lamb's Book of Life.

(Revelation 21:9–27)

There is more. The word of God continues to describe the new heaven:

And he showed me a pure river of water of life, clear as crystal, proceeding from the throne of God and of the Lamb. In the middle of its street, and on either side of the river, *was* the tree of life, which bore twelve fruits, each *tree* yielding its fruit every month. The leaves of the tree were for the healing of the nations. And there shall be no more curse, but the throne of God and of the Lamb shall be in it, and His servants shall serve Him. They shall see His face, and His name shall be on their foreheads. There shall be no night there: They need no lamp nor light of the sun, for the Lord God gives them light. And they shall reign forever and ever. Then he said to me, "These words are faithful and true." And the Lord God of the holy prophets sent His angel to show His servants the things which must shortly take place.

"Behold, I am coming quickly! Blessed is he who keeps the words of the prophecy of this book."

(Revelation 22:1–7)

As Ralph had studied this Scripture passage as revealed to John, he had put in his notes, "What a city!" The city will be approximately 1,500 miles square. That is about two-thirds the size of the entire United States. Now, that is just the city itself placed upon the newly created earth. The beauty of the new heaven is totally indescribable. Many of the children of God may have not been blessed with wealth or elaborate homes in this life, but God has planned the extravagant for them in the new heaven and new earth. That is what the children of God will move into just after the final judgment!

Most importantly, God is going to come down to the new earth and dwell with his children. He will be in constant access to all the hosts of his new heaven and new earth. In fact, the face of God, which has never been seen, will be beheld constantly in the new heaven. These promises of God are just as sure as any other of the multitude of promises he has made and which have been proven to be true.

Ralph had concluded the lesson document with these words, "My friends, all of us have unwisely missed the rapture when Jesus returned in the air to resurrect the bodies of all who had died with faith in him as savior. He brought their souls with him, and body and soul were reunited in the air, into a glorified being. Also, at the same instant, all those living who were right with God, were instantly changed into glorified bodies and caught up to meet the Lord in the air to enjoy the marriage supper of the lamb. That is where Madeline is right now and the reason I found her gone. And many of your family members and friends are likewise gone," Ralph emphasized.

"Because of sin in our hearts or lives, we were not prepared and ready to meet the Lord, as Jesus had emphatically stressed. However, God has graciously saved us by faith and trust in him. We have missed the blessings of the marriage supper, but if we maintain faith in God, live for him, and die in the faith, heaven will soon become the home of our soul. And when Jesus returns in the Revelation, our bodies will be resurrected, rejoined with our soul and spirit, to reign with the Lord forever.

"It is important that we all live true to God, endure severe persecutions, encounter the tortures of the great tribulation, and possibly face martyrdom for our faith. But do it! There is assurance of hope and an eternal heavenly home. It will be worth anything we may have to endure in this life. God bless you and keep you true to him! If I do not see you again in this life, I will see you on the other side in the great multitude clothed in white, awaiting the final consummation of all things promised and assured by God himself!" All of this Ralph had highlighted and wanted stressed.

For the next three weeks, Todd, Faye, Jim, and Sue worked diligently to distribute Ralph's final document to every believer they knew or could recall. It was a life-threatening effort since the Antichrist was urging frantic tactics against all believers. Ralph's documents would be hidden inside the clothing of the persons attempting to distribute them.

Peddling their bicycles around the area to deliver the document was time consuming as extreme caution was necessary. All of them were sure that sooner or later, they would be confronted by the agents of the Antichrist, arrested, and probably martyred. However, they considered the rewards of their efforts worth it. After all, getting out of the horrors of the great tribulation would be a blessing as the Bible had stated:

> Then I heard a voice from heaven saying to me, "Write; 'Blessed are the dead who die in the Lord from now on that they may rest from their labors, and their works follow them."
>
> (Revelation 14:13)

So they continued on in their efforts to distribute faith-building materials. When the Antichrist was informed that the successful efforts of believers was going unchecked, he ordered a mass roundup of all known and suspected believers everywhere. That order reached the east coast of Florida, where Ralph had ministered. Almost immediately, the agents of the Antichrist began arresting believers. Todd and Faye, along with Jim and Sue, were some of the first called upon and arrested. In addition, most of their friends who had met and worshiped with them were arrested. The interrogations were intense, and every believer was promised freedom if they would renounce their faith in God and pledge allegiance to the Antichrist.

A few, whose faith was weak, faltered, choosing life rather that martyrdom. The brief life they chose would be filled with tortures of the remaining events of the great tribulation, and eternal torment in the fires of hell. Most of the believers, who had learned from Ralph's studies and trainers, maintained an unwavering faith in God. They chose instant death, by the swing of a sword, rather than turn their backs upon the God who had graciously and mercifully saved them. Knowledge that the next instant after death they would join the great white-robed multitude in the presence of God, as he had promised, buoyed them up:

After these things I looked, and behold, a great multitude
which no man could number, of all nations, tribes, peoples,
and tongues, standing before the throne and before the
Lamb, clothed with white robes, with palm branches in
their hands... Then one of the elders answered, saying to
me, 'Who are these arrayed in white robes, and where did
they come from?' And I said to him, 'Sir, you know.' So he
said to me, 'These are the ones who came out of the great
tribulation, and have washed their robes and made them
white in the blood of the Lamb." Therefore they are before
the throne of God, and serve Him day and night in His
temple. And He who sits on the throne will dwell among
them.

(Revelation 7:9, 13–15)

Suddenly, a chorus rang out in the execution waiting room,
extolling God for the fact that they would soon be with him in
his heaven. None of the persecutions they had encountered or
the death they were about to die could rob them of victory over
death. They joyously sang of being able to soon see Christ and be
with him forever.

Their guards shouted, "Shut up." But there was no silencing
these followers of Christ, who were soon to see him and be with
him. Louder and louder, they kept repeating the chorus. Finally,
in sheer disgust, the guards left the room yet amazed at the
courage of these converted followers of Christ.

The horrors of the great tribulation will grind to an end
with the appearing of Jesus Christ coming to this earth in the
Revelation. The massive attack of the armies of the world, led
by the Antichrist, will be defeated by Christ and the hosts of
heaven. Then Christ will set up his earthly kingdom and reign
for a thousand years as King of kings and Lord of lords. And the
finality of all things will unfold much as Ralph discovered and
taught from the Word of God in spite of the torturous turmoil of
the great tribulation.

The final word to all who read this book, whether you agree with it or not, is that Jesus Christ is returning soon, and you can be ready. What a wonder and reward it will be to meet him in the air and be with him forever. You can be one who is gone!

Bibliography and Recommended Reading

Beacon Bible Commentary. Kansas City, Missouri: Beacon Hill Press, 1967.

Cahn, Jonathan. *The Harbinger.* Florida: FrontLine Charisma Media/Charisma House Book Group, 2011.

Clarke, Adam. *Clark Commentary.* New York: Abingdon Press.

Jeremiah, David. *I Never Thought I'd See the Day.* New York, Boston: Faith Words, 2011.

———. *What in the World Is Going On?* Nashville, Tennessee: Thomas Nelson, 2008.

Jeremiah, David and CC Carlson. *The Handwriting on the Wall.* Published by Nashville, Tennessee: Thomas Nelson, 1992.

Lindsey, Hal. *The Late Great Planet Earth.* Michigan: Zondervan, Grand Rapids, 1970.

Price, John. *The End of America.* Indianapolis, Indiana: Christian House Publishers, Inc., 2009.

Spence, HDM and Joseph S. Exell, eds. *The Pulpit Commentary.* Grand Rapids, Michigan: Wm. B. Erdmann's Publishing Company, 1950.

The New King James Version. Thomas Nelson, Inc., 1982.

Richardson, Don. *Secrets of the Koran.* Ventura, California, USA: Regal Books, From Gospel Light, 2003.